An Irresistible Kiss

"Oh, Anne, we're alone, so why can't you at least be honest with me?"

"Because I have given my word that I will marry the Duke of Wroxford, and I mean to stand by that word."

"Even though *I* am the one you love?" Gervase held his breath, but still she didn't say the words he needed.

He was anguished. "What have I done that you have not shared? We *shared* those caresses, Anne."

She was in turmoil. "Why are you doing this? What possible good can come of your interference?"

Oh, if only he could tell her that he was the real Duke of Wroxford, and that none of her fears would be of any consequence at all if she would only say she loved him!

She met his gaze. "Please leave, Mr. Danby."

"Oh Anne," he whispered, putting his hand to her chin and raising her lips toward his.

"Just go," she breathed.

"No, Anne, I'm going to *make* you admit the truth." Her body was taut and anxious as he slid an arm around her waist, and his kiss allowed her no quarter at all. Never before had he used his experience so passionately, ̶o̶r̶ ̶s̶o̶ ̶d̶e̶l̶i̶b̶e̶r̶a̶t̶e̶l̶y̶.̶

Anne could feel he̶r̶

"Please, don't. Plea̶

for she knew her wea̶

D1089573

SIGNET REGENCY ROMANCE
Coming in July 1998

April Kihlstrom
An Outrageous Proposal

Melinda McRae
The Temporary Duke

Andrea Pickens
Code of Honor

1-800-253-6476
ORDER DIRECTLY
WITH VISA OR MASTERCARD

The
Faun's Folly

―――――

by

Sandra Heath

A SIGNET BOOK

SIGNET
Published by the Penguin Group
Penguin Putnam Inc., 375 Hudson Street,
New York, New York 10014, U.S.A.
Penguin Books Ltd, 27 Wrights Lane,
London W8 5TZ, England
Penguin Books Australia Ltd, Ringwood,
Victoria, Australia
Penguin Books Canada Ltd, 10 Alcorn Avenue,
Toronto, Ontario, Canada M4V 3B2
Penguin Books (N.Z.) Ltd, 182–190 Wairau Road,
Auckland 10, New Zealand

Penguin Books Ltd, Registered Offices:
Harmondsworth, Middlesex, England

First published by Signet, an imprint of Dutton NAL,
a member of Penguin Putnam Inc.

First Printing, June, 1998
10 9 8 7 6 5 4 3 2 1

Copyright © Sandra Wilson, 1998
All rights reserved

 REGISTERED TRADEMARK—MARCA REGISTRADA

Printed in the United States of America

Without limiting the rights under copyright reserved above, no part of this
publication may be reproduced, stored in or introduced into a retrieval system, or
transmitted, in any form, or by any means (electronic, mechanical, photocopying,
recording, or otherwise), without the prior written permission of both the copyright
owner and the above publisher of this book.

BOOKS ARE AVAILABLE AT QUANTITY DISCOUNTS WHEN USED TO PROMOTE PRODUCTS OR
SERVICES. FOR INFORMATION PLEASE WRITE TO PREMIUM MARKETING DIVISION, PENGUIN
PUTNAM INC., 375 HUDSON STREET, NEW YORK, NEW YORK 10014.

If you purchased this book without a cover you should be aware that this book is
stolen property. It was reported as "unsold and destroyed" to the publisher and
neither the author nor the publisher has received any payment for this "stripped
book."

Chapter One

Anne shivered as she stood in the arched doorway to see her parents off at the outset of their hastily arranged visit to Dublin. It was not a journey they'd undertaken lightly, for it involved traversing the Irish Sea, which was of uncertain temper at the best of times, let alone at the depths of winter. As if to emphasize the hazards lying ahead, the February wind moaned beneath the barbican and rustled the ivy that grew so profusely on the courtyard walls. The draft also rattled the trapdoors that gave into Llandower's ancient cellars, as if someone were trying to open them from below. It wasn't a pleasant notion, and Anne shivered again.

Mr. George Willowby, a large, bluff Irishman whose charming manner concealed great sadness in his past and constant financial worries in his present, assisted his wife into the waiting traveling carriage, then turned to his daughter. "This April twentieth will be the first of your birthdays that your mother and I have missed."

"Father, I do not think the world will end on account of the omission. Besides, I've grown up now, and promise not to cry," Anne replied with a fond smile.

"Are you sure you'll be all right here on your own?" His Irish origins were easily detectable, even though he hadn't set foot in his native land in more than thirty years.

"Quite sure. Besides, I won't be alone, I'll have the servants." She nodded toward the nearby kitchen door, where the plump housekeeper, Mrs. Jenkins, and the gardener, Joseph Greenwood, both of whom she'd known all her life, stood watching the leave-taking with the general boy, Martin.

Her father sighed. "All three of them, and one a mere child."

"They are sufficient, and before you harp on about it yet again, yes, with their help I *can* see to the running of

Llandower for a few months. After all, it isn't exactly a huge estate."

"Nevertheless, we shouldn't be leaving you alone like this."

"It's unavoidable when there hasn't been time to appoint a new agent," she reminded him. The sudden retirement due to ill health of the old and valued Mr. Ayers had caused innumerable difficulties, but she was confident of being able to manage.

He gave her a hug. "Oh, if ever a father was blessed with a jewel for a daughter, I am." Then he added, "And if ever a fellow was undeserving of such a prize for a wife, it is the new Duke of Wroxford!"

She drew away. "Some might say that a duke is far too good for the daughter of one of his tenants." Her voice was almost lost as the chill wind gusted again, cutting through her brown dimity gown and woolen shawl.

Mr. Willowby looked into her wide gray eyes. "I'll never understand this match, Anne. Why has Gervase Mowbray offered for you? It has something to do with his late father's one and only visit here last summer, hasn't it?"

"Has it?" She met his gaze squarely, wishing he would realize by now that she had no intention of telling him the truth about her startling contract.

"Oh, come on now, it *must* have! I wish I understood what's going on. One of England's greatest catches elects to marry a woman he still hasn't met, and who brings him nothing because her father only just manages to keep out of debt, then he does all in his power to postpone matters by toddling off to Italy with his cousin. It's unlikely to say the least."

"Don't look for reasons, Father, just accept that the daughter you thought was on the shelf has somehow managed to make the sort of dazzling match of which fairy tales are made."

He searched her face. "I thought you were on the shelf because you wished it so in order to remain here."

"You think I love Llandower *that* much?" she asked with a wry smile.

"Yes, I do," he replied seriously.

She glanced around. "It's true that I love it here, but then so do you."

He didn't reply, but kissed her cheek.

She gave a quick laugh. "Anyway, I shall soon be mistress of one of the grandest Palladian houses in all England."

"Oh, Anne, I wish I could be at ease over this match. For instance, what of his penchant for actresses? Can you accept *that*?"

Anne drew a long breath. "If we're to believe rumor, it was only one actress, and anyway I'd be a fool indeed if I expected such a man to be celibate."

Her father hesitated, then nodded. "I suppose so, and once you are a duchess, you will rank among the highest in the land. Why, I imagine you will even secure an invitation to Princess Charlotte's wedding!"

"What wedding? She blows so hot and cold one wonders if she wishes to make the Prince of Orange her husband at all. Besides, I doubt very much if the duke will have returned by then, so I do not for a moment think I will be attending anything as important as a royal wedding. Now then, *please* climb into the carriage and go, or you will not reach the first inn before nightfall.

Anne's mother leaned out rather crossly, the ribbons of her blue velvet bonnet fluttering wildly around her still pretty face. "Oh, do come on, George. After all, it's *your* brother who has seen fit at last to extend a long overdue olive branch!"

Anne understood how her mother felt, for this journey to Ireland had resurrected some very painful memories. Long ago George Willowby, eldest son of a well-to-do Irish landowner, had been disowned after being accused of selling family property to pay off gambling debts. Penniless and disgraced, he'd come to England, where he'd married and taken over the tenancy of Llandower, the small Monmouthshire castle he'd grown to love deeply, even though it was far from profitable. He never spoke of the events that had brought him across the water to England, but the tortures of the past still shadowed his eyes from time to time. Now it had all been dragged to the fore again by an urgent message summoning him to Ballynarray, the family estate outside Dublin, where his only remaining relative, a brother, was ill.

Mr. Willowby gave Anne another hug, then clambered into the vehicle, stepping first onto the block of Roman masonry that he always used as a mounting block, and which had been dug up in the grounds of Llandower. The carriage sank on its springs as he sat heavily on the worn leather seat. Then Anne closed the door, and the coachman tugged his hat low over his forehead before stirring the team into action.

The servants shouted their farewells, and the narrow court-yard took up the echo of voices, hooves, and wheels as Anne hurried to the ancient gatehouse, from where she waved her handkerchief as the vehicle passed the windswept hedges of the great maze. She watched the carriage drive through the lit-tle park that bordered the River Wye, which was not only renowned as one of best salmon rivers in Britain, but also one of the most beautiful. Along its banks there were weeping willows and tall undulating reeds. There was also a small jetty, where several rowing boats swung on water that in sun-light sparkled like diamonds, but which today was dull and gray. In a few weeks the whole scene would be bright with spring leaves, blossom, and daffodils, but in February it was bleak and cheerless, and as the carriage passed out of sight, she hurried gladly back into the fortified manor house, for such Llandower was, even though it gloried in the name of castle.

Once in the entrance hall, she paused just to inhale the beloved smell of the old building, which the Mowbray family had outgrown in their meteoric rise to a dukedom. Now it was deemed worthy only of a tenant, while the dukes of Wroxford occupied their grand but soulless estate in Berkshire. Llandower had a soul, and a heart, and sometimes Anne could almost imagine the ancient stone was breathing. When she left, it would be the hardest wrench imaginable, but the old duke had made it impossible for her to stay. Blinking back sudden tears, she crossed the hall and hurried up the staircase to the warmth of the blue tapestry drawing room, where the first thing that confronted her on entering was her own reflec-tion in the mirror above the fireplace.

She saw a slender but plain woman in brown dimity, who in two months' time would be all of twenty-nine. Apart from her long-lashed eyes, which were an arresting and handsome green, there was little to commend in the future Duchess of Wroxford. Her complexion wasn't pale enough to be fashion-able, her mouth was too wide, and her dark golden curls, al-though a pleasing enough color, were an unmanageable mane that resolutely refused to bow to the dictates of brush, comb or pin. She snatched off her mobcap so that the mutinous tresses in question tumbled willfully around her shoulders.

Oh, the number of times she'd striven to achieve a fashionable coiffure, only to eventually admit defeat by resorting to a cap of one sort or another. What a drab nonentity she was. No wonder her father had expected her to remain unmarried! And as for the opinion of London society, well she would always remain a very average, very provincial creature who did not warrant the miraculous good fortune of a contract with the handsome eighth Duke of Wroxford. If only what she'd said to her father were untrue, and the match was indeed the stuff of fairy tales, but it wasn't in the least romantic, rather was it a duty she could not avoid. She did not know how Gervase regarded it, but didn't doubt he was being coerced as well.

With a sigh Anne moved closer to the fire and held her hands out to the warmth. Flame light flickered on the brass fender and set rosy shadows leaping over the sky silk walls of the small but elegant room. Her mother's touch was everywhere, for Jane Willowby had stitched all the tapestry for the chairs and cushions. In the alcove to one side of the fireplace there stood a tall lamp holder in the form of a beautiful life-size wooden sculpture of the water nymph Penelope. Made of the palest and most flawless of local beech, she wasn't the work of an expensive London craftsman, but of Joseph Greenwood, the gardener. An indirect descendant of none other than the great Grinling Gibbons himself, Joseph had inherited some of his forebear's brilliance, and had carved Penelope for Anne's parents on their twenty-fifth wedding anniversary. The wooden nymph had a delicacy and grace that seemed truly ethereal, as if she would at any moment set aside the tray and candelabra she held above her head, gather the filmy skirts of her gauzy gown, and slip silently from the room to find the nearest pool or river in which to swim. She had once been very badly scratched, but Joseph had gone to work on her, and now her wooden surface was pristine once more.

Originally Penelope had a partner, the god Mercury, who had seduced her in mythology, but poor Mercury had come to grief when Joseph's highly inflammable beeswax polish mixture had been heated a little too much. The resultant fire had not only severely burned Mercury's nether regions, but also half the kitchen at Llandower, and since then Joseph had taken much greater care with his hazardous wax and turpentine brews!

A log shifted, and a cloud of sparks fled up the chimney,

reminding Anne that the security of Llandower would do the same if she declined to marry Gervase Mowbray. Her father had been right to link her match with the late duke's visit, for it had all begun then. The old man, who had never before visited the property where his family had its roots, suddenly chose to do so the previous summer. Anne had soon become aware of his pensive glance, which made her feel as if she were being assessed, which indeed proved the case, for prior to his departure he had sought a private meeting with her. He told her that if she agreed to marry his son and heir, Llandower would immediately become her father's property; if she refused, George Willowby's lease would not be renewed at the end of this coming summer. She had no idea why the late duke had been so determined that she should be the next duchess, but faced with such an ultimatum, she felt she had no option but to agree. What pressure the duke had put upon his son she did not know, but it was clearly equally as forceful, for a man like Gervase Mowbray would never have *chosen* such an insignificant bride.

Anne reached up to take a small bundle of letters from behind a candlestick. Each missive was brief and impersonal, but amounted to the only contact she had ever had with the man she was to marry. Written on costly parchment, they all bore the impressive seal of the Mowbray family, whose badge was a representation of the Llandower maze. The last one had been sent a few months ago, shortly before Gervase's departure for Italy with his only cousin, Hugh, and on impulse she read it aloud, adopting the pompous tone she imagined Gervase to possess.

"Wroxford Park, December 1st, 1815.

"Miss Willowby, I trust this note finds you well. I also trust that my decision to oblige my cousin, Hugh, by accompanying him to Italy for six months will not cause any inconvenience with regard to our betrothal, the formal celebration of which will take place immediately on my return.

"With all courtesy. Wroxford."

How warm and charming his communications were, she thought wryly as she refolded the letter and replaced the bundle behind the candlestick. It was clearly an afterthought to even inform her of his intention to go abroad, and it was equally clear that he did not care about her opinion. On the evidence of his letters, the new Duke of Wroxford was a man of few words, and even less consideration for the feelings of others. Was this how it would be on their marriage night? Would he write a note to say he trusted that what was about to occur would not cause her any inconvenience? Perhaps she should have a written reply in hand, stating that she trusted it wouldn't be either!

She was certain that Gervase Mowbray was going to prove as pompous, cold, and disagreeable as his letters, and if that was indeed the case, one day she would take him to the little ornamental rotunda in the center of the maze, then desert him, leaving a note trusting he wouldn't be put to too much trouble finding his way out of the puzzle that was his family's proud badge!

She glanced away then, for it was all very well to be facetious, but the fact remained that she *was* going to marry him, and the moment she did, her body became his property. She wasn't ignorant about what happened during lovemaking, because at the age of ten she had watched two lovers in a cornfield. Spying upon the fashionable lady and gentleman hadn't been a deliberate act, for she'd been innocently gathering honeysuckle when an elegant carriage had suddenly pulled up on the other side of the hedgerow. Because she was out when she shouldn't have been, she'd instinctively ducked down out of sight among the summer leaves, and oh, the things she'd learned that day. . . .

Like every other bride since time began, she had always dreamed of surrendering her virginity, hoping it would be a joyful initiation with a husband she loved. Instead, she was entering into a cold contract in which love played no part, with a man she did not know, and who seemed to lack all consideration. What manner of marriage really lay ahead? Not a matter of ecstasy and soft sighs in a sun-drenched cornfield, with the scent of honeysuckle all around and the sweet song of skylarks tumbling in a clear blue sky . . .

Chapter Two

That evening in Naples, Gervase Mowbray, eighth Duke of Wroxford, stood in the window of the third-floor lodgings he and his cousin, Hugh, had taken in the Riviero di Chiaia. His dark hair was a little tousled from sleep, and his hands were thrust deep into his pockets as he leaned against the embrasure. It was dusk, and the darkening February sky was lit by the eerie red glow of snow-capped Vesuvius, some six miles away to the east.

Even with his shirt undone and his neckcloth tossed idly on the crumpled bed behind him, Gervase was effortlessly stylish, with the mark of Bond Street evident in every fine stitch. The white of his full-sleeved shirt was almost stark in the fading light, and the cut of his trousers outlined his slender hips and long legs to complete perfection. He had made one gesture against fashion since leaving England, and that had been to let his hair grow. It was now long enough to be in frequent need of pushing back from his forehead, which he did by running his fingers through it. Together with his lazily seductive smile, this unconscious gesture gave him an irresistibly romantic air, as was proved by his numerous conquests across Europe.

He was thirty-two years old, and over six feet tall, with a lean, strong, well-proportioned shape that always showed to advantage in the close-fitting clothes that were the order of the day. His handsome face was tanned from the Mediterranean sun, and his blue eyes were swift and shrewd, their glint giving the lie to any notion that a man of such style and fashion might be easily fooled, as many a French and Italian ostler had found to their cost during the journey from England.

The elegant Riviero di Chiaia was separated from the shore of the famous Bay of Naples by the magnificent Royal

Gardens, where the lilacs were in full bloom and lanterns of every color had been lit. He watched as masked revelers, some in gorgeous costumes, poured through the gardens and along the elegant cobbled street. It was Carnival, and tonight was also one of the several festivals of Bacchus that took place during the course of the year. Neapolitans seized every excuse to follow their ready inclination to eat, drink, make love, and generally enjoy themselves, and right now all four could be accomplished behind the anonymity of masks. Merrymakers thronged the city, music played everywhere, and from time to time fireworks glittered and flashed against the heavens.

Gervase suspected there was more to tonight's particular revelries than met the eye. Neapolitans were superstitious enough to hedge their bets where religion was concerned, and he sensed that many of them still made obeisance to the ancient pantheon of Roman gods. Now that darkness had fallen, and the festivities had begun, there was almost a sound of panpipes in the air, enticing the unwary into folly. How many of the coming hours' high jinks would be regretted by the morning? How many women would wish they'd resisted the lure of seduction? Come to that, how many men would wish they'd resisted the urge to seduce?

English voices drawled below the window, and Gervase glanced down to see a group of young masked noblemen leaving the Royal Gardens to enter a carriage at the curb opposite. It sometimes seemed there were as many Anglo-Saxons in Naples as there were Neapolitans, for the city was compulsory for the *gran turisimo*, and Carnival was the most sought after time of year to visit.

The door opened suddenly, and Gervase's cousin, Hugh, entered. "Ah, you're awake," he declared, crossing to the wardrobe and opening it to search through the elegant clothes hanging there as if they were his own.

"So it would seem," Gervase murmured, watching him with some irritation.

"Then you'll accompany me to the theater tonight after all?"

"The questionable delights of the San Carlo hold no appeal," Gervase replied, thinking of the Neapolitan insistence upon making so much noise throughout performances that actors had to shout to be heard. "But I'll dine with you afterward at our usual place along the street."

"Suit yourself, but if it's macaroni again, I swear I'll expire." Hugh went on sifting through Gervase's wardrobe. The cousins were very alike, possessing the same height and coloring, but Hugh was less good-looking, and didn't possess the immense charm of which Gervase was capable when he chose. Hugh was also from the less wealthy branch of the Mowbray family, a fact Gervase knew he bitterly resented, although the resentment was always hidden behind smiles. Hugh had hidden depths, and some of those depths were better left unplumbed, Gervase thought, for there were aspects of his cousin he found hard to like. Hugh was not a man to rely upon in an emergency, nor to place faith in if one's life depended upon it, but for all that, he was Gervase's only living relative, and so had to be tolerated. However, tolerating someone was one thing, being cooped up with him constantly for six months quite another. This European visit had been a mistake, and the veneer of friendship between the cousins was beginning to wear thin.

"Is there something you require, Hugh?" Gervase asked a little tetchily as Hugh went on sifting through his clothes.

"I was looking for your greatcoat. I thought I'd take a stroll before the theater, and although the lilacs are out and the days are warm, the evenings soon prove to be February after all." What Hugh said was true, for although as a whole the Neapolitan climate was clement at this time of year, at night it still became quite cold; indeed frost and ice were not unknown. "Ah, here it is." He lifted out Gervase's best greatcoat, a fine ankle-length garment of charcoal wool with an astrakhan collar and gleaming silver buttons that bore the maze badge of the Mowbrays. Belatedly, he thought of seeking Gervase's permission. "May I?"

"I suppose it would be churlish to refuse."

"Is that what you said to your father when he confronted you with the Willowby creature?" Hugh asked with lightning change of subject.

The sudden barb was there, and it found a mark. Gervase flushed a little. "I bowed to his wishes because it was the only way to make certain of my birthright." He could hear the old man's voice now. *That's my final word, Gervase. Your recent entanglement with that actress creature caused me great con-*

cern, so I wish to be certain that the right sort of woman becomes the next duchess. I have found that woman in Anne Willowby, and she is the price you will have to pay for wasting your life thus far. There is nothing you can do about it, for my will has already been altered, and it is binding. You marry Miss Willowby, or forfeit your right to the title and all that goes with it.

Hugh turned to look at him. "No doubt you fear such a rustic will embarrass you before the *ton*."

"Since I have never met Anne Willowby, I cannot form an opinion. She may be very accomplished for all I know."

"I can't understand that you haven't even wanted to see her."

"I resent her too much to wish to have any contact more intimate than the written word. She is clearly a fortune hunter who somehow, although God knows how, managed to wrap my father around her scheming finger."

"If she was simply a fortune hunter, don't you think she'd have trapped *him* into marriage, not you? The purse strings are usually held by the reigning duke, not the duke-in-waiting," Hugh pointed out practically.

Gervase shrugged. "Perhaps she tried and failed. Who can say?"

"You can't postpone the match forever, you know. I seem to recall that the terms of the will dictate marriage within a year."

"I'm aware of that, but until those twelve blessed months are up, I intend to stay free, which is why Italy seemed so blessed a haven."

"Seemed? Past tense?"

"It begins to pall. One can examine only so many ruined temples, admire so many reliefs, gasp at the beauty of so many busts."

"Ah, now when it comes to *busts* . . . !" Hugh gave a sly grin.

"I was thinking of the marble kind."

"I know, but I am more drawn to soft, warm busts, especially when attached to the person of the delightful Teresa del Rosso." He was referring to their landlady's daughter, a doe-eyed coquette of voluptuous proportions, who had thus far spurned his determined attentions.

Gervase sighed. "I'd forget her if I were you," he advised. Why couldn't Hugh see that Teresa simply wasn't interested in him? And why couldn't he also see the wisdom of steering well clear of a young woman who clearly possessed a vindictive nature. One fell foul of Teresa del Rosso at one's peril.

Hugh's smile became fixed, for Gervase had offered exactly the same advice concerning Kitty Longton, the fascinating Drury Lane actress Hugh had wanted from the first moment he'd seen her.

Gervase recognized the expression on his cousin's face, and was irritated. "Oh, for heaven's sake, don't hark back to Kitty again, for she was *not* the injured angel you choose to believe!"

"No? Then why will you not say why you ended things with her so very cruelly?"

"*Cruelly?*" Gervase gave a brief laugh. "My dear Hugh, believe me when I say *I* was not the cruel one."

"Then tell me what happened."

Gervase hesitated, but then shook his head. "No, Hugh, for it is none of your business. Suffice it that Kitty Longton was guilty of such a harsh and unfeeling act that when I found out about it I could no longer bear to be in the same room as her. That she was a whore with ambitions to marry into the aristocracy I had always known, and it made no odds, but that she was a whore entirely without heart or conscience I did not know, and the difference it made was too great by far."

"Tell the truth, Gervase. She was no more than a passing fancy to you."

"Are you suggesting I used her and then cast her aside without a second thought?"

"Didn't you?"

"Not in the way you think, although it's true she didn't exert her fascination over me for very long. A man's self-esteem is not best served by a woman who is determined to parade in the hoops and diamonds of court dress, nor does he feel comfortable when she shows herself to have little discretion. A daring expanse of bosom is embarrassing and vulgar outside the confines of the bedchamber, a fact to which Kitty would not pay heed, no matter how often it was pointed out. Desire soon wilts under such circumstances, I promise you, and it wilted still more when I learned unpleasant details from her past." He looked away, remembering when he had reached the final straw where the lovely actress was concerned. Quite by chance he'd discovered that when her parents died, rather than encumber herself with her ten-year-old brother, she had consigned the boy to a disreputable orphanage, where he had died a year later of a deadly chill brought on by the cruel conditions there. Such monstrous callousness was beyond comprehension, especially as Kitty could well have afforded to show compassion for the child.

Jealousy devoured Hugh. After Gervase, Kitty had set her calculating cap at Sir Thomas Fanhope, a dashing sporting type who was very much available on the marriage mart, but financial difficulties had soon obliged him to leave her bed in order to marry the heiress to a Staffordshire pottery fortune, a selfish only child whose doting father still controlled the purse strings. Fanhope, like Hugh himself, still loved Kitty, but Gervase, upon whom the gods smiled as usual, fully escaped the tortures of heartbreak. Women always flocked to Gervase. It had happened with Kitty, and no doubt would happen with Teresa del Rosso and the serving girl at the inn along the street . . .

Overcoming the moment of steel-bright hatred he really felt for Gervase, who was all that stood between him and the dukedom he coveted, Hugh slipped into the coat and admired his reflection in the cheval glass in the corner. "You have an eye for clothes, I'll give you that, Coz," he murmured.

"It's as well, since you wear them almost as much as I do," Gervase remarked.

"What are cousins for?" Hugh replied, taking a black velvet mask from his trouser pocket and slipping it over his head.

Gervase raised an eyebrow. "You intend to follow the rites of Bacchus Night to the full?"

"Naturally," Hugh replied, reaching for Gervase's hat, gloves, and cane. "You don't mind, do you? Only they do complement the coat so perfectly."

"That is why I chose them," Gervase murmured. "No, I suppose I don't mind—well, not that much, anyway."

A moment later, Hugh strolled out, looking for all the world as if he, not his cousin, were the Duke of Wroxford. As his footsteps died away along the passage, Gervase heard the sounds of merrymaking in the street outside. Paganism seemed to tingle tangibly in the air as he reached for the half-finished glass of sweet white Lachrymae Christi wine on the table nearby. Lachrymae Christi, Christ's tears. Well, those tears might indeed be shed before tonight's somewhat profane reveling was done, he thought as he resumed his slouch against the window embrasure.

As Hugh emerged from the lodging house to stroll among the exuberant Bacchus Night revelers on the lamplit pavement, he was sure he could hear the menacing rumble of Vesuvius in the distance. But the sound was faint because of the singing and dancing, the throbbing of guitars and tambourines, and the fireworks bursting above the rooftops. In spite of the merrymaking, he was very much on his guard, for Naples possessed an army of beggars known as *lazzaroni*, most of whom were skillful pickpockets, and he had no intention of becoming one of their victims.

He hadn't gone far when he noticed Teresa del Rosso ahead of him. Her shapely ankles twinkled tantalizingly from beneath the hem of her warm gray-striped gown as she hurried along, and she held her long woolen shawl over her raven hair. As he watched, she turned into the dark alley that led, he knew, to the wine store kept by her mother. Without hesitation he followed her.

The alley was dark and deserted, and when Teresa heard his steps, she turned nervously. She saw his tall shape outlined against the light from the street at the far end of the alley, and by the coat thought she recognized Gervase. Her dark eyes softened, and her pretty lips curved into the sort of knowing smile that proved her chastity had long since been consigned to the realms of distant memory.

"I hoped you would not resist much longer, signor," she murmured, holding out a hand and melting back into the dark shadows of the store doorway.

Hugh felt desire begin to surge unstoppably through him, and he dropped Gervase's cane as he went to her. He knew it was a case of mistaken identify, that she would not have welcomed him at all had she known who he really was, but for Gervase she was prepared to surrender all. Bitterness heated Hugh's lust, and he knew he would punish her for wanting his cousin, not him.

She was soft and yielding, her lips parting beneath his, and there was nothing innocent in the way she pressed into his loins in order to feel his arousal. He trembled as she undid her bodice to reveal those breasts he'd yearned for from the moment he'd arrived in the Riviero de Chiaia. Even in the darkness he could see their plump firmness and the way her nipples turned up eagerly for him. He lowered his head to kiss them, but as his lips brushed the perfumed sweetness of those delectable mounds, the remnants of restraint vanished into the night. His gloved hands were rough as he wrenched up her skirts, then unbuttoned his trousers to take her without further ado.

He hurt her, and she was at last seized with fear. She tried to call for help. *"Aiuto! Aiuto!"*

He clamped his hand over her mouth and forced her against the door, but then an old woman entered the alley, advancing toward the courtyard with shuffling infirm steps. At first Hugh thought she'd come in response to Teresa's choked cries, but then he heard the chink of keys and realized she was coming to unlock the wine store. With a stifled curse he straightened his clothes, but was careful to keep a hand over Teresa's mouth as he did so. The old woman was still yards away as he looked coldly at Teresa, his eyes shining behind his mask. "I will say you invited my advances, so say nothing unless you wish your mother to learn how many men have sampled her supposedly virginal daughter these past few years," he whispered harshly in the formal Italian he'd learned at Cambridge University. Then he retrieved the cane before walking swiftly away. He didn't even glance at the old woman, who paused with a start as he suddenly emerged from the shadows.

Still under the impression that he was Gervase, Teresa gazed hatefully after him. She knew it would be foolish to accuse him because he would carry out his threat, and the last thing she wanted was for her strict mother to find out how immoral her daughter's conduct had become. Stepping forward quickly, she seized the old woman's arms. "You'll say nothing, Maria, nothing at all! Do you understand?"

The old woman shrugged. "It is none of my business that you are a whore, Teresa del Rosso. I am paid to look after the wine store, not guard your morals."

A particularly rowdy group of revellers passed the mouth of the alley. They were dressed as fauns and bacchantes and were chanting Bacchus's name as they brandished wine bottles aloft. One of them was playing panpipes, and a new light entered Teresa's eyes. The Englishman would not escape, for there were still ways to punish him, old ways that went back into the mists of time.

Chapter Three

As Hugh left the scene in Naples, faraway to the northwest at Llandower, Anne was seated in the drawing room, finishing her needlework. Her hair was unpinned, and she wore a dark red velvet gown flushed to the color of warm wine by the flickering fire, which flared now and then as the blustering gale drew mournfully down the chimney. The dismal wet weather had continued all day, and she'd been obliged to light Penelope's candelabra a little earlier than she would have liked.

At last the final stitch was done, and she held her work up to admire. It was only a plaid shawl, but she'd fringed the thick blue-and-green woolen material herself. Plaid accessories were all the rage now because of Sir Walter Scott, and even in the sticks of Monmouthshire one wished to be as fashionable as possible, but as usual she had modified things to suit her own particular taste. Fringes were always modish, although not as long as this, or as intricately knotted. Maybe ladies of true fashion would look down their noses at it, but she was well pleased with her efforts.

The mantelpiece clock struck eleven, and she closed the workbox, then folded the shawl and placed it neatly on top. Getting up, she pulled the guard in front of the fire, then extinguished all Penelope's candles except one, which she placed in a waiting candlestick. Shielding the little flame with her hand, she went down to the kitchens to talk with Mrs. Jenkins and enjoy a glass of hot milk, as she did every night.

The plump housekeeper beamed as she entered. "Ah, there you are at last, Miss Anne," she declared unnecessarily, dusting a chair with her apron in readiness. As a new maid, she had been present when Anne was born, and although she and her late husband had never been blessed with children of their own, she had come to regard herself as Anne's second mother. She was in her late forties, with soft brown eyes, an unexpectedly youthful pink-and-white complexion, and graying hair that was always concealed beneath a large frilled mobcap. Her apron was starched, and her wine taffeta gown, which once belonged to Anne's mother, made a familiar rustling sound as she went to put a saucepan of milk on the fire.

The other two servants were also in the kitchen, Joseph at the table surrounded by his woodwork paraphernalia, and Martin, thin and nimble, with spiky brown hair and huge dark eyes, was sprawled on the stone floor with the gardener's sly lurcher, Jack. Joseph was a fifty-year-old bachelor, and the sort of slow-moving countryman who was never fazed by anything. Still handsome beneath his full beard and weather-beaten complexion, he adhered firmly to the philosophy that everything—no matter how fantastic on the surface—had a logical explanation beneath. His unflappability sometimes drove Mrs. Jenkins to distraction, for she was of a far more impulsive and busy disposition. She often declared that he was about as animated as one of his carvings, and he called her gullible and twitchy, but he said it in the sort of fond way that hinted there was more regard between them than might at first appear.

Anne was usually able to see the gardener's latest piece of woodwork, but for several weeks now he had always hastily drawn a cloth over it the moment she entered. It was about a foot high by a foot long by four inches wide, but she couldn't even begin to guess what it was, beyond the fact that it was probably a gift for her approaching birthday. Knowing his skill, she did not doubt that it would be perfect in every detail. She glanced at the cluttered table, where his implements, oils, and waxes were carefully laid out. The smell of linseed and turpentine hung in the air, and there were soft cotton squares stained with brown from whatever he'd just been polishing. A double saucepan stood in the hearth, and she knew he'd just mixed some more of his special beeswax polish, three parts bleached beeswax to nine parts turpentine. That the kitchen was still intact meant that on this occasion he'd taken the necessary care.

Mrs. Jenkins persuaded Anne to eat a slice of currant cake, and every mouthful was watched longingly by Martin and

Jack. The former was eventually rewarded for his patience, but the lurcher received not a single crumb because the housekeeper rightly held it responsible for the disappearance of many a tidbit from the kitchens. Mrs. Jenkins had never caught the crafty dog in the act, but she vowed that if ever she did, heaven help its mangy hide. Joseph left the animal to its own devices. If it got caught, it only had itself to blame, and if it got away with the crime, then Mrs. J. would have to be more vigilant in future.

The evening ritual over, Anne retired at last to her bedroom, which wasn't by any means Llandower's finest chamber in the house, but which had the best view over the maze and grounds toward the Wye. Comfortably furnished in her chosen green-and-gold brocade, with a capacious bed in which she could snuggle on nights such as this, it was warm and welcoming as she stood at the washstand to pour water from the porcelain jug into the bowl. The wind still blustered as she extinguished the candle and curled up to try to sleep. Fire shadows moved gently on the walls, leaping now and then as another gust of wind tossed rain against the window.

She was tired after a few days that had been hectic from the moment the messenger had arrived from Ballynarray, but sleep would not come. She lay in a half world between slumber and wakefulness, her thoughts wandering over all manner of subjects before inevitably coming to rest on the one thing that made her deeply apprehensive about her coming match—the physical yielding that Gervase Mowbray could, and would, demand of her. Beneath the bedclothes she put her hands to her breasts, a gesture that was half defensive, half wondering. What would her first night as Duchess of Wroxford really be like? Not a romantic occasion of shared tenderness, that much was certain, but would he treat her kindly? Would the consummation be gentle, or would he just take her roughly and consider his duty done?

As she drifted on the boundary of sleep, it seemed she was no longer at Llandower, but in a much grander bed in the principal chamber at Wroxford Park. The door was opening, and her bridegroom was coming in. In her imagination he was tall, but he had no face as he stood looking down at her. He wore a silk dressing robe, and as he loosened the belt she saw he was naked beneath. . . . In her imagination his body was pale, lean but muscular, and very beautiful, as had been the unknown gentleman in the cornfield all those years ago. He was saying something to her, but his voice was a distant echo, and she couldn't understand. Her heart was pounding, and her mouth was dry as he climbed in beside her. He pulled her toward him in the candlelit darkness and whispered something, but again she could not hear. Then he took her hand and drew it to the hard, upstanding shaft that showed how ready he was to complete this marriage of convenience. He pressed into her palm, and the blood thundered through her veins as her fingers closed tentatively around him. Wild emotions ran through her as she felt his heat and urgency, and she wanted to do all the things those other lovers had done, but as he pulled her into his arms and put his lips to hers, the fantasy was shattered by a sudden fierce gust of wind that blew her bedroom window open. It banged back upon its hinges as if it would fly away on the storm, and the curtains billowed as an icy draft swept into the room, where she was very much alone in her bed.

For a moment she lay in confusion, but as the window banged again, she flung the bedclothes back to get up. Her hair and nightgown were tugged by the gale, and rain spattered her face as she leaned out to seize the window catch. In the darkness below she could see the shivering hedges of the maze and the convoluted path that twisted and turned back upon itself in a pattern known as the City of Troy, because it was said to be a plan of that city's defenses. The ornamental rotunda in the center of the maze was pale and white, holding her attention for a breathless moment before her fingers felt the catch and she managed to close the window again.

Far away in Naples at that moment, Bacchus Night was in full swing as Gervase and Hugh sat in a relatively quiet candlelit corner of the inn farther along the street from their lodgings. Signora del Rosso did not provide meals, and neither cousin had wished to persuade her to do so, for she was a dragon of the highest order—coughed up by Vesuvius as indigestible, as no doubt would be her cooking, was Gervase's opinion.

Macaroni had indeed proved the order of the day, and it had been brought to their table by the saucy maid who from the outset had made her interest in Gervase only too obvious. Ignoring Hugh, she kept leaning across in such a way that the lighted candle on the table treated Gervase to frequent glimpses of the contents of her tight bodice. Her dark eyes invited, and when he'd tossed her some *scudis*, she'd caught them deftly. *"Grazie,"* she'd whispered, as if thanking him for pleasuring her in love, then she'd very pointedly slipped the coins between the breasts she'd made so certain he noticed.

Later, as the cousins lingered over their postprandial wine, Gervase glanced around the dining room, in which he and Hugh were among the few not to be wearing Carnival costumes. Disguises ranged from animal masks and skins, through several Harlequins and Columbines, to clothes from previous ages, including, he noted with interest, a large number of bacchantes and fauns—or were they satyrs? No, he decided, they were fauns, for satyrs were the Greek counterpart. Not for the first time that evening he wondered how lightheartedly the Neapolitans really regarded their ancient gods. Was it possible that Bacchus was still worshipped in fact as well as fiction? Yes, he decided, looking around again.

Hugh hadn't had a good evening. His visit to the theater had only served to remind him of Kitty Longton's preference for Gervase, and his jealous resentment had been further fanned by the serving girl's obvious liking for the same unfairly privileged cousin. He had drunk more than was wise and was only just on the right side of pleasantness, although his true state hadn't yet become apparent as he used the candle on the table to light one of his, or rather Gervase's, Spanish cigars. His deep antagonism was hidden behind a warm smile and tone as he addressed his cousin. "What are your plans after this? Do you intend serving the serving girl? Or will you perhaps languish alone dreaming dreams of sweet Anne Willowby?"

It was another of the little close-to-the-mark gibes that Gervase found so irritating. He didn't exactly dream dreams of Anne Willowby, but he certainly lay awake wondering what manner of bride she would turn out to be. He kept trying to banish her from his mind completely, but at night, when he was alone, she crept in and wouldn't go away. He also wished now that he *had* called upon her, for at least then he would be able to put a face to the name. Pouring some more wine, he swirled the glass. The wedding night would probably be the one and only time he shared her bed, and he only hoped he'd be able to rise to the occasion! What if the head of the Mowbray family proved to be a limp bridegroom? What if the consummation proved to be a disaster like that of the Prince Regent and Caroline of Brunswick?

Hugh saw his pensive expression and enjoyed the effect his comment had caused. He was about to spitefully press the point a little more when the maid returned to replenish the jug of wine. Before leaving, she bent to whisper in Gervase's ear. "If you wish, I will make tonight special for you, signor . . ."

Gervase hesitated. Her attentions all evening had only mildly stirred his interest, but Hugh's sharp reminder about the unwanted bride awaiting his return to England suddenly made the Neapolitan girl of exquisite desirability. So he gave her one of his lazily seductive smiles and nodded.

Her eyes shone, and she bent even closer to put her parted lips softly to his, but then there was a stir at the far end of the dining room, and she straightened to see what it was about. The other diners had suddenly fallen silent, and all eyes were upon a slightly built man, cloaked and hooded, who'd just entered. Someone whispered a name—Sylvanus—and on hearing it the girl gave a nervous gasp and hurried away. The name had the same effect on everyone else too, for there was a scraping of chairs, and in a few moments the only persons left, apart from the strange new arrival, were the two Englishmen and a local shopkeeper who was too drunk to know what was happening.

Without removing his long voluminous cloak or even tossing his hood back, as one might have expected now that he was no longer outside, the stranger approached the cousins' table. It seemed to Gervase that his steps were oddly light, almost like the pattering of little hooves, and when he spoke, his voice was peculiarly high and nasal.

"Allow me to introduce myself; my name is Sylvanus," he said, and as he inclined his head, all they could see of his face was the faint gleam of his eyes behind a mask, and a chin that was adorned with a beard that put Gervase in mind of a he-goat.

Hugh rather rudely waved the man away without speaking,

but Gervase responded courteously enough. "Good evening, Signor Sylvanus."

"Just Sylvanus. I trust Naples is to your liking?"

Gervase smiled a little. "How could Naples fail to be to our liking?"

Sylvanus made a sound of approval that was almost reminiscent of a goat's bleat. "Ah, yes, for it is the fairest city in all Italy, as so many of the more discerning of your countrymen are pleased to agree. Tell me, gentlemen, have you seen all the sights? Have you visited Pompeii?"

"Naturally, and we've been to Herculaneum, the Cavern of the Sibyl, the island of Capri, Virgil's tomb, and we've climbed Vesuvius—twice," Gervase added, wondering what the man's purpose was, for clearly there was one.

"All things classical are precious to the British, are they not?" Sylvanus said then.

Ah, now we come to it, Gervase thought. The fellow has some fake treasure or other to hawk. "We admire your heritage, sir, for it is our own," he replied.

Hugh wasn't inclined to be even vaguely polite. "Be off with you, whoever you are, we don't want to be bothered by someone trying to sell something," he said, tapping the ash from his cigar carelessly onto the otherwise spotless table.

"I am not selling anything, sir," Sylvanus replied with studied courtesy.

"How true, for we aren't buying, nor are we about to empty our pockets of *scudis*. You've made a mistake in choosing us, for we are armed and not easy targets, so if you are just another of the *lazzaroni*, you would be better advised choosing other victims."

Gervase could have sworn he heard Sylvanus stamp his foot with annoyance—or rather, he thought he heard the thud of a small hoof upon the stone floor—but if the strange little man was momentarily angered, he was soon in command of himself again. "You do me wrong, signor, for my purpose is to your advantage. You may think you have seen all there is to see around Naples, but I will wager there is one place you have never even heard of, let alone seen."

"I doubt it," Hugh answered superciliously, gazing at the man through a curl of cigar smoke.

"I speak of the grove where lies the wedding diadem great Bacchus gave to his beloved Ariadne. It fell from her fingers moments before she died, and now lies at the bottom of a pool, and Bacchus in his heartbreak decreed that it should never be retrieved because hers were the last fingers to touch it. Of course, if a human were to find it . . ." Sylvanus's high-pitched voice died away tantalizingly.

Hugh gave a disparaging snort. "I'll warrant you make a handsome living this way! How many fake diadems do you sell each year, eh?"

"I have already said that I do not sell anything, sir!"

The cloaked figure bristled so comically that Gervase would have given much to see the expression on his face. However, it was time to pour oil on the troubled waters, before Hugh's unpleasant temper got the better of him completely. Gervase gave Sylvanus a placatory smile. "You must forgive my cousin, sir, for I fear he is a little in his cups," he murmured, giving Hugh a warning look.

Hugh scowled, but to Gervase's relief took the hint and said nothing more.

Sylvanus turned his attention upon Gervase. "The story of the diadem is not a myth, signor, and if you wish to be the first of your countrymen to visit the grove, you must follow the track that leads up beyond the disused church with the broken spire. You will find your way straight to your destination."

Hugh had begun to pour himself some more wine, but irritated now, put the jug down with a thud. "Just go away and take your nonsense with you before I do something you may regret!" he growled, for Sylvanus had gotten right under his skin.

"You cannot harm me, sir," was the quiet reply.

Hugh began to rise furiously from his chair, but Gervase restrained him. "For God's sake sit down!"

Hugh hesitated, then sat down again, but Sylvanus suddenly seemed intent upon goading him. "Could it be that you are afraid of Bacchus, signor?" he taunted.

"I'm not afraid of a nonexistent Roman god!" Hugh would have leapt up again had not Gervase held him back.

Sylvanus shrugged. "Are you so sure he does not exist, signor?"

"Yes."

"Then prove it by going to his sacred grove at dawn and risking his wrath by searching for the diadem."

"Risk the wrath of Bacchus? The only risk I will be taking by going to your damned grove is that of ambush by you and your *lazzaroni* cronies!"

"You have my word that this has nothing to do with the *lazzaroni*, or indeed with any form of robbery. Sir, I am telling you of the greatest lost treasure in all Campagna. Can you imagine the fame and fortune that will be yours if you find it? Or are you indeed too timid?"

"I'm not afraid of anything!"

"Then come to the grove at dawn."

Gervase would endure no more and looked a little coldly at Sylvanus. "Sir, I don't profess to know what your real purpose is, but I know its effect, so I would be obliged if you would remove your person and allow us to finish our wine in private."

But Hugh had taken the bait. "All right, I'll go there—we *both* will!" he said recklessly, dragging Gervase into it as well.

Having clearly achieved what he came for, Sylvanus hurried away without further ado. His steps again pattered like little hooves, and as the street door closed behind him, Gervase looked uneasily at Hugh. "*We* aren't going anywhere at dawn, Coz. You may have been incited into scrambling around Italian groves, looking for mythical diadems, but you can leave me out of it."

Hugh grinned as he stubbed out the remains of the cigar. "You'll come," he said with quiet confidence.

Gervase would have felt more uneasy still if he'd known that in the street at that moment Sylvanus was with Teresa, in whose native tongue he was as fluent as he was in English, but then his race was fluent in every known language, except that of cats and dogs. His tone was piqued, for this was not the first time he'd come at her bidding, and he felt imposed upon. "Teresa, if I do what you want, I must have your word that my indebtedness will be discharged once and for all. Do you promise?"

"Of course, Sylvanus," she replied.

"I do not like your demands of me, you know," he grumbled, his head revealed for a moment as his hood was blown back by a sudden breeze. He was snub-nosed and ugly in a rather appealing way, his ears were pointed, and from his forehead protruded two stumpy little horns.

"You have my word I will not do it again," Teresa said soothingly.

"If my master should discover . . ." Sylvanus made an anxious bleating sound, for he knew that in becoming embroiled in Teresa's scheming he was guilty of the utmost folly.

Teresa rightly thought he was on the point of trying to wriggle out, so she spoke swiftly. "Remember that I saved you from drowning. You *owe* me, Sylvanus!"

He scowled, forced to recall his terror when he had fallen into the deep pool in the grove. Yes, he did owe her his life, for his kind was supposed to haunt water, and therefore to have no fear of it, but he was the only one who couldn't swim! However, greater than his dread of water was his dread of his master's fury should any of this business with the Englishmen come to light.

Teresa was persuasive, for she was determined to have her revenge for what had been done to her tonight. "Provided you do it as we agreed, no one else will ever know anything."

Sylvanus shuffled reluctantly. "Oh, all right," he said at last.

"It must be both of them, mind, for the duke did but carry out what his equally vile cousin has thought of doing ever since they entered my mother's house. They are as bad as each other and must both be punished."

Sylvanus was a little perturbed. "Are you *quite* sure it was the duke who assaulted you? I mean, he doesn't seem the sort of man who would stoop to such a thing, but his cousin, oh, yes, *he* is one I can well imagine would force himself upon a woman."

"It was the duke—I recognized him," Teresa insisted.

Sylvanus gave in reluctantly. "Very well, if you are so certain . . ."

"I am."

"It will be done at dawn." A wind sprang up along the Riviero de Chiaia, and Sylvanus glanced toward the wooded heights above the city. "It's time I went back to sleep. I shouldn't be down here at all, and without sufficient sleep I'm not as vigilant as I should be."

He turned to push his way through the crowds. As he went, the hem of his sweeping cloak lifted, revealing his rough brown goat fur and cloven hooves, for Sylvanus was a faun, and the master he served was great Bacchus himself. Fauns were able to cause uncontrollable desire between men and women who might otherwise loathe each other, and they could turn men to stone; at dawn he would be lying in wait for the two Englishmen, ready to use the latter power to exact a terrible fate upon them both.

Chapter Four

The dawn air was cool as Gervase and Hugh rode up the track behind the church with the broken spire. Both men wore winter clothes, Gervase the greatcoat that had led Teresa to believe him to be her assailant, and Hugh a mock-military coat for which he still owed his tailor. Gervase wished he hadn't allowed Hugh to persuade him to come on what might prove a hazardous exercise, but it was too late now.

Behind them the moonlit bay was dotted with the torches of fishing boats, and Naples itself was still ablaze with lights. The city rose from the quays, tier upon tier of houses that in daylight were bright terra-cotta, yellow, coral, and parchment, and from time to time occasional distant fireworks could still be heard. But up here the only sound that really mattered was the disturbing rumble of Vesuvius to the east.

Violets and anemones scented the air as the track wound up through groves of oranges and olives, then the shadows became purple and mysterious as evergreen trees, oak, and cypress closed in around the track. The atmosphere was strange and alien, and the horses were nervous, tossing their heads now and then as if something frightening lurked nearby. At last the track petered out into nothing, seeming to offer no certain way to go—except back down the mountainside. The trees whispered all around, and suddenly the lights of Naples were nowhere to be seen.

Gervase reined in to scan the gently moving foliage, and his breath was silvery in the dawn cold. A shiver passed through him. "Fanciful thoughts come more easily in places such as this. I vow I can almost believe in Pan's power to strike unreasoning terror into men's hearts." He removed his hat to run his fingers through his hair, then looked at Hugh. "Right, Coz, this is *your* expedition, so which direction do you select? Back to the Riviero de Chiaia, I hope?"

"That Sylvanus fellow said we would find our way straight to our destination, and having come this far, I intend to test his claims," Hugh replied.

"So he did, and if one believes that, one will believe anything, including the existence of Ariadne's diadem." Gervase smiled.

Hugh flushed. "I'm not here because I believe in any diadem."

"No, *we're* here because *you* were drunk and allowed yourself to be goaded." As he replaced his hat, Gervase recalled those moments at the inn. Just why had the stranger set out to lure them up here? Maybe it would prove to be an ambush after all, but somehow he didn't think so. No doubt all would soon be revealed. He kicked his heel to move his horse on, but the animal balked, and so he dismounted. "It seems my nag doesn't wish to proceed," he murmured, tying the reins to a low-hanging branch.

"Flea-bitten Neapolitan jades," Hugh muttered, alighting as well.

The two men made little sound as they walked through the springy grass. In spite of the night chill, the scent of flowers was almost heady, especially the violets that bloomed so freely in the hollows. The trees moved softly overhead, and Vesuvius grumbled in the distance, but then the sound of trickling water carried to their ears. Instinctively they made toward the sound, and suddenly the trees thinned into a grove where a spring splashed gently into a deep shining pool.

Gervase smiled. "Behold, the sylvan resting place of Ariadne's diadem," he said softly.

"It's just a grove," Hugh observed disappointedly, although what else he had expected he didn't know.

They approached the pool and looked down at the shimmering surface, from where the moon and stars gazed back as clearly as if from another universe. Suddenly the hitherto constant rumble of Vesuvius was briefly stilled, and in the fleeting silence Gervase thought he heard something.

He put a hand on Hugh's arm. "Do you hear that?"

"What? Oh, you mean Vesuvius has stopped. Yes, I hear."

"No, it's something else. There it is again. It's like . . . well, it's like someone snoring."

Hugh gave him a look. "Someone *snoring*? You're imagining things."

Vesuvius's rumble recommenced, and Gervase heard nothing more.

Hugh bent to dip his hand in the pool to drink, and as he did so, something in the depths caught his eyes. "Good God," he gasped, staring down.

"What is it?"

"There's something down there—I can see it glittering. There are colors—red, green, blue." Hugh straightened excitedly. "The diadem! Gervase, it's the diadem!"

"Hugh, you're still in your cups, there *is* no diadem."

Hugh pointed into the pool. "Look down there and still say that," he challenged.

With a sigh Gervase did as he was asked, and to his astonishment saw a small rainbow of iridescent colors that had nothing to do with the stars.

Hugh clutched his shoulder excitedly. "You have to go down for it, Gervase!"

"Me?"

"Yes, you can dive better than I can, and besides, we both know I'm less than sober."

"Yes, but . . ."

"Do it, Gervase, otherwise we'll never know. What if it *is* Ariadne's diadem?"

Gervase hesitated, but then began to unbutton his greatcoat. The dawn air made him shudder as he undressed, but he knew Hugh was right—unless they examined it in full now, they would wonder ever after what it had been. Taking a deep breath, he dove into the icy water, cutting the surface so cleanly that he hardly made a sound.

Down and down he swam, his skin taut with the shock of the cold. His lungs felt as if they would burst by the time he was within reach of the enticing little rainbow. His questing fingers closed over a hard, intricate surface that was wedged tightly between two rocks. He tugged, and at first it wouldn't budge, but suddenly it came away in his hand, and he kicked for the surface.

He burst into the pale gray air again, waved the trophy aloft, then swam to the bank to toss it onto the grass at Hugh's feet. There Ariadne's diadem lay, its gold gleaming, its precious stones ablaze in the early light. It was still perfect, as if it had fallen in the water but a few minutes earlier.

Hugh stared at it, then looked incredulously at Gervase, who was still in the water. "Dear God above . . ." he breathed.

Gervase stared at it, too. The magnificent craftsmanship was ancient, and it was studded with jewels so rare that he could not begin to identify some of them. Even if it wasn't the wedding crown that had slipped from Ariadne's dying fingers, it was certainly a priceless treasure from the time of the Romans.

Hugh picked it up with trembling hands. "Sweet Jesu," he whispered, his eyes gleaming with anticipation of the fortune such an item would fetch.

Gervase reached up to him. "Help me out," he said.

Hugh hardly heard, for excitement suddenly bubbled so irrepressibly through him that he laughed and gave a loud whoop of triumph.

The sound echoed around the grove, awakening Sylvanus in his hiding place among the roots of a tree. The faun sat up sharply on his snug bed of leaves, and in the process banged his little horns and pointed ears on a protruding root. For a moment his rather comical face was a picture of sleepy confusion, but then his dreams of pursuing and ravishing nymphs fled, as with a start he realized that the diadem he was supposed to guard with his life was in danger. He should have been lying in wait for the two Englishmen, not sleeping! With a bleat of dismay and fury he scrambled out into the dawn-lit grove, making so much noise that both men heard.

Hugh thought he saw one of the *lazzaroni* in costume, but Gervase's lips parted as he beheld the creature with the head and upper body of a man, and the legs and tail of a goat. Since the night began he had seen revelers dressed this way, but this was no disguise; what he was seeing now was the real thing!

Still bleating, Sylvanus scampered toward Hugh, his hands outstretched to grab the diadem. In the brief ensuing grapple, during which Hugh held on tightly to the prize, the frenzied faun slithered close to the water's edge. Gervase had the presence of mind to seize one of the creature's cloven hooves and haul him into the pool. Struggling in alarm as his lower half was dragged into the water he dreaded so much, Sylvanus pointed a quivering finger toward Gervase. Mystical words in a strange, unknown language began to ring shrilly from the faun's lips.

Gervase clung to the bank with one hand and stretched the other desperately toward Hugh. "For God's sake, help me out!" he cried.

But an instinct for self-preservation cut through the remains of Hugh's alcoholic haze. He had no intention of putting himself at risk in order to save his loathed cousin, and with sudden, savage decision, he brought his heel crashing down upon the hand Gervase was using to hold the grass.

Gervase let go with a gasp of pain and disbelief, and his eyes cleared in a moment of final understanding of the depth of loathing and jealousy that had always consumed Hugh. Then the faun finished his dreadful incantation, and as Hugh began to run for his life with the diadem, the blood became slow and cold in Gervase's veins. His limbs began to petrify. His flesh turned to the whitest of marble, and there was nothing he could do, no movement he could make, but his mind was still alert and clear as he sank slowly to the bottom of the pool. He'd become as perfect a Roman statue as any yet found.

Hugh glanced back in time to see Sylvanus trying to clamber from the water, but no sign of Gervase. Had he drowned? What other explanation was there? He ran on and didn't look back again as he reached the horses. Within moments he was riding like the wind for Naples, still telling himself that it was a mere mortal who'd attacked them.

Sylvanus was desperate to pursue Hugh, but his frantic scrambling only made the bank so muddy that his clawing fingers found nothing to grip. The dawn was lightening by the moment, and he wasn't permitted to leave the grove in daylight. Hugh was going to escape with the diadem! With a huge effort the faun tried to think sensibly, and after a moment edged farther along the bank until he reached a dry portion, then he pulled himself out next to Gervase's discarded clothes. But he knew it was already too late to chase Hugh, for there was too much light.

The guardian of the grove lay facedown on the grass, his hands clenched into frustrated, frightened fists. How was he going to explain his incompetence and stupidity to Bacchus? The gravest of punishment lay ahead, for the god was going to be very angry.

Sylvanus got up and with a spurt of anger kicked Gervase's costly clothes across the grass. Then, his little goat tail down, he crept despondently back to his hiding place. There he curled up in a ball on his bed of leaves.

Sylvanus hastened secretly to Naples as soon as darkness fell again and was dismayed to learn from Teresa that Hugh had already taken passage for England. Gervase's disappearance had been explained by a very convincing tale of an ill-fated nighttime excursion to Vesuvius, during which Gervase had slipped and fallen into the smoking, red-hot crater. The British consul had believed the story, and so had the Neapolitan officials whose palms had been discreetly crossed with silver, in order that a death certificate would be issued the same day. Hugh had been able to set sail immediately, not only with the priceless diadem, but also with every hope of becoming the next Duke of Wroxford. Sylvanus knew there was nothing more he could do, and so returned dejectedly to the grove, where he collected Gervase's clothes and took them in a neat bundle to his lair to await Bacchus. But it was to be two long months before retribution came.

And while Hugh made good his escape to England to claim his cousin's wealth and title, Gervase remained at the bottom of the pool, fronds of weed wafting gently around him. He was marble to the very heart and believed he would remain there forever.

Chapter Five

Hugh arrived in London on a fine April day a week or so before Anne's birthday. He found a capital that was ringing to the news of the betrothal of Princess Charlotte, heiress to the throne, and Prince Leopold of Saxe-Coburg, the Prince of Orange having been supplanted in her affections. The wedding was set to take place at the beginning of May, and the jostling for invitations was quite shocking. Also shocking were the rumors about the famous poet Lord Byron, whose wife had left him because his dealings with his half sister were of such an intimate nature, but none of this meant anything to Hugh, whose preoccupation was solely upon the golden future that had suddenly opened up before him. With this in mind, he swiftly secured a meeting with his late uncle's lawyer, Mr. Critchley, senior partner of Messrs. Critchley, Faulkner, Oliver, and Danby.

Lilac was in full bloom, just as it had been in Naples in February, and the air was warm and pleasant as Hugh strolled through Mayfair to keep the appointment. He was the picture of restrained mourning elegance. Weepers trailed from his arms, and his eyes were suitably downcast, but he hummed lightheartedly because he was entirely without conscience regarding the cousin he believed had drowned at the hands of a deformed Neapolitan beggar. In fact, it would be true to say that he was probably the happiest man alive, because not only was he sure of Gervase's title and wealth, but also of Kitty Longton.

She had taken only a few hours to woo once she discovered that he now had every expectation of being confirmed as the next Duke of Wroxford. Suddenly, the formerly *un*interesting Hugh Mowbray was very interesting indeed, although her final capitulation had not been the matter of abandoned passion it appeared, for it followed his frustrated and rash declaration that if she would only be his, he would make her his duchess the moment a decent period of mourning for Gervase had been observed. Hugh didn't suspect her of the same cold calculation he himself displayed; indeed he was so besotted that he believed her when she swore she had finally realized he was the one she had loved all along. In truth, he and Kitty Longton were splendidly matched, for they were both so deeply unpleasant that they fully deserved each other.

Since leaving Naples, his only disappointment had been the diadem, and—had he known it—this was simply due to an error by a jeweler's assistant. The person in question had imbibed too much at luncheon and was alone in the fashionable Bond Street shop when Hugh entered. After casting his somewhat blurred vision over the rare stones and priceless workmanship, the assistant declared the diadem to be a paltry item of little consequence. Since the shop in question was second only to the royal jewelers, Hugh did not doubt that he was being told the truth, so without seeking a second opinion he disappointedly returned the matchless piece to the pocket in his traveling valise and forgot all about it.

Ariadne's wedding crown therefore did not figure anywhere in his thoughts as he was shown up to Mr. Critchley's second-floor room. The portly, red-faced lawyer presided at a vast desk, behind which was a window with a fine view over Hyde Park, where the sun had attracted a throng of fashionable carriages and riders. Mr. Critchley and his partners boasted the most exclusive clientele in London—mere honorables hardly figured at all—which meant that where Hugh was concerned the lawyer was at first guilty of a certain snobbish condescension. His attitude swiftly improved at the revelation that the "grief-stricken" young gentleman in black was not merely the nephew of the seventh Duke of Wroxford and the cousin of the eighth, but apparently the *ninth* duke himself! From that moment the startled lawyer listened very attentively indeed to the harrowing tale of how Gervase had met his demise in the mouth of Vesuvius.

When Hugh finished, Mr. Critchley wiped his forehead with a silk handkerchief. "What a tragedy, what a terrible, terrible tragedy," he muttered, pouring two glasses of brandy from the decanter on his desk.

"If I had been more agile, maybe I would have been able to save him, but my foot slipped, and all I could do was watch as he fell into the crater." Hugh managed to make his voice catch, then reached inside his coat for one of the cigars he'd been careful to filch from Gervase's things before leaving Naples. "I trust you do not mind if I smoke? I find it calms my distress."

"Of course, sir, of course." The lawyer got up to light a spill at the fire, and held it for Hugh, who made certain his hand trembled convincingly. His acting was accomplished, for the lawyer pressed one of the brandy glasses concernedly into his other hand. "Drink this, sir, for you have suffered a dreadful ordeal. I can understand that you blame yourself, but there was clearly nothing you could do. Vesuvius chose to claim the duke, and that is the end of it."

"I fear so," Hugh replied, draining his glass in one gulp.

"Well, the death certificate issued in Naples cannot be argued with, and in the absence of any other heirs, you, my dear sir, are now the ninth Duke of Wroxford."

"It is not an inheritance I accept gladly, Mr. Critchley," Hugh declared sanctimoniously.

"I realize that, for you are still consumed with grief for the cousin you loved, but nevertheless it is your duty to accept your destiny."

"I realize that," Hugh answered earnestly.

The lawyer resumed his seat and toyed thoughtfully with the stem of his glass. "There is one problem—at least, it *may* be a problem. Tell me, is there a lady in your life, sir?"

"A lady?" Hugh repeated blankly.

"Are you married? Betrothed, maybe? Or do you have an understanding with anyone?"

Hugh became very still. "Why do you ask?"

"No doubt you knew that your late lamented cousin was to have been engaged to Miss Anne Willowby of Llandower in Monmouthshire?"

"Yes." Hugh was puzzled. Where was this leading?

"Well, the match was a condition of the seventh duke's will, and although the eighth duke died before the betrothal actually took place, I'm afraid the stipulation remains in force as far as you are concerned."

Hugh was thunderstruck. "I beg your pardon?"

"In order to inherit, you will have to marry Miss Willowby."

Hugh stared at him. "If this is a jest . . ."

"No jest, sir, merely a statement of legal fact. To inherit the Wroxford title and fortune, you must make Miss Willowby your bride." The lawyer spread his hands apologetically. "I fear that is how it must be, sir."

The ash fell from the end of Hugh's cigar. His mind was racing, for this certainly had no place in his scheme of things. "Isn't there *any* way out of it?" he asked then.

"Sir, if there was, you may be assured that your late cousin would have found it." Mr. Critchley's displeased gaze followed the gray-white ash to the floor, where it scattered only too visibly upon the costly Axminster carpet. The lawyer cleared his throat. "Do I take it that you consent?" he asked after a moment.

Hugh could only nod, for what other choice did he have?

"I will write to Llandower immediately. Shall I inform the Willowbys that you will leave within a day or so?"

"Leave? For Llandower, you mean?"

"Yes."

"Whatever for? My cousin certainly wasn't obliged to go there." Hugh intended to postpone things as long as possible.

Mr. Critchley shifted a little uncomfortably. "Forgive me for having to point this out, sir, but your cousin was wealthy in his own right—through his mother—so he could afford to delay. I fear you do not have the same . . . er, cushion, so to speak . . . so you do not get anything until the clause is met."

Hugh knew when he was up against it. "Oh, very well, yes, I will leave within a day or so." He was mindful of his wish to appear in a good light, so he went on. "Maybe it would be appropriate if I wrote as well? If I use your facilities here, it can be sent with your letter." And it will cost me nothing, was the unspoken addendum.

Mr. Critchley was impressed. "Excellent. By the way, perhaps I could presume to recommend a certain hostelry in the neighborhood of Llandower? It's called the White Boar, and although five miles away, is a clean and comfortable establishment with an excellent table. I know of it because my widowed and somewhat eccentric sister fancies herself a writer of Gothic novels and has become a devoted Wye Valley sightseer in recent years. The area is a magnet for artists, poets, and writers of all description, for it possesses the requisite gorges, mountains, rapids, castles on crags, lush meadows, and woodland, et cetera. She always stays at the White Boar and speaks of it most highly."

"Then I will stay there too, sir. Thank you for your advice."

"Not at all, sir, not at all."

They both rose to shake hands, but as he went to the door Hugh paused, glancing down at his cigar as if searching for the right words to say something exceedingly delicate. "Mr. Critchley, I am curious to know what would happen if . . . heaven forfend . . . Miss Willowby should expire? I mean, we now know that the clause applies to whoever becomes heir to the dukedom, but what of the lady? Will *her* heir—a sister perhaps—have to obey it as well?"

The lawyer was a little startled. "No, the will is most specific in naming Miss Willowby as the bride concerned, so her demise would negate the clause entirely. Where the bridegroom is concerned, however, it merely refers to the heir to the dukedom. So if you in turn were to pass on, which also heaven forfend, of course, the dukedom will become extinct."

Hugh did not hum beneath his breath as he strode bitterly back to Kitty's house in Knightsbridge. His cane lashed angrily from side to side, and his fashionable spurs rang on the fine pavement as he considered the full implication of his late uncle's will. At first he contemplated making himself so obnoxious that not even regard for her beloved father would induce the Willowby woman to throw herself onto such an odious marital pyre. But such a course offered an uncertain conclusion, for what if, come what may, she remained determined on the match? Then there was Kitty to consider. The advent of another bride was bound to mean forfeiting the sensuous favors he had lusted after for so long and had only just begun to enjoy! The answer was simple. Anne Willowby had to go.

When he arrived at the house and told Kitty what had happened, she wasn't at all pleased; indeed she was so beside herself at having her dream snatched from under her nose again, that it took a great deal of persuading to prevent her from immediately having him thrown out. The chestnut-haired actress was hardly able to believe that once more she was apparently being cast aside because a titled lover needed to marry elsewhere, and in furious silence she swept up to her rose brocade boudoir, intending to slam the door in Hugh's face should he dare to follow. He pushed his way past, and they faced each other at the foot of the sumptuously draped four-poster in which she had given her all to an unconscionably long list of gentlemen. A rather florid watercolor hung above the headboard, depicting a bacchanalia of naked nymphs and other mythical beings cavorting in a grove, and from behind one of the trees there peered a creature very like the beggar in the grove above Naples. Its eyes seemed to rest mockingly on Hugh as he implored the furious actress not to reject him.

Still too angry to trust herself to speak, Kitty flounced to the window and twitched the lace curtain aside to look down at some boys playing with hoops in the street below. Her rich red-gold hair spilled smoothly about her shoulders, and her primrose muslin robe parted to reveal a shapely thigh. Her full, pink-tipped breasts were clearly visible through the diaphanous material, as was the slenderness of her tiny waist. She was twenty-six years old and unbelievably beautiful, but the sweetness of her visage belied the sourness within. There was nothing soft or caring about her, nothing gentle or endearing, just a magnetic voluptuousness she didn't hesitate to use to her own advantage. Most men found her irresistible, unless, like Gervase, they discovered what she had caused to happen to her tragic little brother.

Hugh was at last able to put into words the thoughts he'd had on leaving Mr. Critchley. "Kitty, I swear you will have the world itself if you will only wait until I can bring about Anne Willowby's demise."

Kitty's lustrous hazel eyes swung from the boys, one of whom reminded her sharply of her brother. "Bring about her demise?" she repeated incredulously, a hand creeping to the creamy expanse of bosom revealed by the plunging décolletage of her robe.

"Yes, for it is the only certain way of being rid of her."

"You're prepared to go to such a length?" Incredulousness began to give way to a thrill of erotic excitement.

"I will do anything to keep you, Kitty."

"I've never had a man want me *that* much," she breathed. A new light had begun to gleam in her eyes, but then her gaze sharpened once more. "When will you do it?" she demanded.

"I swear it will not be long. I have undertaken to leave for Llandower within a few days."

"Do you promise you will do it?"

"Yes, oh, yes," he whispered.

She smiled a little. "I really believe you will," she murmured.

Encouraged, he ventured to approach her, slipping his arms around her waist and burying his face in her hair. "I want you, Kitty," he whispered, becoming aroused by the perfumed softness of her body through the diaphanous robe.

She pressed back against him. "And you'll still make me your duchess?"

"Yes, oh, yes . . ." His hands moved up to cup her full breasts. She pushed her nipples into his palms, savoring the desire kindled by his wicked promise, and his arousal became almost unendurable. "Oh, Kitty, Kitty . . ."

She turned to link her arms around his neck. "Make love to me, Your Grace," she whispered.

He caught her up in his arms and bore her to the bed, where she lay with impatient eagerness, her fiery copper hair spreading over the pillows. Hugh was conscious of the watercolor and the creature gazing at him from behind the tree, but he didn't glance up as he hastily tore off his clothes, then lowered himself into Kitty's waiting arms.

Chapter Six

Several days later, Anne was on the point of setting out for a late ride when the letters arrived from London. She had been kept busy all day with problems on the estate, and had just spent three long hours in her father's study composing letters to importunate creditors who had heard of her match and thought the Willowbys were suddenly overladen with wealth, so she was in much need of a little relaxation. She wore her nasturtium riding habit and a black top hat from which trailed a long white lace scarf, and she was just pulling on her gloves by the table in the hall when Martin hurried in with the mail he'd intercepted.

The letters were both addressed to her father, but since she was empowered to act on his behalf in everything during his absence, she read them both. The contents caused her to sit down a little weakly beside the table as she tried to marshal her thoughts. Gervase was dead, and instead she was expected to marry the cousin he had accompanied to Italy? It was hard to take in. For a long moment she didn't know what to think, but then common sense prevailed. She didn't know *either* of them, and she still had to save Llandower for her father if she could, so what earthly difference did it make which man she married? That was that then—she would go to the altar with the ninth Duke of Wroxford instead of the eighth, although heaven alone knew what her parents would make of this latest development.

At least Hugh Mowbray was going to call in a few days' time, which was more than the late unlamented Gervase had ever done! She glanced again at his letter. It was couched in the sort of courteous and considerate terms she'd always looked for in vain from Gervase, and when she recalled the frosty missives tucked behind the candlestick in the drawing room, she could only hope that Hugh Mowbray lived up to the

promise that seemed evident in this single communication.
The thought of Gervase's letters dispelled any fleeting idea
she might have entertained about wearing mourning for him,
for he didn't deserve so much as a single black ribbon!

Anne knew she would have to wait until later to inform
Mrs. Jenkins of the new duke's impending visit, because the
housekeeper had gone to visit her sister in Peterbury, so she
tossed the letters on the table, then hurried out to the courtyard, where Joseph was waiting with her favorite roan mare.
The evening shadows were already beginning to lengthen as
he helped her onto the mounting block so that she could slip
easily onto the sidesaddle. After telling him she intended to
ride east to see if the bluebell wood was in full bloom yet, she
kicked her heel and urged the mare out of the courtyard. But
she hadn't ridden far when she changed her mind about the
bluebells, for she'd set out later than she intended and
wouldn't reach the woods before darkness fell. So instead she
decided to ride north along the river as far as the bridge carrying the Peterbury road.

The Wye was beautiful at any time of year, but it was particularly so in April when the hawthorn was in bloom and the
meadows were full of cowslips. She reined in for a while by
the jetty, where willows draped their fresh-leaved fronds in
the current and tall reeds swayed in the slightest breeze. The
rowing boats bumped together from time to time, as if impatient to skim out on the swift water again, and flowers filled
the spring evening with fragrance. Suddenly, she remembered
her seventh birthday and the wonderful moonlight picnic she
and her parents had enjoyed on the jetty. After a fine feast
prepared by Mrs. Jenkins, they'd rowed a few hundred yards
downstream to the medieval stone-edged spring known as St.
Winifred's Well, which lay on the opposite bank just before
the river formed white rapids as it carved its way through a
rocky but leafy gorge. Everyone had enjoyed it so much that
the exercise had been repeated every year since . . . until now.
Sadness swept over her then, for she knew that once she was
Duchess of Wroxford, there would never again be a birthday
picnic on the jetty or a moonlight trip to St. Winifred's Well.

She glanced at Llandower. If there was a paradise on earth,
it was here, she thought, and it was up to her to do all in her
power to save it for her father. She wondered how her parents
were. Was the visit to Ireland going well? Or was it an unmit-

igated disaster? She wished she knew, but there hadn't been any word at all since they'd left.

She rode on, observed only by the cattle that grazed in the rich meadows. The sun's rays were slanting with crimson when the bridge came into view several hundred yards ahead, and everything was so calm and peaceful that it seemed nothing could possibly happen. But happen it did, for suddenly there was a flash of lightning—at least she thought it was lightning. The mare reared, and Anne screamed as she was flung from the saddle. The Wye flashed in the setting sun as she fell on the very edge of the bank. She wasn't hurt and wanted to get up again immediately, but a strange lassitude came over her. It was a delicious, irresistible weariness, and she had to close her eyes and sleep. The last thing she remembered was the heady scent of cowslips and the sound of the mare returning to Llandower.

It was no ordinary sleep, of course, and far from being a natural occurrence, the lightning was the result of divine intervention, for at the very moment Anne had set out for her ride, in far-off Italy an angry Bacchus had come at last to punish Sylvanus for what had happened to Ariadne's diadem.

The Mediterranean evening had already closed in as the ever-young god of wine, pleasure, and wild nature arrived in the grove to deal with his bungling minion. Tall, handsome, and dazzlingly golden, the purple-robed deity led a panther on a silver chain and was attended by a mischievous retinue of scores of fauns. A wreath of vine and ivy leaves around his forehead, he carried a long wand topped by a bunch of myrtle, and his eyes were ablaze with fury as he commanded Sylvanus to come forth from his hiding place.

The terrified faun crawled out on all fours, and his goat tail trembled in the air as he pressed his face to the grass. "Have pity on me, oh, mighty Bacchus, oh, Great One . . ." he whimpered.

The panther growled, and Sylvanus forgot his fear for a moment in order to give the animal a look of loathing. As far as he was concerned, it was little more than a large tomcat with airs and graces above its station.

Bacchus poked Sylvanus with his wand. "Save your attention for me, Faun!"

Sylvanus cowered again, and the gathered fauns began to

snigger at his discomfort, although they were immediately silenced by Bacchus's baleful glare. Then the god stretched out a foot and pushed Sylvanus to the edge of the pool. "You've let me down, Sylvanus," he accused.

"F-forgive me, Master," Sylvanus whimpered, eyeing both the god and the shining water that was once again within inches of him.

"Forgive you? Why should I do that? Your task was to guard the grove, but you failed! Now my Sweet One's crown has been taken, and all because of your folly, Faun! Can you give me one good reason why I should spare you?"

"Give me one more chance, Lord, and I vow I will redeem myself!" Sylvanus pleaded.

Bacchus bent to stroke the panther. "You are not a cat with nine lives, Faun, merely a worthless creature who has displeased me. Your time has come."

Sylvanus squeaked with terror and hid his face again. "Please! I beg of you! Remember that the Lady Ariadne liked me, and would not wish to see me die!"

Bacchus had raised his staff, but then paused. "You presume by mentioning her name," he breathed, glancing up at the deep turquoise sky, where the first evening stars had begun to appear. He had commemorated his adored Ariadne in the constellation known as the Corona Borealis, named after the very wedding diadem this inept failure of a faun had allowed to be stolen!

Sylvanus's tail shook with dread. "Let me save the diadem for you, Liege, let me go after the Englishman and punish him as I punished the duke!"

"That is another thing. The man you turned to marble is innocent of attacking the woman Teresa."

Dismayed, Sylvanus clasped his arms over his head. His goat tail became very still, and he drew his hooved feet up until he could have been rolled into the pool like a ball.

Bacchus snapped his fingers and nodded at one of the other fauns, who immediately ran to Sylvanus's hiding place and returned with Gervase's clothes, which were placed respectfully at the god's feet. The silver buttons of the greatcoat winked in the half-light, their maze pattern very clear to see. "Ah, the defenses of Troy, how well I remember them," the god murmured, touching one of the buttons with the end of his staff. A flood of knowledge immediately swept through him. He saw the maze at Llandower Castle and the old duke issuing his ultimatum to Anne. He saw Gervase being told he must marry Anne if he wished to retain his inheritance. He saw how very much the match was resented by the man who now lay entombed in marble at the bottom of the pool, and he saw also Hugh, the new Duke of Wroxford, lying in the arms of Kitty Longton. Last but not least he saw Anne riding through the early evening sun along the bank of the Wye.

A thoughtful expression entered the god's eyes, and he prodded the terrified faun. "Get up," he commanded.

Sylvanus couldn't move.

"Get up!" Bacchus ordered, poking him more harshly.

Sylvanus uncurled and rose unwillingly to his hooves, then stood with his head bowed as he awaited sentence.

"You're right to remind me that my Sweet One liked you, and for her sake I will indeed give you another chance, but don't think I intend to let you off lightly." Bacchus hooked the greatcoat with the end of his staff and tossed it toward Sylvanus, who caught it. "Touch one of the buttons," the god commanded.

Sylvanus obeyed, and the knowledge flooded through him, too.

"There are conditions to be met before you will have fully redeemed yourself in my eyes, Faun. You will go to the place called Llandower Castle, where the diadem will soon be brought. It must be given *willingly* into your hands, do you understand?"

"Yes, Master."

"But before you can receive the diadem, you must help the other man complete *his* task."

"What other man?" Sylvanus was puzzled.

The god pointed at the water. "The wrong cousin was punished for what was done to the woman Teresa, but even so he *was* guilty of trying to steal the diadem, so I am going to send him to England as well. He will have to assume a new identity and win the heart of the bride he treated so badly. He will remain a statue by day, but at night will be turned into flesh and blood again in order to woo her. Without ever knowing who he really is, she must tell him she loves him. It will not be easy to make her confess, for she is a young woman of great integrity who now considers herself honor-bound to the man called Hugh. There is only one circumstance that will afford any advantage at the moment—the lady is temporarily alone because her parents have gone to Dublin. There will be several days, or rather nights, before Hugh arrives."

"What if she cannot be won?"

"Then the duke will remain a statue throughout eternity, and you, Faun, will stay in England with him, provided I spare your miserable hide, that is," the god said harshly, and the other fauns sniggered again, for they always took mean delight in each other's misfortune.

Sylvanus swallowed, resigned to what lay ahead. "What is to happen to the man called Hugh?" he asked then.

"His fate I will leave to you and the duke. If you both succeed in your allotted tasks, you will have the pleasure of punishing him as you both see fit."

Sylvanus shuffled his hooves. "When are you sending us?"

"At this very moment," Bacchus replied. "However, first I must make one thing clear. You are not to employ your power to make men and women irresistibly drawn to each other. What the duke achieves must be done without your intervention, is that clear?"

"Yes, Master."

Bacchus pointed his staff at the grass and conjured into existence a marble plinth that was about four inches high. Then he pointed the staff at the pool. "I grant you the power of communication, Englishman. Have you heard everything?"

Gervase had indeed heard and was able to reply through thought. *"Yes."*

The answer seeped up through the pool to Bacchus and the fauns. "Do you accept my conditions?" the god inquired.

"Yes." Gervase felt he had no choice; besides, it offered the only way to escape from this dreadful petrified imprisonment.

Bacchus waved his staff, and the water bubbled and seethed as Gervase began to rise slowly to the surface. Naked, white, and dripping, with weeds draped around his arms and another more private portion of his anatomy, he was suspended in midair for a moment, before being drawn to the bank and deposited on the low plinth, for all the world as if he graced the garden of a villa in ancient Rome. He gazed in amazement at the golden magnificence of the young god, whom he had expected would be a much older personage, grown fat from a surfeit of wine. He was also startled to see the immense gathering of fauns peering curiously at him from behind their master. The panther growled, and Gervase flinched, at least he would have done so had he been capable of even the slightest movement.

Bacchus eyed him critically from head to toe, then used his staff to remove the water weed that was draped so embarrassingly around Gervase's more outstanding lower regions. "Hardly Hercules, but nevertheless a fine enough specimen of humanity," he conceded, "although whether Miss Anne Willowby will ever think so remains to be seen."

"Is there no other way I may make amends for my part in the theft of the diadem? Must I really win her love?" Gervase asked.

"Yes, you must, but be warned that you have been wrong to dismiss her as a schemer." Bacchus told him briefly about Anne's reasons for entering into the match, knowledge of which he had absorbed from the buttons on the greatcoat.

Gervase felt chastened, for he'd said some very harsh things about her. *"I concede that I was at fault, but can you tell me why my father chose her in the first place?"*

Bacchus smiled. "Oh, yes. Her great probity revived memories of his first wife."

So that was it. Gervase's mind cleared. His mother was his father's second wife and had always known that she stood in the shadow of her predecessor.

Bacchus turned to Sylvanus. "Well, Faun, it is time to commence. Pick up the duke's clothes."

The faun obeyed.

"Now climb upon his back."

Sylvanus gaped. "Climb? But—"

"It is the only way to be absolutely certain you both arrive in exactly the same place at exactly the same moment. Climb!" The god's staff quivered at the faun, who hastened to do as he was told. It was no easy matter with an armful of clothes and a pair of riding boots to contend with, for his cloven hooves found little purchase, but at last he managed to haul himself up to put his arms around Gervase's neck and his furry goat legs around his waist, and stuff the clothes between himself and the cold marble.

Bacchus looked at Gervase. "By the way, I have caused Miss Willowby to fall from her horse and then into a deep sleep perilously close to a riverbank. She will slip into the water and drown unless you reach her quickly. Do not forget that she must live if you are to be released."

As both Gervase and Sylvanus wondered to what purpose the god had done such a thing, Bacchus gestured again with his staff, and a great wind sprang up from what had been utterly still. The flowing purple robe billowed, and the company of fauns shrank together as the water of the pool was whipped up into countless little waves. Sylvanus clung on with all his might, and Gervase felt the plinth shudder a little, then suddenly the wind snatched them both, whirling them high into the evening sky.

There was a roaring and rushing of air, and Naples and its bay fell away behind. The twist of smoke from Vesuvius meandered heavenward for a time, but then Italy itself was lost from view as they swept northwest. They were so high that the air was bitterly cold, but although Gervase felt nothing through his shell of marble, poor Sylvanus's teeth chattered. He bleated wretchedly, scrabbling with his hooves as he lost his grip for a moment. How he wished he was back in his cozy hiding place. More than that, how he wished he could swim, for then he would never have landed in Teresa del Rosso's debt, and none of this would have happened!

A journey which should have taken weeks was over in a few minutes. Suddenly, England was below them, clearly visible in the northern twilight. Sylvanus peered down at an alien landscape of neat fields, lush meadows, and scattered villages, with trees that were just beginning to show their cloaks of spring green. They flew above a river that flowed from north to south like a silver ribbon, through a beautiful tree-clad valley that was sometimes rich farmland, sometimes tree-hung cliffs and rocks. Sylvanus saw a gorge with white rapids, a dell with a stone-edged spring, then a house in grounds where there was a maze that was laid out in the same pattern as Gervase's buttons. In the very center of the maze stood the sort of little white rotunda that cried out for the finishing touch of a statue, and Sylvanus knew instinctively where Bacchus intended them to end their journey.

They plummeted downward, spinning and swinging wildly from side to side as if some great power were trying to pinpoint an exact spot. In the final moments the faun looked upstream and dimly saw a young woman in a nasturtium riding habit lying on the very lip of the riverbank, then to the east he saw two bobbing lanterns as old Joseph, Martin, and the lurcher set out in the wrong direction toward the bluebell woods to look for Anne, whose riderless horse had returned only moments before.

Gervase and Sylvanus arrived with a thud on the floor of the rotunda. After the rushing of air, suddenly everything was silent. Beyond the maze rose the moonlit rooftops and battlements of Llandower Castle, and in the distance they could hear the searchers calling Anne's name.

Chapter Seven

The rotunda consisted of a domed roof supported on elegant Corinthian columns, and between two of them it was walled to provide some protection from the prevailing southwesterly winds. Otherwise it was open to the elements, which Sylvanus knew only too well as he slithered down from Gervase's back.

For an English spring evening, the temperature was mild and pleasant, but a faun from the Mediterranean found it disagreeably damp and cold. His teeth chattered as he hastily donned Gervase's greatcoat, which was far too big for him, before taking the rest of the clothes and throwing them across an ivy-covered stone bench that stood in the shelter of the walled portion of the rotunda. Then he paused for a moment, sniffing the air a little curiously before he turned to Gervase and brought him to life by reversing the magic words he'd used in the grove.

"Come on, for your Miss Willowby is in danger. I saw where she is, so I know which way to go," the faun said, and trotted to the edge of the rotunda, where he waited impatiently for Gervase to dress in the now rather crumpled pine green riding coat and cream breeches.

Gervase felt oddly normal as he pulled on his top boots. He wasn't stiff or awkward; indeed it was as if he hadn't been marble at all. He straightened at last and looked in dismay at the high, seemingly impenetrable hedges of the maze. "Miss Willowby may be in danger, but first we have to find our way out of this damned puzzle."

"It's no problem to me because I'm familiar with the defenses of Troy, but I must say I'm surprised that anyone can wear a plan of the maze on his buttons and not know it by heart."

"I don't spend my time contemplating my buttons," Gervase pointed out a little testily, fumbling with the tying of his neckcloth, which was not at all easy in the dark and without a mirror.

Sylvanus's lips twitched, but he said nothing more.

"Before we go, there's one thing I'd like to ask."

"What?"

"Why has Bacchus put Miss Willowby in such unnecessary danger?"

The faun shrugged. "I have no idea, but my master never does anything without a purpose." With that he turned up the collar of the coat and left the rotunda. His hooves crunched on the gravel, and as the costly hem of the greatcoat dragged on the ground behind him, Gervase pictured his Bond Street tailer's reaction to such sacrilege. There wouldn't be sufficient sal volatile in the whole of London to bring the poor fellow out of his swoon.

Sylvanus's sense of direction was unerring, and a few minutes later they emerged from the maze close to the archway into the castle courtyard. The castle was quiet because old Joseph and Martin were out searching for Anne, and Mrs. Jenkins had yet to return from her sister in Peterbury. An owl hooted somewhere, and the sweet-scented cowslips in the park were pale in the moonlight as the faun led the way toward the river.

Gervase found it difficult to keep up, for Sylvanus's goat legs were much faster than his own, but he didn't fall too far behind as they hurried north past the jetty and through the riverside meadows. At last the faun saw the bridge ahead and Anne lying inches above the waiting water. He thought she moved slightly, and with a muted bleat of dismay he made a greater effort, for he was only too well aware that if she fell into the river and drowned, neither he nor Gervase would be able to meet Bacchus's terms. Keeping a wary eye on the lurking river, the faun pulled Anne safely from the brink, watching her closely to see if she was about to awaken, for it wouldn't do at all if she were to come around to see him, but she seemed deeply asleep.

Gervase hurried up, and for the first time looked upon the face of the woman he had to win if he was ever to regain his true form. He saw she was slender and unremarkable, with untrammeled dark blonde curls that had escaped their pins when she'd fallen from the horse. The riding habit she wore was stylish enough, but at least three years old, and the top hat

that lay nearby wasn't quite what would have been admired in
Hyde Park, although he had to concede that he found the addition of a lace scarf, rather than the more usual muslin or
gauze, rather appealing.

The sound of hooves clattered from the road, and Sylvanus
put an urgent hand on Gervase's arm, pushing him down
among the cowslips that filled the night air with scent. They
lay there in silence as two farmers rode across the bridge.

As the hooves dwindled away into the darkness again, Gervase got up and glanced across the meadow to where a small
barn stood against the hawthorn hedge. It would afford shelter
while he and Sylvanus wondered what to do next. He still
didn't know why Bacchus had chosen to place her in such a
hazardous situation, and apart from that he hadn't had time to
invent a new identity *or* a plan for wooing her. Stooping to
gather her into his arms, he carried her to the barn, where he
rested her gently on the remains of a pile of hay from the previous year's harvest.

Sylvanus collected her hat and followed, then they both
stood looking down at her in the moonlight. The faun
hunched himself in the greatcoat. By the Furies, how cold and
hungry he was! *And* how he hated being hundreds of miles
away from Italy! He glanced out at the night, where stars now
studded the sky. At least he could see the Corona Borealis,
just as he could from his grove.

"What now?" Gervase asked.

Sylvanus shrugged. "*I* don't know; *you* are the one who
must woo her."

"Which is all very well, but I haven't had time to collect
my thoughts, let alone anything else." Gervase ran his fingers
agitatedly through his hair as he gazed down at her. From the
first moment he'd heard Anne Willowby's name, he'd been
convinced she was a brazen adventuress of some sort, certainly a schemer, but the truth was very different. He didn't
know where to begin.

The faun hung the top hat on a protruding nail and watched
Gervase a little crossly. Why did humans always make such
heavy weather out of everything? All this man had to do was
seduce a woman. There was nothing to it. Fauns seduced
nymphs all the time! Sylvanus hopped impatiently from hoof
to hoof. Gervase needed a nudge to send him on his way, and
since virginal ladies were notoriously easy to shock, it would

be simple enough to prevent this one from remembering anything. Oh, if only Bacchus hadn't forbidden him to use his power to cause overwhelming sexual desire. If it weren't for that, this whole business would be over and done with before dawn! Bacchus had to be obeyed, of course, but all the same, it was a very tempting thought. The faun's lips twitched. His master was hundreds of miles away—would he find out about a few minutes' disobedience? Sylvanus decided to take the chance, and after a sly glance up at the Corona Borealis, he snapped his fingers.

As Anne stirred and began to open her eyes, her subconscious re-created the cornfield fantasy that had always meant so much to her. As a result, the first thing Gervase felt was that the spring night had brightened into the warmth of a summer day. He seemed to be standing by a hedgerow at the edge of a waving sea of golden corn, beneath a cloudless sky where skylarks sang. His nostrils were filled with the seductive scent of honeysuckle, but as he looked into Anne's wide green gaze, he neither knew nor cared that the hour, the seasons, and even his own common sense had been turned topsy-turvy. An erotic charge swept irresistibly through him, and he knew such a powerful sense of attraction that his whole body throbbed with excitement. He was conscious of the sweet invitation of her lips and the captivating curve of her breasts beneath the tight-fitting jacket of her riding habit, and he couldn't help sinking to his knees to put a loving hand to her cheek. She sighed and moved against his fingertips, and his heart tightened with intense joy.

Gervase's face was an anonymous blur, yet Anne knew she loved him more than anyone else in the world. She was reliving the caresses seen all those years ago, and the gratification was exquisite. She smiled sensuously and began to unbutton the jacket of her riding habit. So firm and taut were her breasts that she needed no stays or other undergarments to give shape to her figure, and her nipples were pert and upturned. Her breath caught with almost feline pleasure as he cupped both in his palms. Her hand crept tentatively to his thigh, then slid slowly up to enclose the fierce erection that now strained the front of his breeches. After a few moments' hesitation, she dared to stroke the steely shaft through his clothes, and his groan of desire intensified her own. Her whole body ached for the consummation she knew was about to take place.

The exquisite sensations passing through Gervase were almost painful. He wanted to be inside her, to feel her warmth encasing him, to feel his own final capitulation. He lay down and pulled her against him, finding her lips in a kiss that flamed so fiercely through them both that he felt he would lose his senses. Her mouth was sweet, and for a moment their tongues slid together. She pressed her body to his, molding to his shape so perfectly that she might have been fashioned just for him. His erection felt as if it would explode as she moved against it.

Suddenly, out of the clear starlit sky, there came a blinding flash of lightning. It struck a tree in the hedge behind the barn and lit everything with vivid electric blue. Bacchus had been watching after all. Gervase and Anne became frozen in mid-caress, their sensuous embrace caught as if upon a canvas, and Sylvanus gave a bleat of dismay as he at last realized why his master had put Anne in danger. It had been to create the very circumstances that might tempt a foolish faun into using forbidden powers. And he, Sylvanus, had fallen into the trap!

Confirmation of this came immediately. *"You have been found wanting yet again, Faun!"* Bacchus's voice was inaudible to anyone except Sylvanus, who squeaked with dread.

"Be merciful, O Great One!" the faun begged, his teeth chattering so much he could scarcely be understood.

"I was merciful the last time," Bacchus reminded him severely.

"I've learned my lesson, I *swear*!" Sylvanus bleated tearfully.

"I doubt if you will ever learn, Faun," came the weary reply. *"Can't you be trusted to do anything—except the wrong thing?"*

"B-but if you put an end to me now, the duke will be on his own." Sylvanus could only hope to appeal to what remained of the god's better nature.

There was silence, and Sylvanus prayed that this boded well. "It won't happen again, Master, please believe me," he pleaded, his tone only just short of wheedling.

In spite of the faun's undoubted culpability, Bacchus was disposed to be charitable. *"Very well, but you have had your final warning. Disobey me again and it will definitely be the last thing you do!"*

"Yes, Master!" Sylvanus whispered with relief. He waited for the god's next words, but there was only the silence of the English spring night. The faun stole a glance up at the sky, but all was quiet again.

Then soft sighs made him glance down, and he saw that Gervase and Anne, freed from their brief immobility, were once again pursuing their white-hot passion. The faun was horrified. "Stop! Oh, please stop! Bacchus is very angry with me!" Their kisses continued unchecked, and at last he remembered to snap his fingers.

The bewitchment ceased immediately, the summer cornfield was no more, and Gervase looked around in confusion as Anne went suddenly limp in his arms and sank back into the deep sleep of before.

Sylvanus swallowed. "I'm sorry."

Gervase began to realize what had been happening, and after laying Anne gently back on the hay, and doing up her buttons again, he scrambled to his feet. He tried to muster his scattered thoughts as he stared down at her in the moonlight. What in God's name had he been thinking of? He turned furiously on the guilty faun. "That was *your* fault?" he cried.

"Yes," Sylvanus replied, unable to meet his accusing gaze.

"But what is she going to say? As soon as she comes around, she'll remember and . . ." Gervase couldn't finish, for it seemed the end of everything almost before it had begun! He'd never succeed with her after this!

"She won't recall anything, so don't worry about that. Besides, if anyone should be worried, it's me. Bacchus knows I disobeyed him and has issued a final warning."

"He knows?"

"Didn't you see the lightning? Oh, no, I suppose you wouldn't have because—" Sylvanus broke off and turned as a new sound drifted through the night. It was the swift rattle of a pony and trap approaching along the Peterbury road, and instinctively the faun knew that it signaled Anne's imminent awakening. Without further ado he grabbed her hat from the nail and ran from the barn toward the bridge. Halfway across the meadow he unwound the lace scarf and draped it prominently over a hawthorn bush, then at the bridge he tossed the top hat into the middle of the road, where the trap's lamps would pick it out immediately. Dashing back to the barn, he grabbed Gervase by the arm. "Come on, we mustn't be seen!" he cried, and together they ran along the riverbank to the hedge of the next meadow, where they hid to watch what happened.

The pony trap was conveying a rather nervous Mrs. Jenkins home after her visit to her sister. She had been chattering quite happily until the bolt of lightning startled her into silence. Now she glanced uneasily up at the flawless sky and shrank a little closer to her unruffled brother-in-law, who was too wise a countryman to be surprised at anything Mother Nature chose to do. Lightning out of a clear sky? Why not? There were stranger things at sea. So he stoically tooled the stocky pony along the lane, watching the animal's pricked ears and fat rump, but then he reined in surprisedly as the top hat was suddenly picked out by the dim beam of light from the lamps.

He climbed down to inspect the hat, and as he brought it to the lamp, Mrs. Jenkins recognized it and gave a cry of dismay as she clambered down as well. "It's Miss Anne's! Oh, no, was she struck by the lightning?"

"Don't be daft, woman, for if that had happened, she'd be lying here all crisped to a cinder!" he replied.

"Oh, mercy on us, don't say such things!" cried Mrs. Jenkins, now in more of a fluster than ever.

As they glanced around, a strong stir of wind fluttered the white scarf on the hawthorn bush. Mrs. Jenkins's dismay increased. "That's her scarf—only Miss Anne wears lace like that!" she gasped, and gathered her skirts to hurry into the meadow.

"Come back, woman," grumbled her brother-in-law, but she took no notice, and so he followed her, grumbling all the time about foolish old fowls that flapped about anything and nothing.

There was another gust of wind, and this time it rattled a loose timber on the barn. Mrs. Jenkins's gaze flew toward the sound, and as she looked, she heard a soft moan. Alarmed, she ran toward the barn, where she found Anne beginning to stir.

"Oh, Miss Anne, Miss Anne, whatever has happened?"

"I don't really know," Anne confessed, her brow wrinkling in puzzlement. Why on earth was she in the barn? She didn't remember anything, except riding along the riverbank toward the bridge.

"Are you injured?" asked the anxious housekeeper, kneeling down beside her.

"No, except for a little bruising. To be truthful, I simply feel as if I've been asleep." She also felt strangely warm and relaxed, as if something exceedingly agreeable had just taken place, although for the life of her she couldn't imagine what that something might have been!

Mrs. Jenkins's brother-in-law stepped closer to help Anne to her feet, and she smiled a little foolishly as she brushed the hay from her riding habit. "I feel perfectly all right," she assured them both.

"Are you well enough to walk to the trap?" the housekeeper asked.

"Yes, I'm sure I am."

Sylvanus and Gervase had observed everything from the safety of the hedgerow, and at each gust of wind the faun had shivered, for he knew it was the work of the god of wild nature. Once Anne had been helped back to the trap, which then continued swiftly along the road toward Llandower, the secret watchers emerged. Sylvanus breathed out with relief as the pinprick of light disappeared along the land. "Well, she's safe now," he declared.

Gervase gave him an angry look. "And still a virgin, although no thanks to you!"

"*I* didn't touch her!" protested the faun indignantly.

"Maybe not personally, but you certainly saw to it that *I* did!" snapped Gervase, overcoming a strong impulse to bring a clenched fist down upon each of Sylvanus's horns in turn.

The faun shuffled penitently. "I know, and I'm sorry. I just couldn't help trying to use a shortcut. You see, I knew that you and she would be helpless to resist my power, and I foolishly thought my master wouldn't be watching, but he was. He *knew* I'd be disobedient again, and I proved him right. I'm a very bad faun."

"I'll go along with that statement," Gervase replied with feeling as he ran his fingers through his hair. "Tell me something, Sylvanus, is there anything you *can* do properly? Apart from incite two total strangers into conduct that would surely have culminated in full intercourse if it hadn't been for divine intervention! How *dare* you make me do what I did in that damned barn! I didn't feel in control, thanks to you, and it wasn't a feeling I appreciated. In future I want to be left to my own devices.

"Don't worry, you will be!" The faun thought a moment, then gave a cheeky grin. "I must say she was more enthusiastic than I expected. You're in luck, you know, for she's far from being cold!"

"So it would seem," Gervase murmured, remembering every little caress, every little sigh. He looked at the faun. "Why did I think we were in a cornfield?"

"Cornfield?" Sylvanus shrugged. "I don't know, unless, of course, she has a deep longing to make love like that. Yes, that's probably it."

"Really?" Gervase raised an eyebrow. Miss Anne Willowby was becoming more interesting by the moment.

"She's almost as sensuous as a nymph. Almost, but not quite," the faun added approvingly.

Gervase didn't reply. Sensuous? Yes, she was that, more sensuous than any woman he'd ever held. As they began to walk back toward Llandower, he wondered a little more about the cornfield, and whether or not a specific lover figured in the scheme of things. At this thought a pang of something akin to jealousy struck through him, for whoever Anne Willowby imagined herself to be with, it wouldn't be the late unlamented Gervase Mowbray, who had treated her so casually and arrogantly.

He knew he had no right to feel jealous—indeed he could hardly believe that was how he was feeling—but something had happened to him from the moment he looked into her wonderful eyes.

Chapter Eight

After spending the remainder of that night in the rotunda talking with Sylvanus—learning of the lies Hugh had told the Neapolitan authorities, and learning too a great deal that was new to him about Roman mythology, but failing to decide upon a course for winning Anne's heart—Gervase was obliged to resume his place on the plinth at dawn. Sylvanus curled up on the bench in the greatcoat, grumbling constantly until at last he fell asleep.

Not long after dawn the weather changed for the worse, becoming cold, windy, and very wet. A Monmouth doctor was summoned by Mrs. Jenkins to examine Anne, and left again shortly afterward having found nothing wrong with her. Anne informed the housekeeper about the letters she'd received from London, and of her decision to accept this new ninth duke. The rather startled Mrs. Jenkins could only wonder anew what lay behind the match, for as sure as eggs were eggs, it wasn't love!

The day went on, and the presence of the statue remained undetected. No one glanced out from Llandower's upper windows or came into the maze as the previous autumn's leaves were whisked from nooks and crannies and whirled through the wild air. Gervase didn't feel anything as the rain lashed dismally along the valley, but the unhappy, long-suffering faun huddled in the greatcoat. All Sylvanus could think of was the much warmer Italian home he wouldn't see until this wretched English business was over and done with. There was one consolation, however, and that was an unexpectedly welcome scent that carried now and then on the wet gusting air. At last the faun sat up to sniff attentively.

Gervase's curiosity was aroused. *What is it?*

"I can smell Roman incense. I thought I detected something last night when we first arrived, now I'm sure. There's a temple hidden here somewhere underground." The faun's nostrils twitched wistfully, and he got up to patter to the edge of the rotunda, staying just out of reach of the downpour. "I hope I'm right, because it would provide the perfect shelter for me until I can go home. I'll have to look for it."

"How?" It seemed to Gervase that finding a hidden temple wouldn't exactly be easy.

"By following my nose," Sylvanus replied simply, then gave a sigh. "Oh, I'm so hungry that my insides are rumbling. It's no good, I'll have to find some food."

"You're going to leave the maze in daylight?" Gervase was startled.

"I can't wait any longer. Besides, I need to sleep, and I can't do that when I'm hungry. Don't you want to eat too?"

"I'm not in the least hungry," Gervase replied.

The faun thought for a moment. "No, I suppose you might not be. My power does that sometimes." He turned up the collar of the greatcoat, and before Gervase knew it, he'd stepped out into the rain, his little hooves crunching on the wet gravel as he disappeared among the high hedges.

By the time Sylvanus reached the edge of the maze he was more wretchedly cold than ever. Wet and dripping like the hedges, he slipped unseen across the deserted courtyard, where the hitherto faint scent of incense became so powerful that he paused to test the air again. He sensed that the smell came from beneath the wind-rattled trapdoors leading down into the cellar, but then he espied Mr. Willowby's mounting block, and with a faint bleat he hurried across to it. His moments of fond Roman memories were short-lived, however, for his rumbling stomach reminded him how hungry he was, and with a sigh he went to the nearby kitchen door, listened closely for any sound of someone inside, then carefully lifted the latch.

Peering in, he saw some currant buns and a Madeira cake Mrs. Jenkins hadn't long ago set out to cool. Licking his lips, he darted in to devour as many buns as he could. He wasn't a tidy eater, leaving crumbs all over the scrubbed table, and he broke the cake into so many pieces that its original shape could have been anyone's guess. After that he drank the entire jug of milk he discovered on the cold slab in the pantry, dipped eager fingers into some gooseberry preserves, and then stuffed the greasy remains of a cold roast chicken into the pockets of Gervase's greatcoat to take back to the maze for later. Then he glanced through the doorway that gave into the rest of the castle. He saw a passageway leading to the entrance hall, and halfway along it a door into the cellars. From the entrance hall there wafted yet another delicious smell— the distinctive and delicious fragrance of water nymph! The faun's lustful eyes lit up, for naiads were his favorite nymphs. He was sorely tempted to follow the enticing scent, but then a door banged upstairs and he heard Mrs. Jenkins's busy footsteps approaching.

Drawing hastily back into the kitchens, he was confronted by Joseph's lurcher, which had slunk in to steal some of the buns. Alarmed to find a creature he couldn't identify as either man or beast, Jack began to bark frantically, silenced only when a well-aimed goat hoof sent him flying. For a split second Sylvanus considered turning the stupid creature into marble, but then decided that a solidified lurcher was perhaps not the best thing for the housekeeper to find on the kitchen floor, so he gathered the greatcoat and ran. Jack followed at a safe distance and contented himself with barking furiously at the entrance to the maze long after Sylvanus had vanished inside.

Mrs. Jenkins arrived in the kitchens to find the devastation of crumbs on the table. Her eyes darkened. "Just wait until I lay my hands on that mangy mongrel!" she muttered darkly, hearing the distant barking.

Anne, in the meantime, was seated by the fire in the drawing room, where the dismal weather made it dark enough to light Penelope's candles. Her hair was brushed loose, and she wore a green fustian gown, with her new plaid shawl around her shoulders. She was holding a cup of hot chocolate in both hands as she puzzled about what had happened during her ride. How had her hat gotten into the road, and her scarf onto the hawthorn bush? And how had she been found in the barn? There was a horrid blank in her memory, and it was most disconcerting.

She sipped the chocolate. Maybe she'd been knocked on the head after all, for she felt generally rather odd today. It wasn't an unpleasant oddness; indeed an almost lazy warmth seemed to pervade her entire body, and when she'd opened her eyes this morning, there lingered a very sensuous dream containing all the elements of the erotic tryst she'd observed so long ago. Warm color flushed her cheeks, and she glanced wryly at the wooden nymph, whom she was occasionally wont to address. "I'm afraid I was very shameless in my sleep last night, Penelope," she murmured.

The naiad gazed back at her, and Anne was about to sip the chocolate again when Jack began to bark outside. As the barking continued, she got up to go to the window. The scene was blurred by rain, but she could just make out the lurcher dashing up and down by the entrance to the maze. After a moment Joseph came from the kitchen gardens, gave a sharp command, and the dog ran to him. Then Anne had the uncanny feeling she was being watched. She hesitated, trying to look through the rain-washed glass, but she saw nothing untoward. With a sigh she resumed her seat by the fire.

Gervase's marble eyes had been upon her. It was a long time since he'd experienced kisses that were such a bewitching blend of innocence and sensuality, and on seeing her again now, he pondered the irony of his situation. If only he'd come here to Llandower at the outset, by now he might have been married to her and enjoying to the full the charms he'd begun to appreciate so very much last night. As things were, it might be Hugh who first possessed her.

His wistful thoughts broke off as Sylvanus arrived breathlessly back to the rotunda, made himself as comfortable as possible on the bench, and explained what had happened. They decided that when darkness came and Gervase was brought to life to properly commence his campaign of seduction—the exact form of which was still unresolved—the faun would go down through the cellar trapdoors to look for the temple. After that—he'd find the water nymph! Eyes glittering with lusty anticipation, the faun ate some of the chicken, then wiped his hands on the greatcoat before curling up to sleep.

Gervase was resigned as his costly coat was subjected to further ignominy, for he knew that the unfortunate garment would never again achieve its former glory. His tailor would expire of the vapors if he knew.

Rain was falling in London as well, and the Knightsbridge street where Kitty's house stood was deserted. Firelight flickered over the painting of the bacchanalia as the actress lay naked on the bed, watching Hugh as he used the cheval glass to accurately tie his gray-and-white striped neckcloth in the complicated *Irlandaise* knot. Kitty's eyes were calculating. After her bitter disappointments with Gervase and Sir Thomas Fanhope, he was the best hope she'd had of a voucher into the aristocracy, and now that it was the eve of his departure for Llandower, she felt he should be made to think his hold upon her was only fragile.

She caught his eyes in the glass. "I will be very late back tonight," she murmured.

He turned in surprise. "But it's the last night before I leave!"

"That cannot be helped. After the performance of *Julius Caesar*, there are the first rehearsals for the next production." She plucked at the coverlet on the bed, pouting her lips and avoiding his eyes in a way she knew would unsettle him.

"What rehearsals?"

"The next production. *Harlequin Undone*, I believe it's called. Some such name, anyway."

He came to the foot of the bed. "Why haven't you mentioned this before?"

"It just slipped my mind, I suppose."

He searched her eyes. "There aren't any rehearsals tonight, are there? What are you really doing?"

She didn't reply.

He came closer, then reached down to put a hand to her cheek, and forced her to look at him. "I will have the truth, Kitty. Who are you seeing?"

"It's none of your concern."

"How can you say that when I've promised to make you my duchess!"

"Maybe you have, but as yet another woman stands in the way. Besides, how do I really know you'll honor your word to me? Men are untruthful when it comes to getting what they want. The one I'm meeting tonight was untruthful to me in the past, promising me all and then marrying another. Now he's being equally untruthful to his new wife in order to try to win me again."

Hugh's mind raced over the possible candidates. "Fanhope? Is *that* who you're seeing?" He was startled, for Sir Thomas was known to go in dread of a wife who was as hard and cold as her family's famous pottery.

Kitty remained enigmatically silent.

Hugh sought to belittle his unexpected rival. "Well, you

would be advised to take any of his financial promises with a pinch of salt, for I hear that his father-in-law's finances are becoming somewhat precarious, and since Fanhope has no money of his own . . ." He shrugged. "Besides, if he and his wife aren't already out of town, they soon will be. Staffordshire calls, I understand."

"But before he leaves . . ." Kitty smiled. The truth was that the Fanhopes had left for the country the day after Hugh had arrived in town; indeed Sir Thomas had been so bold as to call upon her in order to tell her. Poor Thomas, how much he regretted marrying the Queen of Pots.

Hugh put his hands to her bare shoulders, caressing her with his thumbs. "How can I prove that I will marry you? You ask the impossible, Kitty, and I think you know it. I *must* make overtures to this rustic milkmaid, but you are the one I want."

"I so want to believe you, Hugh, but I can't help my doubts."

"Oh, my darling, if I could make you my bride today, believe me, I would, but that would mean forfeiting the title and fortune." Suddenly, he thought of something and caught her hand to pull her from the bed. "Come here."

"What . . . ?"

He ushered her before the mirror and made her stand there while he went to the chest of drawers in the corner. He bent to remove the lowermost drawer, then took out something he'd hidden underneath. It was wrapped in soft maroon cloth, which he unfolded to reveal the diadem.

Kitty's breath caught as the amazing jewels caught the firelight, winking and flashing with myriad rainbow colors. Their light was reflected in her eyes as she stretched out a trembling hand to touch the exquisite gold workmanship. "Oh, Hugh, it's the most beautiful thing I ever saw. Where did you get it?"

"I bought it in Naples for you." As he glanced at the precious stones, Hugh still found it hard to believe they were only clever paste, for if ever anything looked like the genuine article, this clever gewgaw did.

"You bought it for *me*?" Kitty's lips were soft and curved with pleasure.

"Yes, to wear at our wedding." He slipped it on to her head, then turned her toward the mirror again. He stood behind her, his hands to her waist, his cheek against her hair. "I saw it and thought of you, my beloved. I always intended to try to win you when I came back to England, and I needed a jewel that was fit for your head. This is that jewel. It cost me all I had, but it was worth every coin." Behind her in the mirror he could see the painted faun stared disconcertingly at him. Kitty's expression was rapt as she admired herself in the diadem. "I'll wear it onstage later, for it is the most perfect thing for Caesar's wife," she breathed as the jewels glinted with a magnificence that was almost unearthly.

Hugh's hands slid up to enclose her full breasts. "Now say you still doubt me," he whispered, his lips soft against her hair.

She was still admiring her reflection. "I doubt you less," she conceded.

"Promise you won't see Fanhope."

She gazed at the flashing jewels. "I promise," she whispered.

"It's the last performance of *Julius Caesar* tonight; why don't you tell them you don't wish to begin new rehearsals just yet, and come with me to Llandower instead?" he urged recklessly.

She turned her head in surprise. "Are you serious? What if your Miss Willowby should find out?"

"The inn is five miles away." He bent his head to kiss the tender flesh between her neck and shoulder.

She smiled a little, for the thought was novel. "Very well."

He kissed her hair. "I'm going to make you the Duchess of Wroxford, and if I have to drown Anne Willowby in the River Wye in order to do so, then I will."

A sensuous surge of triumph swept along her veins. "Make love to me now," she whispered.

As he hastened to oblige, the painting of the bacchanalia suddenly fell off the wall. It slid behind the bedhead, but Hugh still felt as if the faun were watching him, and chilling memories returned of events in the Neapolitan grove. The pounding weapon at his loins wilted, and Kitty gave a tut of annoyance. "Well, that's the end of *that*!" she declared, going to put on her robe. She flounced from the room, the diadem still on her head.

Chapter Nine

As daylight faded once more into darkness at Llandower, the wind drew audibly down the chimney in Anne's bedroom. About to go to bed, she wore her nightgown, her thick hair loose about her shoulders. The window casement rattled, threatening to burst open again, so she went to see that it was properly closed. Something made her open it first, though. Her hair was blown in confusion, and the rain dampened her face as she looked out.

For a moment the moon shone from between the fleeing clouds, and to her shock she saw what appeared to be a statue in the rotunda, but then the moon disappeared again. She closed the window, grabbed her rose woolen wrap, then hurried to her parents' room, where her father's telescope stood at the window. Opening the casement, she trained the glass upon the rotunda and saw there was indeed a statue. But how could that be? When had it been put there? Why hadn't anything been said? Above all, why hadn't she noticed it before?

Nothing less than an immediate investigation would do, so in spite of the wildness of the night, she returned to her own room to put on her boots and cloak, then went down to the courtyard to take the old lantern that hung creaking by the main entrance, and which was always lit at nightfall. Raising her hood and ignoring the unsettling rattling of the trapdoors opposite, she hurried beneath the archway toward the maze, where the hedges gleamed with moisture in the swaying light of the lantern. Her cloak billowed as she followed the complicated but well-remembered route toward the rotunda, where Gervase and Sylvanus had slept on longer than anticipated.

Her hood fell back as she paused at the edge of the little clearing, and her unruly hair blew free as she held the lantern aloft. The dim rain-dashed light swung over the rotunda, revealing the unmistakable shape of a naked man sculpted from solid white marble. So her eyes hadn't deceived her! She was totally at a loss. Surely her father would have said if he'd purchased it? And anyway, there would have been quite a to-do when it was carried through the maze, so how could she possibly not have known? Joseph must know something about it, or maybe even Mrs. Jenkins. She would ask them first thing in the morning. *Someone* had to know where it had come from, and when.

She went closer, and with each step the lantern revealed more detail of the statue's perfect male lines. Beyond the arc of light, Sylvanus didn't stir on the bench. He was far away in Italy, having just pursued and caught the daintiest, most delightful, most compliant water nymph any faun could wish for—indeed she was perfect. He sighed contentedly in his sleep, but the soft sound was lost in the bluster of the wind.

Anne reached the statue and put a tentative hand on one of the marble arms to make certain she was not imagining the whole thing. It was hard, cold, and very real beneath her fingers. Gervase awoke with a start. The light of the lantern slanted awkwardly, giving everything a nightmarish quality, but the warmth of her fingers told him he was very much awake. A spurt of alarm immediately fled through him as he feared she had after all recollected events under the wanton influence of Sylvanus's power, but then he relaxed as he saw no hint of recognition on her face, just puzzlement about a statue that had no business being where it was. Briefly, he wondered how she had come to find out in the middle of the night, but this curiosity was soon supplanted by the sheer pleasure of seeing her again. Those few incredible moments in the barn had changed everything for him, because in spite of everything he'd expected to the contrary, the dashing, sought after, sophisticated Duke of Wroxford was strongly attracted to the provincial nobody he'd once so bitterly resented. Pray God he could achieve the task Bacchus dictated, for if ever he'd wanted anything, it was to be free to resume his birthright and take Anne Willowby to wife.

Anne's astonishment about the existence of the statue was temporarily supplanted by interest in the identity of the long dead Roman. Was he one of the emperors? Or a great general? There was no name on the plinth, but she concluded that at the very least he'd been noble. Whoever he was, he was certainly very handsome indeed. She had been trying not to look at those male regions ladies aren't supposed to see until their wedding night, but there hadn't been a woman yet who could resist the temptation. She blushed a little as she allowed herself the considerable impropriety of looking directly at his masculinity.

Gervase's first embarrassed instinct was to cover himself with his hands, but solid marble couldn't cover anything, so all he could do was stand there, his parts very much on display! His only consolation was that he was certainly not deficient in that area.

Anne felt self-conscious too, even though she thought she was looking only at marble. That day in the cornfield the man had looked so soft, pliable, and unaroused at first, but how magnificently he had changed! She closed her eyes briefly as a sense of yearning passed keenly through her. She was a year short of thirty, and had never been truly kissed, let alone made love to! Life had been set to pass her by until the old Duke of Wroxford chose her for his son. Now it would be Hugh Mowbray who initiated her into the carnal delights of the flesh—at least she prayed they would be delights. If he was gentle and understanding, she knew she could be the sort of wife any man would want. She had a latent passion that was just waiting to be released, and oh, how she longed for that moment.

Gervase wished he knew what she was thinking. Why had she closed her eyes like that? Her lips had curved just a little, and her lashes cast dainty shadows in the light from the lantern. How he would have liked to bend down and kiss that sweetly generous mouth. How he would like to run his hands through her wonderfully unmanageable dark golden hair. How he would like to show her what pleasure his maleness could really give!

Suddenly, she heard a slight scuffling from the shadows by the bench at the rear of the rotunda, and she turned swiftly toward the sound. She raised the lantern uneasily, but there was nothing there. Unless . . . She saw what appeared to be a heap of something—more leaves, perhaps? Were rats sheltering there? Almost immediately she discounted the notion, for the rotunda was far too exposed and drafty to appeal to rats; however, it was better to err on the side of caution. With a shudder she caught up her cloak to hurry away.

As the bobbing light of her lantern disappeared into the maze, Sylvanus got up and shook the coat. "She gave me quite a start. For a moment I thought she was going to find me," he said.

"*So did I,*" Gervase replied.

"What made her come, I wonder?"

"*I don't know, I was asleep, too. Suddenly she was here.*"

The faun came over to him, then grinned knowingly. "Well, I'll warrant she woke you well and truly awake by the time she'd finished."

"*I've never felt so vulnerable in my life,*" Gervase muttered as Sylvanus murmured the incantation that softened his marble casing into flesh once more. The bitter cold of the night swept immediately over him, and with a low curse he hurried to the bench to put on his clothes. Then he sat on the bench and ran his fingers through his hair to push it back into place as best he could. "I feel scruffy and in need of a good wash," he complained.

"You look all right to me," replied the faun, retrieving the cold chicken and sitting next to him to eat a little more. "How shall we go about things tonight?" he asked.

"I have no idea," Gervase replied, shaking his head to a proffered leg.

"Aren't you hungry yet?" the faun asked in surprise.

"Yes, but not for something you've seen fit to shove into my coat pocket, and then keep on the floor. You clearly have more goat in you than you think."

Sylvanus sniffed. "Suit yourself," he said, and tore off more meat with his teeth.

Gervase was silent for a moment, then looked at him. "Sylvanus, there's one aspect of this that bothers me. I know you were able to make her forget what happened last night, but now that she's seen the statue, what will happen when she comes face-to-face with me in the flesh? You saw how closely she examined me! Surely she's bound to realize the statue and the man are one and the same?"

"Yes, but it wasn't your face she was interested in," the faun replied slyly.

"Very amusing, but you know what I mean."

Sylvanus rubbed one of his horns thoughtfully, but then shook his head. "No, she won't recognize you. When you're a statue, your hair clings around your forehead, but when you're as you are now, the first thing you do is push your hair back. You look quite different."

"Different enough?"

"Yes. Anyway, the worst she will think is that you *resemble* the statue. Let's face it, she's hardly likely to leap naturally to the conclusion that you and the statue are one and the same!"

"Unless she comes here at night again, and there's no statue because I'm elsewhere," Gervase pointed out, looking at the deserted plinth.

The faun had no answer for that. "Well, we'll just have to hope she stays inside," he said dismissively. "Look, what's the point of picking over what *might* happen? We've got to concern ourselves with what *is* going to happen, and by that I mean your campaign of seduction. How are you going to go about it?"

"I still haven't really thought." Under normal circumstances Gervase would not have been too concerned at having only a few days in which to accomplish a seduction, but these were not normal circumstances, and he'd never before had to succeed with a woman because failure would mean an eternity of marble!

"You'd better decide quickly, for it won't be so easy once your cousin arrives." Sylvanus dropped the remains of the chicken behind the bench, then drew a long breath. "If the lady were a nymph, I would simply chase and ravish her, but that's what fauns are supposed to do, and anyway it's what nymphs expect of us. They're quite insulted if we don't."

"Most illuminating, but it doesn't solve my problem. I can't simply throw myself on Anne Willowby and expect all to be well. Damn it, I can't even think how to approach her in the first place. Have you any ideas about what story I can concoct? My mind's still a complete blank."

The faun swung his hooves to and fro thoughtfully, then wiped his hands on the front of the coat. "Well, I suppose you *could* pretend to be an agent from your father's lawyers. I mean, she knows the deeds will have to be transferred if the marriage takes place, and so may not see anything amiss in such a story."

Gervase stared at him. "That's inspirational!" he declared in astonishment.

"I *do* have some good ideas, you know!" Sylvanus replied crossly, but then shivered as a stronger gust of wind brought a scattering of rain right up to the bench. "Oh, this damp cold is torture! I can't possibly stay outside another night. I'll have to find that temple. I'm almost certain it's somewhere below the castle itself. Are you coming to help me look? We'll probably think more about your cover as we go along." He got up and trotted to the edge of the rotunda.

"I suppose so," Gervase replied resignedly, and got up as well.

"Just watch out for that stupid dog."

Sylvanus led the way out of the maze.

Chapter Ten

Gervase and Sylvanus left the shelter of the maze and crossed to the gatehouse, where the noise of the stormy night was emphasized by the crowding walls of the castle. Water gurgled along gutters and down drainpipes, and ivy leaves shone in the swaying light of the lantern, which Anne had replaced on its hook. Everything seemed to be deserted, and there was no sign at all of Joseph's lurcher.

Sylvanus sniffed the air again, then followed his nose across the courtyard to the double trapdoors. Lifting one, he clambered inside and disappeared from view down a ladder. Gervase knew it would be as black as pitch in the cellar, so he brought the lantern, then went down after the faun. The air was musty, and the flagstone floor very uneven as he followed Sylvanus's damp hoofprints between stacks of garden tools, rows of cider casks, and empty racks. He could hear a scrabbling noise from the darkest shadows ahead, and as he drew near, he saw the faun clawing desperately at one of the farthest flags.

"Help me get this up," Sylvanus cried, striving to get his fingers beneath the heavy stone.

"You'll never raise it like that," Gervase said. "Wait, I saw a crowbar with some garden tools." He went back, found what he was looking for, then returned.

Sylvanus almost snatched it from him, and in a few moments the flag was lifted free of its neighbor. As it fell aside with a thud, a dark hole was revealed beneath, and although Gervase couldn't smell anything, the faun gave a sigh of pleasure as the heady scent of incense drifted up. Sylvanus promptly disappeared down some worn steps into the subterranean darkness.

As Gervase followed, the lantern revealed a mosaic floor of Dido and Aeneas hunting on horseback. The temple had been hacked from the solid rock, where rusty torches and incense burners were still fixed to wall brackets. A spring welled silently from a wall fissure, filled a polished stone bowl containing coin offerings, then splashed gently over to vanish into another fissure. At the far end of the temple there was a blue marble altar on which stood a chalice and two dishes, almost as if the worshippers had only just departed, except that everything was covered with dust and cobwebs.

In an alcove behind the altar was a gilded likeness of the goddess Minerva, to whom the temple was dedicated, and Sylvanus was making very low obeisance to her. His forehead pressed to the floor and his goat tail aloft, he muttered a prayer in Latin. When he'd finished, he scrambled to his hooves again and pattered across to Gervase, who'd waited at a respectful distance. "This is perfect. I shall be able to sleep very comfortably here."

"Well, good for you," Gervase muttered, thinking of his sparse plinth and the openness of the rotunda.

"Provided I behave respectfully, Minerva will not mind if I sleep here, but I will have to make it safe from the dog. It will smell my presence as surely as I could smell this temple, so I'll deter it from the trapdoor."

"How?"

The faun smiled. "I'll put something there that looks like a snake. Anything will do, even a piece of rope. It always works."

"Really?" Gervase had never heard of such a thing before.

Sylvanus patted his stomach. "I'm hungry—let's find something to eat. There's a way up into the kitchen passage; I saw the door when I explored earlier."

Gervase was reluctant as he followed the faun back up out of the temple. He still didn't feel quite ready for the risky business of actually going into the living quarters of the castle, even in the dead of night, but Sylvanus had already found the door.

The faun's capacity for rash curiosity was to the fore again, and before Gervase could stop him, he'd opened the door, but instead of going to the kitchen, he went the other way to the entrance hall. Gervase hastened uneasily after him. "Come back!" he whispered, but the faun took no notice as he crossed toward the staircase.

Gervase was becoming angry. "Sylvanus, if you don't come back, I swear I'll leave!"

The faun paused on the bottommost step and looked reproachfully at him. "Can't you smell her fragrance?"

"Fragrance? Whose?"

"The naiad's."

Gervase stared at him. "The *what*?"

"Don't you know what a naiad is?" Sylvanus was shocked.

"Yes, a water nymph. I'm just startled that you think there's one here."

"Oh, there is. She's up there somewhere." Sylvanus pointed up to the next floor, then before Gervase knew what was happening, he'd hurried up into the shadows of the second story.

Gervase followed as quietly as he could, but it seemed that every floorboard creaked like the shriek of a barn owl, and every door passed might be flung open at any moment.

Sylvanus's nose was unerringly accurate, leading him directly to the drawing room, where he found Penelope standing so prettily with her candle tray. Falling hopelessly in love at first sight, the faun moved delightedly around her, examining her from every adorable angle, and reaching out at last to put a tender hand to her cheek.

Gervase put the lantern down and looked at the room. He immediately recognized the bundle of letters tucked behind the candlestick. Feeling as he did now, he could hardly believe he'd ever put pen to paper in such a way. If ever a man was paying a price for leaping to conclusions, he was. Simply by giving Anne Willowby the benefit of the doubt, he would have avoided rushing off across Europe with Hugh, and thus avoided the predicament he was in now. Oh, the benefit of hindsight. He was so engrossed in his regrets, he didn't notice Sylvanus suddenly dive behind the curtains at the window, nor did he hear the door swing open. The first he knew of anything was when a blunderbuss jabbed imperatively between his shoulder blades, and a rough male voice demanded to know his name.

"Who might you be, then? Eh? And what are you doing here in the middle of the night?"

It was Joseph, his legs protruding inelegantly beneath his nightshirt, and behind him stood Mrs. Jenkins, her plump face pale and startled in its frame of white-frilled night bonnet.

"I, er . . ." Gervase didn't know who stood behind him and

didn't dare turn around and risk the blunderbuss being fired. He saw the telltale trembling of the curtain that told where Sylvanus had gone, but he also saw the hem of the greatcoat peeping out. If the owner of the blunderbuss should see and investigate, the Lord alone knew what his reaction would be discovering a faun! The seconds hung as his mind raced confusedly.

Joseph poked him with the blunderbuss. "Your name, before I blow a great hole in you!"

Mrs. Jenkins gasped alarmedly and hurried away. "Miss Anne! Oh, Miss Anne!" she cried.

"Put the lantern on the table and turn around." The blunderbuss was removed as Joseph stepped back a little, but he kept it aimed at his captive.

Gervase obeyed slowly, being careful as he did so to move farther from the window, so the gardener was less likely to notice the greatcoat. "There's no need to be hasty," he said in what he hoped was an amiable tone.

"Don't think I'm a country bumpkin who can be gulled by a toff," Joseph growled. "I'm ready to fire this thing right into your rascally hide if need be, so have a care."

"I won't do anything rash, I promise."

Female footsteps hurried back along the passage as Mrs. Jenkins returned with Anne, who was still fastening her wrap. Her dark blond curls were tousled, and her green eyes wary as she faced Gervase. For a heart-stopping moment she stared at him as if in half recognition, but then she seemed to dismiss any notion that they'd met before. "Who are you, sir?" she demanded.

At last he found inspiration. "Charles Danby. Your servant, Miss Willowby."

He was sure a shadow of disappointment crossed her eyes, but then it was gone. "You know who I am, Mr. er . . . Danby?"

"*Certes,* madam, for I am the junior partner of Messrs. Critchley, Faulkner, Oliver, and Danby," he bowed, praying she did not ask for proof of identity.

She was incredulous. "You have been discovered breaking into these premises in the middle of the night, and yet you claim to be a *lawyer*?"

"I haven't broken in, not in the true sense of the phrase, for I've been sent to examine the castle accounts prior to the betrothal taking place." Oh, how thick and fast the untruths came now!

She was ice-cold. "And what, pray, do my father's accounts have to do with the betrothal? The forthcoming contract may be a matter of convenience, but it is certainly not one of fortune, and since the duke will be able to examine them himself in a day or so, I would rather you told me the truth."

Joseph and Mrs. Jenkins glanced at each other, for this was as close as Anne had ever come to admitting the nature of her match with the duke.

Gervase's eyes didn't flicker at the mention of Hugh's expected arrival. "The duke knows nothing of accounts, Miss Willowby," he said.

Anne continued to hold his gaze. "I still do not believe your story, Mr. Danby—if that is indeed your name."

"I swear I am Danby the lawyer, and that my intentions are entirely legal," he insisted.

"Since when has it been legal to break into people's homes, sirrah?" she asked coolly.

Her poise under such circumstances was truly impressive, Gervase thought admiringly, even as his mind skimmed over a suitably convincing story. "Miss Willowby, I admit I've acted foolishly, but in truth I thought there was no one in. I was under the impression that you and your family had gone to Ireland, and I thought to conduct my business during your absence. I'm staying at an inn in Monmouth because I have other business in the area, and I set out in good time to reach here in daylight so that I could explain myself to your servants, but when I dismounted to examine one of my horse's shoes, the wretched creature bolted and left me stranded in the rain. It was nearer to walk here than to go back, so that is what I did. I arrived a few minutes ago, and rather than awaken everyone, I simply entered to get on with things. I thought it the most prudent, discreet, and practical procedure."

Anne's eyes flashed, and she tossed her hair back. "Oh, *did* you! Well, sirrah, I would call your actions reprehensible, not prudent, discreet, or practical! How *dare* you enter my home uninvited, and how *dare* you presume to examine my father's accounts without his express permission!"

"You are right to censure me, Miss Willowby," he conceded.

"And how did you know about the visit to Ireland?" she asked suddenly.

"I beg your pardon?"

"How did you know?"

His mind went horribly blank, and he ran his hand through his hair. "I, er . . ."

"Well, sirrah?" Her eyes followed the unconscious gesture.

"I believe your father notified Mr. Critchley of his intentions." He met her gaze squarely.

She hesitated for the first time. "Well, I suppose that *is* possible," she conceded.

"I have told you the truth, Miss Willowby," he insisted, conscious that at last he was gaining a little credibility.

She suddenly made up her mind. "You may lower the blunderbuss, Joseph, before it goes off and sprays not just Mr. Danby but the entire room."

Gervase breathed out with relief, for he was out of danger, and had successfully embarked upon his false identity. But it remained to be seen whether or not Anne Willowby's heart could be as easily won as her trust.

Chapter Eleven

Joseph was reluctant to let his prey off the hook. "I'm not sure that's wise, Miss Anne. . . ."

"I don't think Mr. Danby has come here to murder us in our beds," Anne replied, and then turned to Mrs. Jenkins, who had hovered in the doorway throughout. "Please prepare the south room."

The south room was the one kept aired for unexpected guests, so the implication was not lost upon the appalled housekeeper. "*Surely* you do not mean to offer this man hospitality, Miss Anne?"

"I can hardly turn him out into the rain."

As the housekeeper's lips parted to give any number of reasons why Mr. Charles Danby should be ejected forthwith, Anne sternly forestalled her. "I feel obliged to offer hospitality, and that is the end of it, Mrs. Jenkins."

The housekeeper hurried reluctantly away, and Anne looked at Gervase again. "Since you represent the late duke's lawyers, you may stay here tonight, but the surrendering of my father's ledgers is a matter to which I will have to give further thought. I trust you understand?"

"I do indeed, Miss Willowby, and thank you for your graciousness. I am aware that I do not deserve it."

"No, you certainly do not." She came a little closer suddenly, searching his face in the light from the lantern on the table. "Your face seems very familiar—have we met somewhere before, Mr. Danby?"

"I don't believe so, Miss Willowby," he replied with commendable poise. He could smell her perfume, warm like summer roses.

She continued to look closely at him. "If you say we have not, then we have not, but it is a fact that I feel I have at least seen you somewhere in passing." She turned to the gardener. "Please conduct Mr. Danby to his room, Joseph."

"As you wish, Miss Anne."

Something occurred to her. "Joseph, what can you tell me about the statue in the maze?"

"There's no statue in the maze, Miss Anne," he replied in astonishment.

"Yes, there is—it's in the rotunda and I examined it tonight. Maybe Mrs. Jenkins knows something?"

"If a statue had been taken into the maze, *I'd* know about it." Joseph hesitated. "Mayhap you dreamed it, Miss Anne."

She shook her head. "I was very much awake. Oh, well, I don't intend to argue about it now, but tomorrow you and Mrs. Jenkins must see for yourselves."

"Yes, Miss Anne."

"Now please conduct Mr. Danby to his room."

"Miss Anne."

Her eyes moved to Gervase for the last time. "Good night, Mr. Danby."

"Good night, Miss Willowby." As he took her hand and raised it to his lips, the physical contact aroused so many echoes of the sweet emotion they'd shared in the barn that he was hard put to quell the instinct to catch her close and kiss her. He saw a soft flush of color enter her cheeks, but as he began to wonder what she was thinking, she lowered her eyes and slowly withdrew her fingers.

When he had accompanied Joseph from the room, Anne closed her eyes. Her heart was thundering wildly in her breast, and not just from the delayed shock of finding an intruder in the house. The truth was that she thought Mr. Charles Danby the most devastatingly attractive man she'd ever encountered, and for a moment on first seeing him she had hoped he was Hugh Mowbray, who was, after all, expected to call at any moment. Maybe it was unlikely that the Duke of Wroxford would enter Llandower uninvited, but then was it any more likely that his lawyers' representative should do the same?

Charles Danby. Everything about him, including his name, rang through her with the clarity of a bell, even the way he'd run his fingers through his hair. He seemed so familiar, so . . . beloved. Oh, heavens above, this was madness, and yet it was how she felt. She pondered what he thought of her, and then she smiled a little resignedly, for she did not doubt that he considered her a very unlikely and unworthy future Duchess of Wroxford. Her glance moved to the letters on the mantelpiece. It didn't matter what she thought of Charles Danby, or what he might think of her, for she was to be betrothed to Hugh Mowbray, and nothing could change that. Tears pricked her eyes suddenly, and without further ado she picked up the lantern and left the room.

Sylvanus immediately peeped from behind the curtains. Satisfied that all was now safe, he came out of hiding. Having observed and correctly assessed the expressions on Anne's face, he was sure that Gervase was now well on his way to a happy conclusion where she was concerned, which left a certain libidinous faun with a little free time on his hands! The long greatcoat dragged behind him as he hurried over to Penelope, whose delightful wooden curves shone in the faint light from the fire. He was about to take some disgraceful liberties with her person when he paused a little crossly, for it was rather dull sport when she remained immobile. It occurred to him that the power to turn *marble* to living flesh—and vice versa—might also apply to wood. There was only one way to find out. He said the words.

For a moment it seemed nothing would happen, but then before his delighted eyes she began to move. The sheen of the beechwood, already palely beautiful, softened to the blush pink of a living woman, and her long silvery hair spilled forward as she lowered her tray to place it on the table next to Anne's workbox. She was dainty and graceful, her perfect little figure outlined by the clinging but revealing folds of her gauzy gown, but as Sylvanus reached out eagerly to do what came naturally to all fauns, to his astonishment she dealt him a stinging blow to the cheek.

"Don't you *dare* presume!" she breathed furiously, keeping her voice low for fear of being heard elsewhere.

Rubbing his cheek, he gaped at her. "Why did you do that?" he asked in genuine amazement.

"No one does that to me unless *I* wish it!"

Sylvanus blinked, but then recovered a little. "You're not supposed to object," he complained.

"Well, I do. I'm not here simply to do as *you* wish."

"Yes, you are—it's what nymphs are for!"

But as he reached out again, she slapped him a second time,

so hard that he stifled a bleat that was half pain, half sheer disbelief. She faced him haughtily. "I have a mind of my own, and *I* decide who can and cannot touch me!" Her critical glance swept over him. "Besides, have you any idea how ridiculous you look in that huge coat?"

Sylvanus glowered. "You'd wear it if you weren't used to this northern cold."

"I doubt it, for I have more pride in my appearance."

"More vanity, you mean." Sylvanus looked her up and down. "You're not a real nymph at all, are you? I suppose I should have known."

"I *am* a real nymph!" she cried, forgetting to keep her voice down.

"Shhh!" He looked around uneasily, but as all remained quiet, he returned his attention to her. "What's your name?" he asked.

She relented sufficiently to reply civilly. "Penelope. What's yours?"

"Sylvanus."

"How did you get here?"

He told her everything, and she was intrigued. "So Charles Danby isn't Charles Danby at all?"

"No." He looked at her again. "There's more than one Penelope—which one are you?"

"I'm Mercury's Penelope. At least, I was." She sighed.

Sylvanus's jealousy pricked. "Was? If he deserted you, I'm not surprised. No doubt, your tongue proved too much for him."

"As a matter of fact he was burned." She explained about the unguarded saucepan and her lover's dreadful fate the day Joseph's special beeswax mixture had set fire to the kitchen.

Sylvanus was now well and truly jealous. "Well, your precious Mercury was clearly no more real than you are," he declared.

"I'm going to kick your horrible hairy goat legs for saying that!" she cried.

As she raised a foot to carry out the threat, Sylvanus quickly pronounced the spell. She could do nothing except return to the candleholder, resume her former pose, and harden into wood again. "Can you still hear me?" he asked. There was silence, so he rather ungallantly pinched her arm, but then fauns weren't known for their manners. There was still no response from a naiad who was now just silent, obedient wood. He grinned infuriatingly and planted a very deliberate and insulting kiss on her stiff lips, but as he drew back to survey her again, he was conscious of considerable disappointment. He wanted her to kiss him back, but right now that seemed very unlikely to ever happen. He looked at her in perplexity, for he'd never encountered a nymph quite like this before. He hesitated, then kissed her again, but much more gently this time. Maybe she had a temper like a Fury, but she was very, *very* pretty. With a wistful sigh, he hunched himself in the greatcoat and went to find Gervase.

In London at that moment Kitty was leaving the Theatre Royal in her best lime green silk evening gown and matching cloak. The diadem glittered in her hair, and she looked very stylish indeed as she swept grandly out of the stage door to a waiting carriage, for it was the eve of their departure for Llandower, and Hugh was taking her to dinner. As he held a hand out to assist her up into the vehicle, an ominous roll of unseasonable thunder rumbled across the sky. He glanced up in surprise, because heavens that a moment ago had been a flawless vista of stars, were now obscured by a thick bank of clouds that billowed above London like a flowing purple cloak.

A moment later, a strong gust of wind got up from nowhere, tugging at Kitty's clothes and hair and ruining her careful curls. As she cried out in dismay, the wind became more fierce, whisking dust, leaves, and other street debris into the air. The startled carriage horses moved backward without warning, the coachman was too late applying the brake lever, and the carriage wheel struck the wooden stand supporting a huge water butt next to the stage door. With a splintering creak, the stand gave way, and the butt tipped slowly over. It shattered on the cobbles, and a deluge of old rainwater drenched both Hugh and Kitty. Then, as quickly as it had risen, the wind died away, the bank of clouds disappeared, and stars twinkled once more.

Hugh's fine black velvet evening coat and white silk trousers were bedraggled, and Kitty's exquisite green gown and matching cloak were spoiled beyond all redemption. Dinner was out of the question.

Chapter Twelve

Had he known, Gervase would have been greatly amused by the ruination of his unworthy cousin's dinner plans, and by the suspiciously supernatural reason, but he was many miles away, seated comfortably before the fire in the south room at Llandower. He mulled over what had happened since he'd arrived, and his eyes warmed a little as he thought of Anne. Fate was cruel, choosing not only to heat him with desire for the bride he'd expected to loathe, but also making her a breathtaking mixture of passion and high principles. Such was her nature that she was capable of all the fire and wantonness any man could desire, yet at the same time—for her parents' sake—she would hold loyally to an arranged match, no matter what new love might come her way in the meantime.

There was a soft tap at the door, and he sat up. "Yes?"

Sylvanus came in and trotted to stand in front of the fire, his tail turned to the heat. He was still a little confounded by his experience with Penelope. "I'm not used to counterfeit naiads with waspish tongues," he declared peevishly, clasping his hands behind him.

Gervase raised an eyebrow. "I beg your pardon?"

The faun explained about Penelope.

"Serves you right," Gervase observed with deliberate lack of sympathy, "and to be honest I don't rank your lecherous activities very high on the scale of priorities. I'm much more concerned that in a few hours it will be dawn, and I will have to become a statue again, which means that much as I would like to, I can't really sleep here."

Sylvanus thoughtfully rubbed one of his horns, then gave a slight shrug and pointed toward the little escritoire at the far side of the room. "You said you had other business in Monmouth, so slip away leaving a note explaining urgent appointments. Say you didn't like to awaken her, and you'll come back as soon as you can."

"And when I do return, it will be without a horse, without a change of clothes, and still without a clue as to how I'm going to proceed. The lady is intelligent enough to wonder why I should travel so light, and she is also virtuous—if fauns know what that means." Gervase pointed out dryly, thinking that the obstacles still seemed unfairly stacked against him.

"This one is beginning to find out," Sylvanus muttered.

"So a note is the best you can think of?"

"Well, on the spur of the moment, yes."

Gervase sighed. "What *is* she going to make of me? First I break in, then I break out again, all the same night!"

"I'll tell you what she makes of you—she likes you very much indeed," Sylvanus observed.

"She does? What makes you say that?"

"Faun's instinct. Now then, I'm going to find some food in the kitchen, then I'm going back to the temple to make it comfortable. I saw some rope to make pretend snakes, so I'll be safe from that wretched animal. You'll have to go back to the rotunda now that the statue has been discovered. Here, take this to find your way." Sylvanus tore a silver button off the greatcoat.

"Have you no respect at all for other people's property?" Gervase inquired, again dryly, taking the button.

"Well, the coat's ruined anyway," replied Sylvanus.

"Yes, by you."

Sylvanus chose not to respond, and as the door closed behind him, Gervase pocketed the button and then went to the escritoire to write in a disguised hand, for his natural writing was distinctive enough to ring bells concerning the letters on the drawing room mantelpiece. He was brief and apologetic.

Miss Willowby.

Please accept my apologies, but I overlooked the fact that my other business in Monmouth is scheduled for first thing in the morning, and I do not wish to cause you further interruption by awakening you yet again. I trust I may take the liberty of returning to Llandower within the next day or so.

Charles Danby.

* * *

He left the bedroom, closing the door softly behind him, but as he was about to turn toward the staircase, he noticed a thin line of light beneath a doorway farther along the passage. Was it Anne's room? Unable to resist the possibility of speaking to her alone, he went to knock at the door in question. "Miss Willowby?"

Anne was sitting in bed reading, having found herself far too wide awake to sleep. She was startled to hear him, but as she closed the book and flung the bedclothes aside, a vigilant Mrs. Jenkins emerged wrathfully from the adjoining dressing room, where she'd insisted on sleeping for her mistress's protection. "There, I *knew* that scoundrel up to something!" The housekeeper declared, going to the fireplace for the poker.

Anne got hastily out of bed. "Please be calm, Mrs. Jenkins. I doubt very much if Mr. Danby has anything improper in mind. One moment, sir," she called, as for the third time that eventful night she put on her wrap. Mrs. Jenkins stood behind her with the poker as she opened the door. "What is it, Mr. Danby?" Anne asked, trusting she sounded cool and collected, for a telltale warmth had spread through her the moment she saw him again.

Gervase was a little taken aback to see the housekeeper standing guard with a weapon he did not doubt she was prepared to use. "Er, forgive me for yet another unwarranted intrusion, Miss Willowby, but I fear I have to leave." Anne's perfume drifted distractingly over him again, and her hair was flushed with a halo of gold by the candlelight behind her.

"Leave?" she repeated in astonishment. "But it's the middle of the night."

"I, er, had forgotten that I have important business in Monmouth first thing in the morning. I wrote this note, but then saw the light on in your room and felt it would be churlish to simply leave without speaking."

"But how did you intend to get to Monmouth without a horse?"

Damn, he hadn't thought of that! "I was going to presume greatly by borrowing one from your stables."

Mrs. Jenkins snorted. "So you're a wicked horse thief to boot!" she declared wrathfully.

Anne tossed a cross look at her. "That's enough, Mrs. Jenkins." Then she turned to Gervase again. "You may indeed borrow a horse, Mr. Danby."

He smiled. "I promise you will see your property again."

The smile sent color into her cheeks, and she was glad the candlelight was behind her. "I'm sure I will, Mr. Danby."

"I trust you will be able to overlook what has happened tonight, Miss Willowby, for I assure you my conduct is not usually so unorthodox."

She gave a little smile. "I'm relieved to know it, Mr. Danby."

"When I return, I will come to the door in a much more proper manner," he replied, struggling against the longing to touch her. She was meant to be his duchess, and he wanted to sweep her from her feet and carry her to the rumpled bed behind her. Cupid's arrow had pierced him with an accuracy he could never have anticipated, and he hoped Sylvanus's faun instinct was right. It was true that she blushed and lowered her eyes, and that she was prepared to view him charitably, but such things might have nothing to do with attraction to him and everything to do with her being a trusting innocent.

She managed another little smile. "We will begin again at our next meeting, Mr. Danby."

"You are most kind, Miss Willowby," he murmured, reaching for her hand and drawing it to his lips.

"I will take my leave for the time being, Miss Willowby." Her fingers trembled in his, and he couldn't help putting his lips fully to her skin, albeit for the most fleeting of moments. He thought he heard a soft intake of breath, but he wasn't sure.

"Good-bye, Mr. Danby." Inclining her head, she drew back into the room and closed the door.

He stood there for a few seconds, still struggling with the force of feeling she'd aroused in him, then he walked swiftly away down the passage.

On the other side of the closed door, Anne was leaning back with her eyes closed. Her hand was still alive to his kiss, and her whole body felt flushed with emotion. She listened to his steps dying away into the night and prayed he would return as he'd promised. But it was wrong to feel like this about a man she hardly knew, wrong anyway to have such feelings now for anyone except Hugh Mowbray, to whom she now regarded herself pledged. When next she met the unconventional but exceedingly desirable Mr. Charles Danby, she mustn't betray by so much as a glance that she felt anything more than she should.

Mrs. Jenkins said nothing as she replaced the poker by the hearth. She could not mistake the glow on Anne's face. The dismayed housekeeper did not know what to do, for in her opinion the departed male person was anything but a gentleman! It was as well that the new duke would arrive any day, for mayhap his presence would instill a little common sense into her suddenly foolish young mistress.

Chapter Thirteen

The following morning found Anne, Mrs. Jenkins, Joseph, and young Martin in the center of the maze, surveying the statue. Jack was there too. The lurcher knew the statue wasn't quite what it seemed and pawed Gervase's foot for attention. Gervase wished it would go away, for its nose was damned cold!

Anne was puzzled. "What's wrong with Jack?"

"Hopeful of a tidbit, even from a stone man," Mrs. Jenkins replied tartly, folding her hands in front of her crisp white apron and putting her head to one side to view the statue's lines a little better. "Well, he's a particularly handsome fellow, I must say."

Anne was in agreement with the housekeeper. "Yes, Mrs. Jenkins, he's exceedingly handsome."

Joseph pulled the protesting dog away, then he looked disapprovingly at the statue. "It's not fit to have a fellow standing there as naked as the day he was born!"

Martin sniggered, and as Joseph gave the boy a cuff on the ear, the housekeeper raised an eyebrow. "Just because *you* never looked like that, Joseph Greenwood."

"If it was a *female* standing there without a stitch on, you'd soon have something to say," Joseph replied. "At least I had the consideration to put a gown on that lamp holder I made."

Anne looked impatiently at them both. "What does it matter if it's got clothes on or not? I just want to know when—and how—it came to be here."

The gardener shook his head. "I have no idea at all, Miss Anne."

"Mrs. Jenkins?"

"It's a mystery to me," the housekeeper replied.

Anne looked inquiringly at Martin. "Have *you* any knowledge of it?"

"No, Miss Anne," the boy replied.

Anne sighed. "Come now, one of you *must* know."

But they protested their innocence so vehemently that in the end she had to concede that they were as much in the dark as she was. She was perplexed. "Then it must have been delivered on a day when we were all absent."

"Llandower is never completely empty, Miss Anne—there's always *someone* here," Mrs. Jenkins pointed out. Then she added, "Mind you, now I come to think of it, Mr. Willowby was here alone for a while the day before he and Mrs. Willowby left for Ireland. Joseph took me to market in Monmouth, Martin went home to visit his mother, and you and Mrs. Willowby went to Peterbury to see if the haberdashery had any peach-colored ribbon. Do you recall?"

"Yes, I do, but if my father was here when it came, why didn't he mention it? At the very least I would have expected him to describe the trouble there must have been to carry it through the maze and then erect it."

Mrs. Jenkins cocked her head to one side again, studying Gervase's profile. "He reminds me of someone," she murmured.

Gervase's stone heart missed a beat.

"Now who is it . . . Ah, yes, I recall! It's that rascally Mr. Danby who was here last night. If the hair were to be combed back instead of forward, they could be one and the same."

Gervase felt colder than marble. Had he been found out before he'd really begun?

Anne gasped. "You're right, Mrs. Jenkins, it *is* like Mr. Danby!"

The housekeeper met her eyes, recalling the telltale moments after the mysterious lawyer had taken his leave in the middle of the night. "Will that be all, Miss Anne?" she asked after a moment.

Anne nodded. "Yes, you may all go."

When they'd left, she looked up at the statue again and wondered if the astonishing likeness was why the lawyer had seemed familiar. Slowly, she put a hand up to the marble cheek, unable to prevent herself from imagining Charles Danby like this. How immeasurably enticing was the notion of lying in the lawyer's arms in a summer cornfield. . . . Shocked by the force and eroticism of her thoughts, she caught up her skirts and fled from the rotunda.

Gervase felt suddenly emboldened as he gazed after her, for he knew that Sylvanus had been right—she *did* like him in the relevant way. There'd be no more shilly-shallying; tonight he'd embark properly upon the task of seducing her into loving him. He only prayed the servants wouldn't be in the offing, especially Mrs. Jenkins, who was justifiably watchful and suspicious.

Fate came to his rescue. That afternoon the housekeeper was summoned urgently by her sister, whose kitchen was covered in soot after a chimney fire, and armed with cleansing equipment of every description, she set off with Joseph, who providently offered his assistance too. As soon as they had gone, Martin slipped away across the fields to spend a little time with his family at their cottage about three miles away. Anne was left on her own, and Gervase's coast was clear.

Sylvanus had enjoyed a good sleep in the comfort of the subterranean temple, and as dusk approached, he emerged to call upon Penelope. He left the greatcoat behind because he was mindful of the nymph's taunts, and he paused by a mirror to polish his horns and smooth his goat fur. After admiring himself from every angle, he proceeded toward the drawing room, intending to impress the nymph with his virile faun handsomeness.

Anne had taken a lighted candle to her father's study, which wasn't a very well lit room at the best of times, and was sifting through the accounts to see they were all in order should Mr. Danby insist upon seeing them. With her curls loose and a lacy white shawl around the shoulders of her lavender velvet gown, she examined the ledgers. She didn't glance up as the faun crept past the open door. But on reaching the drawing room, which was lit only by the dancing flames in the hearth, Sylvanus was almost undone because of Mog, Mrs. Jenkins's cat, who was enjoying a clandestine sleep on the cushioned armchair by the fire. At first he didn't realize Mog was there because the cat continued to sleep contentedly, but when the faun's hooves pattered on the polished wooden floor, her ears twitched and suddenly she awoke. Her amber eyes widened with alarm, her fur stood on end, and she erupted noisily from the chair to dash from the room. But Sylvanus had closed the door behind him, and there was no way out. Suddenly, there was pandemonium, with the panic-stricken cat dashing in all directions, knocking ornaments over.

Sylvanus was in a panic too. There was a cat here as well as a dog? And the wretched creature was making so much noise that Anne was bound to hear! For a few moments he simply froze, but then he had the wit to open the door. In a second the cat had rushed out, but Sylvanus had no time to feel foolish in front of Penelope, who must have witnessed everything, for to his further dismay footsteps and the flutter of candlelight announced that Anne had heard and was coming to investigate! Once again he was obliged to dive ignominiously for the shelter of the curtains, and had only just pressed back out of sight as Anne entered.

She halted in astonishment as she saw the scattered ornaments, which included a little porcelain Cupid that had been broken. She'd heard Mog, so knew who the culprit was, but couldn't imagine what had frightened the cat like that. Setting her candle on a table, she straightened the undamaged ornaments, then gathered the broken Cupid and bore him off to the kitchens.

Sylvanus peered from behind the curtains, then fled without a glance at Penelope, who he was sure was laughing at him. He scampered down the staircase and out into the darkening courtyard just as Anne emerged from the kitchen to return to the study. The faun ran into the maze and didn't stop until he reached the rotunda. Then he transformed Gervase from stone again and regaled him with his woes.

Gervase dressed, struggling to tie his neckcloth without the benefit of a mirror. "So all you're saying is that you had a set-to with a cat," he said when Sylvanus had finished.

"Yes, but it was in front of Penelope!" The faun was wretched. "I wanted to look my best to impress her, but I stood there uselessly, and then hid behind the curtain again like a felon. I felt completely foolish and embarrassed."

"Now you know how I feel when I'm a damned lump of stone and people gaze at my more intimate portions!" Gervase replied unsympathetically.

Sylvanus scowled. "You might at least be a little understanding."

"You aren't," Gervase pointed out.

The faun gave a labored sigh and said no more.

Gervase finished his neckcloth. "How does that look?"

"All right, I suppose."

"My success with Anne Willowby is much more important than yours with a naiad, so give me a sensible reply."

Sylvanus tweaked the folds of muslin. "There, that's better."

"Thank you." Gervase looked toward the castle. "Well, at least I've been able to think of a few logical explanations for some of the odd things about Charles Danby, so I feel a little more confident about my strategy."

Sylvanus looked imploringly at him. "If you can leave the drawing room clear, I'd be most grateful."

"I hope you don't expect me to carry Miss Willowby straight up to the nearest bedroom."

"It would solve a lot of problems," the faun replied hopefully.

"In your world, maybe, but not in mine. The ravishing of women is against the law here!"

Sylvanus looked sly. "There wouldn't have been anything forcible in the barn last night."

"Need I remind you about your panic when you realized Bacchus had discovered your continuing sins? So just let me get on with it in my own way, will you? Besides, I really don't want your dubious help; it's a little overpowering, even for me."

Taking a deep breath, Gervase left the rotunda, and without another word Sylvanus meekly followed.

Chapter Fourteen

Anne was just putting one ledger away and taking out another when she heard the knock at the courtyard door. The night was quiet, and she turned in surprise as the sound echoed dully through the house. For once Charles Danby was far from her thoughts as she picked up the candlestick and hastened downstairs. Shielding the dancing flame with her hand, she opened the door and found herself staring into Gervase's eyes. "Why, Mr. Danby . . ."

"I trust I haven't called at an inconvenient moment, Miss Willowby." Gervase replied, conscious of Sylvanus watching him from the dark archway across the courtyard.

"Er, no . . . of—of course not. Have you no horse?" She looked past him at the empty courtyard.

This was the first thing for which he was prepared, although he crossed his fingers that no one had realized there hadn't been a horse missing in the first place. "I rode here leading the mount you so kindly permitted me to borrow, and I've taken the liberty of putting them both in your stables. I hope you don't mind."

To his relief she didn't question him further. "No, of course not. Please come in." She was trembling, and a thousand and one doubts ran through her mind as she stood aside for him to enter. Propriety was *definitely* being flouted this time, for she was completely on her own in the house, but what else could she do? She'd indicated a willingness for him to call again, and it was hardly his fault that everyone else had gone out.

As he stepped past her, he was beguiled by her air of fresh innocence, which was so at odds with the wonderfully wanton way she'd kissed him in the barn. For a reprehensible second he was guilty of thinking that Sylvanus's approach wasn't entirely without merit, for right now it would be very sweet indeed to make passionate love to her between scented sheets.

As she closed the door and turned to face him, her glance moved a little curiously over his clothes, which could hardly be described as being in the prime of laundered excellence. Didn't he have a change of shirt or a fresh neckcloth?

He read her thoughts and had an explanation ready for this as well. "I fear my portmanteaux were stolen en route from London, so I hope you will excuse my somewhat unkempt turnout."

"How terrible for you, sir. Please be at ease, for I'm sure that under such unfortunate circumstances even Mr. Brummel would have found it difficult to remain the picture of sartorial elegance."

"You're most kind."

She wondered about the lateness of his call. Was he hoping to be invited to stay the night again? It was out of the question if he was. "I trust you've taken a room for the night at the Salmon's Leap tavern in Peterbury, Mr. Danby," she said pointedly as she placed the candle on the table and then turned to take his hat and gloves.

"Er, no—I'm staying at an inn a little off the beaten track some miles from the village. I mistook my route and was directed there. It seemed an excellent hostelry, well within riding distance, so I decided to stay there. I forget its name, I fear."

"Oh, you must mean the White Boar."

"Yes, I believe that was its name." Gervase watched her place his hat and gloves neatly on the table. The candlelight burnished her hair, and the soft lavender velvet of her gown clung to her figure as she moved.

She felt she had to make idle conversation in order to counteract the emotions that streamed so treacherously through her veins. She had to be on guard against her own weakness, for he made her feel more aware of her femininity than any other man had ever done. "I'm sure you'll find the White Boar most agreeable, Mr. Danby. Did you know that it is said to be the only inn of that name in the whole of the country?"

"The only one?"

"I believe it dates back to 1485 and the Battle of Bosworth. Richard III's badge was the white boar, and on his defeat all inns of that name thought it prudent to become Blue Boars overnight."

"Except this one?" He smiled into her eyes.

"Yes, except this one. The then lords of Llandower remained loyal to the Yorkists. That was before the duke's ancestors owned the castle, I believe."

"I suppose so." Still he gazed into her eyes—oh, such beautiful, soft, arresting eyes. "So in this neck of the woods Richard's plea for a horse to save his kingdom would have been met gladly?"

"A horse to save . . . ? Oh, yes." Her self-consciousness was affecting as she touched her loose hair. "You sought my forgiveness for your appearance, Mr. Danby, and I fear I must beg the same of you. I thought your business in Monmouth would take much longer, and not only am I on my own, but also completely unprepared for guests."

He longed to tell her that her unpreparedness endeared her to him all the more, but confined himself to more politenesses. "I think unpinned hair is most charming, Miss Willowby, and besides, you were not alone in expecting my other business to take longer, for I was under the same impression. In the end it proved quite trivial. I still have other appointments to keep in the next day or so, but decided to call upon you first. The lateness of the hour is perhaps a little thoughtless on my part, and for that I again crave your tolerance."

"You are a somewhat unconventional lawyer, Mr. Danby."

"And you are a refreshingly unaffected future Duchess of Wroxford, Miss Willowy," he replied in a tone that was gentler than it should have been.

A spark of electricity seemed to pass between them, but although Gervase knew she was as attracted to him as he was to her, he also knew that she would never admit it because there was still the small matter of her loyalty to Hugh. Anger and frustration burned through him as he thought of his cousin, who did not deserve even a kind thought from her, let alone loyalty! He glanced around the hall, trying to think of something to say. "I, er, imagine you will be very sad to leave Llandower, Miss Willowby."

"Leave?"

"On your marriage to His Grace."

"Oh, I see. Yes, I will be sad to leave here." Again their eyes met with a charge that almost seemed to crackle.

"You will be a perfect duchess, if you don't mind my saying so."

She looked away. "I think you flatter me, Mr. Danby."

"I do not seek to flatter, merely to speak the truth."

"You're too kind, sir, which draws me to wonder if it is because you wish to charm me into surrendering my father's accounts?"

It hadn't occurred to him that she might think such a thing; indeed he'd almost forgotten he'd mentioned the accounts at all. "Miss Willowby, I assure you I'm not given to uttering false compliments for ulterior motives."

"I didn't mean to offend you, sir, but I find it hard to believe that anyone who is acquainted with London society could actually believe I will be a resounding success as Duchess of Wroxford. I am dull and unaccomplished compared with the numerous ladies of the *ton* who might have become the next duchess, and since you represent the duke's lawyers, you must know full well that the forthcoming betrothal is a matter of convenience, nothing more."

"You are clearly not looking forward to the future, Miss Willowby."

"No, I am not, sir, although I confess the advent of Hugh Mowbray gives me cause for some relief, for I cannot pretend to grieve over the passing of his late cousin, whose disagreeable manners and character were only too evident in his letters." Gathering her skirts, she proceeded toward the staircase. "Please come up to the study, sir, for you will be relieved to learn that I have decided to show you my father's accounts after all."

Her harsh opinion of him was sobering, and for the first time Gervase realized how deeply his previous conduct had hurt her. All he could say in mitigation was that he'd been convinced she was a schemer, but oh, how bitter the pill of hindsight. The sweetness of her perfume lingered in his nostrils as he followed her, and the whisper of her skirts was like a longed-for caress. He was almost overwhelmed by the tumult of emotion she aroused in him, and wanted to beg her forgiveness for the pain he'd caused. Above all he wanted to tell her the truth and show her that Gervase Mowbray was worthy of her after all, but as they neared the top of the staircase, he glanced back and was just in time to see Sylvanus draw sharply out of sight. Tell her the truth? That there was a faun at Llandower? That the statue in the rotunda was really the eighth Duke of Wroxford, upon whom the god Bacchus had imposed punishment? That Ariadne's diadem actually existed and would soon be brought here? There was no doubt that to even *hint* at all that would be to convince her that Mr. Danby, far from being merely unconventional, was in fact completely mad!

The candle flame guttered as Anne led him into the study. "Please be seated, Mr. Danby," she said, placing the candle where it would throw the most light. As he sat, she indicated the ledgers, then looked inquiringly at him. "Where would you like to begin?"

His mind was a void. Begin? He didn't know. "Well, the beginning, I suppose." He gave a light laugh.

"The beginning? Mr. Danby, my father has been tenant here for over thirty years, so am I to understand that you wish to examine every book since then?"

"Er, no, of course not. The last five years will do."

To his relief she nodded. "Yes, that is what I expected, so I have the relevant ledgers here." She pushed the pile of leather-bound books toward him.

With a weak smile he took the topmost one and opened it. A sea of entries and invoices swam before him, and his heart sank. The inestimable Mr. Willowby was clearly a very methodical man, plague take his honorable hide! Not a single thing had been omitted—there was even a receipt for a shoe buckle purchased in Oxford during a journey from London, and another for a jug of ale at the Three Tuns in Cirencester. Nothing was too insignificant, and Gervase could only be thankful there wasn't a charge for the air one breathed, for as sure as night followed day, Mr. Willowby of Llandower would have recorded every inhalation!

Anne sat with her back to the open doorway, and after a moment remembered her duties as hostess. "May I offer you some refreshment, Mr. Danby?"

"I don't wish to put you to any further inconvenience, Miss Willowby. Besides, I ate at the White Boar." He was actually very hungry indeed, but he was sure she would think it rather odd if he *hadn't* eaten at the inn before calling.

"Then some brandy, perhaps?" She indicated her father's decanter.

"Thank you, that would be most agreeable." He smiled, then pretended to pore knowledgably over the accounts.

She brought him a liberal measure. "I hope the ledgers are in order, Mr Danby. I know my father has always been most particular, but I suppose it is possible he has missed something."

"He is an excellent bookkeeper, Miss Willowby." Missed something? That would be the day! At any moment Gervase expected to find an exact listing of how many blades of grass were scythed in the park during a particular calendar month—and of exactly how many hours of ruminating the cattle enjoyed from the resultant hay!

"Are you a London man, Mr. Danby?" Anne asked suddenly, resuming her seat.

"Er, no, I come originally from Berkshire. Quite close to Wroxford Park, actually."

Her eyes brightened with interest. "Indeed? What is it like? Wroxford Park, I mean."

He was on firm ground here, for he knew all there was to know about the country estate where he'd grown up. As he began to tell her all about it, he saw Sylvanus creep stealthily past on his way to the drawing room.

Chapter Fifteen

Sylvanus paused to tweak his horns and smooth his goat fur, then went boldly across the firelit drawing room to direct the magic words at Penelope. The gauze of her gown hid nothing of her figure as she gracefully put aside her candle tray, and the lustful faun had to physically clasp his hands behind his back to prevent himself from seizing her. Oh, he did like nymphs, especially the dainty ones with silvery hair!

Penelope gave him a haughty look. "I wondered when you would be back. What sort of disturbance do you intend to cause this time?"

He colored. "I didn't do anything—it was that stupid cat."

"Mog is quiet enough usually—she certainly never bothers about me."

"That's because you're just a piece of wood," he replied sulkily.

"Just wood? Is that really so?" She put a playful hand to his cheek and reached up as if about to kiss him, but then she hurried to the window to look out at the Wye, which shone in the newly risen moon. Ever since Joseph had made her, she'd been plagued by the view from this window. Naiads were meant to haunt water, and yet she hadn't even been able to leave the room. Until now. Her eyes were bright as she turned to Sylvanus again. "Can we go outside?"

"Outside?" He was unsure.

"Oh, please."

When she looked at him like that, he couldn't deny her anything. Besides, once outside, maybe she would let him do what he was supposed to do! "Oh, all right, but we'll have to take care because we have to pass the humans in the study."

They peeped warily out into the dark passage, where the faint shaft of candlelight from the study was the only illumination. Gervase saw the two supposedly mythical beings flit silently past the open doorway, but his voice didn't falter at all as he went on telling Anne about Wroxford Park. Sylvanus held Penelope's hand as they went down to the hall, then out across the courtyard. They hurried past the maze into the moonlit park, and Penelope laughed delightedly as she let go of Sylvanus's hand and ran barefoot through the cowslips toward the river.

The faun's pace checked as Penelope ran onto the jetty, and he couldn't bring himself to follow. He lingered at the water's edge, watching anxiously as the nymph sat down to dangle her feet in the river. "Do be careful," he cried.

She tossed him a scornful look. "I'm a naiad, no harm can come to me here. I'd go for a swim if the water weren't so cold. I don't know where this river rises, but it's in a place that's still quite wintery." She wriggled her toes in the current and glanced upstream. Then she looked downstream at a little fringe of trees on the far bank. "There are strong rapids down there and a spring of some sort on the other bank," she murmured.

The Wye gurgled slightly beneath the jetty, the wind rustled the willows, and the reeds sighed mysteriously. "Please come back on dry land," Sylvanus pleaded, his voice assuming the bleating note it always did when he was perturbed.

Penelope looked curiously. "Why are you so afraid?"

"I'm not!" he replied hotly.

She surveyed him as he hovered impotently at the beginning of the jetty. "Oh, yes, you are, I can tell. What's the matter? All fauns can swim, so—" Her voice broke off as she realized the truth. She giggled. "A faun who can't swim! I've never heard of anything so ridiculous!"

"It's not funny—I nearly drowned." His little goat tail drooped ashamedly, and he kicked disconsolately at a knot of cowslips.

Penelope overcame her amusement. "All right, I promise not to laugh again."

"Really?"

"Really." She held a hand out. "Come here."

"No."

"I'll give you a kiss if you do."

He vacillated on the shore, longing for the kiss, but still filled with dread about the water

Penelope smiled. "Come on, silly. I'm a water nymph, and if anything happens, I can save you. Don't you want a kiss?"

"You know I do! I have since I first saw you! And you should be wanting to kiss me!"

"I do."

"Yes?" His tail perked.

"Well, if I wouldn't let you kiss me before, it's because I wasn't about to do something just because I was *supposed* to. As it happens, I quite like you. You make me laugh."

His tail drooped again. "I don't want to be amusing," he muttered.

"Oh, you are silly. Don't you know that I was paying you a compliment? So come here now, otherwise I'll change my mind." She held her hand out again.

Sylvanus put a nervous hoof on the jetty, testing it carefully before putting the other hoof forward as well. He gazed fearfully down at the water shining between the boards. Oh, may the gods watch over him! With a gulp he pattered swiftly toward her, then closed his eyes tightly as he heard her giggle with laughter. Her little fingers linked with his, and he felt the teasing brush of her lips. Then she released his hands, linked her arms around his neck, and kissed him again.

The faun was so transported that he forgot the river. His lusty goat instincts rose to the occasion, and he tried to grab her, but with a light laugh she ran from the jetty and across the park, with Sylvanus in hot pursuit. She flitted from tree to tree, across the kitchen gardens, and even into the maze, but the faun couldn't catch her. It was a scene that had been captured on countless classical friezes and vases, but never before in the depths of Monmouthshire!

Meanwhile in the study, the ledgers had been forgotten as Anne continued to ply Gervase with questions about Wroxford Park. She was avid for details of the great house of which she would soon be mistress, and she hung on to his every word. At last he smiled. "I think you have exhausted my store of knowledge, Miss Willowby."

She smiled apologetically. "Forgive me, Mr. Danby—it's just that I know so little."

"You will soon learn."

"I trust so." She lowered her eyes, toying with the folds of lavender velvet across her lap.

"You *will* be a perfect duchess, you know," he said quietly.

Her gaze flew up. "I would like to believe you, sir."

"Then do so, for I know something of the world into which you will be going, and believe me, you are not the gauche country mouse you clearly believe yourself to be. The man who marries you will be a very fortunate man, indeed."

"Please don't . . ." She got up agitatedly, for the softness in his voice and eyes aroused feelings she knew should not be there.

He got up as well. "Why not?" he said, coming around the desk toward her. "What is wrong with telling you the truth?"

"You know full well, Mr. Danby." She tried to back away, but could only press against the glass-fronted bookshelves that stretched from floor to ceiling.

"What do I know, Anne?" Gervase asked gently.

"I gave you no leave to address me so familiarly."

"True, but I take that liberty anyway." He put his hand to her chin and made her look up at him.

"Please, don't," she begged, her wonderful eyes filling with tears.

"You want me to keep denying what we have both known since we met?"

"Yes."

"And if I will not?"

"Then I must ask you to leave."

"Is that what you want, Anne?" He stroked her cheek with his thumb.

She tried to fend off emotion with common sense. "Is this a test, Mr. Danby? Is it your brief to see if the lady who is to be Duchess of Wroxford is in fact a lady? If I succumb now, will you convey my failure to the duke when he arrives? Is he simply seeking an excuse to cast me aside and have my father turned out of Llandower? Has he found a way around the will? Is that what this is really about?"

"Do you truly believe I would do that?" he asked.

"Why should I not?"

"If you require proof that I am in earnest, I give it gladly," he whispered, putting his hand to her waist and drawing her toward him.

"No . . ." She struggled, trying to deny the sensations that were pounding unstoppably through her, but they were irresistible. He wove a magic that was impossible to withstand,

and her futile protests were stifled as his lips found hers. She was spellbound, trapped forever by a sexual enchantment that drew her to him as if they were two halves of one whole. Never had anything felt more right than being in this man's arms, and yet she was only too aware that it was very wrong. She was destined for Hugh Mowbray, and even to *think* of Charles Danby like this was forbidden, but the relentless onslaught of his kiss rendered her resolve ever more fragile, and her heart ever more open to assault. Reason told her to break free, to order him to leave and thus show that she was worthy of becoming a duchess! Oh, she knew what she *should* do, but instead her lips parted, and her arms moved around him, hesitantly at first, then with a fervor that was a mirror of his own.

He slid his fingers into the scented warmth of the hair at the nape of her neck, and her body was sweetly pliable as he pulled her tight against him. She wove a magic too, and it coiled so unsparingly around him that a kiss that began with gentleness soon became a thing of unfettered passion. His whole consciousness was aroused, as if forgotten corners of his being were suddenly stirring with life again. She was the love he had been waiting for, the echo of his own heartbeat, and for these few seconds she was in his arms, responding to him as she had in the barn, but without prompting by the ancient powers of an interfering faun. He crushed her to him, and in spite of their clothes it was already as if they were one.

He couldn't prevent his arousal, nor did he wish to. It was good to feel her pressing against his hardness, good to know that she could feel him too. He heard her breath catch, partly in confusion, partly in excitement, and he knew she had never knowingly experienced anything like this before. She was untouched, and yet in his arms she came so sensuously to life that, just as had happened in the barn, he longed to take things to a natural and fulfilling conclusion. But he could sense her inner struggle. She was trapped by unbelievably erotic feelings, and at the same time torn with guilt and shock that she could indulge such familiarity with a virtual stranger. She didn't know what was happening to her, and her dilemma made him adore her all the more. Yes, he adored her! He *adored* her!

Anne couldn't tear away. She wanted to, but was prey to a new weakness she hadn't realized she possessed. She could feel his maleness through their clothes, and wild new sensations tingled yearningly through her entire body as she pressed against him. Her body felt warm and seemed to be melting. Oh, what would it be like to be naked now, to press skin to skin, to feel him inside her? Please don't let her succumb any more. Please don't let her craving for Charles Danby lead her into the ultimate folly! But, that was the direction in which these treacherous emotions were luring her. The erotic secrets of the flesh beckoned, and she longed to give in. But it was wrong, so very wrong. . . .

Chapter Sixteen

Penelope was still leading Sylvanus a merry dance in the grounds, but now she decided it was time to placate him a little. Still laughing, she fled back to the castle, across the courtyard, and through the nearest door, which wasn't—as she thought—the main entrance into the hall, but the way into the kitchens, where the only light came from the banked-up fire. The faint glow lay warmly on Mrs. Jenkins's prized array of copper pots and pans, and the only sound came from the rather battered clock on the high mantelpiece. Memories swept over the nymph, for this was where she'd been carved, where she'd been polished and varnished until she shone.

Then Sylvanus raced in, but his hooves slipped on the stone-flagged floor, and he slithered into the pots and pans, which fell with an explosive clatter that resounded through the silent house. The faun and nymph froze in dismay, for they knew Anne and Gervase couldn't help hearing such a racket. Sylvanus seized Penelope's hand again and led the way back across the courtyard to the double trapdoors, which he flung open. After clambering down into the cellars, he held his arms up to Penelope, who didn't hesitate about joining him. The trapdoors closed again, and all was silent.

In the study Anne and Gervase had jumped nervously apart the moment they heard the clatter of the pans, and as Anne looked uneasily toward the door, the shocking and entirely uncharacteristic intimacies in which she'd just been indulging fled temporarily from her mind. "There's someone in the kitchens!" she gasped.

"Maybe Mrs. Jenkins has returned, or maybe it's just the dog chasing the cat," Gervase replied, guessing the perpetrator of the interruption. Damn that faun! Of all the times to cause a diversion!

Anne wasn't reassured. "No, I'm sure someone's down there who shouldn't be!"

Gervase still did not doubt it was something to do with Sylvanus and Penelope, but not to investigate would seem odd, so he picked up the poker from the hearth. He tried to make Anne stay behind, but she picked up the lighted candle and insisted on accompanying him. They went stealthily down through the dark house, but in the kitchen passage they had a fright when without warning Mog leapt from a shelf onto Gervase's shoulder. Anne gave a startled cry, and he dashed the cat aside in alarm, receiving a nasty scratch on the knuckles for his pains.

Gervase reassured her. "It's all right—it was only the cat!"

Considering what had happened in the drawing room an hour or so earlier, it now seemed to Anne only too likely that this disturbance had been caused by Mog as well. An hour or so? Was *that* all the time that had passed? She felt her face go hot as she remembered the unbelievable indiscretions of which she'd been guilty in the interim. If only she'd imagined it all, just as she'd so often imagined herself in the cornfield, but she hadn't; it had been only too real, and Charles Danby now had it within his power to destroy her reputation! The duke was about to arrive, and a single word from this man could ruin her. Regret after shameful regret lanced through her, and she wished with all her heart that she could turn back the clock.

Unaware of her thoughts, Gervase advanced into the kitchens, where gentle firelight flickered over the scattered copper utensils. The room was empty, but then he didn't expect otherwise, nor was he surprised to see the open door into the courtyard. Whoever had done this would have shown a clean pair of heels the moment it happened. Sylvanus and Penelope certainly would! Right now the faun and nymph were probably somewhere in the grounds, or—if Sylvanus had any say in the matter—down in the seclusion of the temple! He placed the poker quietly on the scrubbed table and glanced at Anne. "Since the door is ajar, I fear there must indeed have been an intruder, but whoever it was has gone now, and I doubt very much if they will risk coming back," he said, taking out his handkerchief and wrapping it around his scratched hand. He was anxious to reassure her, since he was personally certain of the culprits. "It was probably just some passing vagrant in search of food, but you need not fear, for I will remain until Mrs. Jenkins and Joseph come back."

At that moment there came the distant but unmistakable sound of the returning pony and trap. Anne had just decided she would ask him to leave without further ado, and so was dismayed, for she didn't want Mrs. Jenkins to know she'd entertained him alone in the house. "The problem is solved, Mr. Danby, for they are here, and so you may go—now," she said, with as much dignity as she could muster.

"Anne, I—"

"Please don't use my first name." She was polite, correct, and, she hoped, remote, although in truth such considerations were a little tardy. It was the proverbial attempt to shut the stable door after the horse had bolted, and she knew it.

So did Gervase, inwardly cursing Sylvanus again. But for these spilled pots and pans, a great deal more progress might have been made in the study before the servants returned. He tried to regain the lost ground. "If you still fear that my actions have been prompted by a plot to discredit you, let me assure you that is not so. I concede that I did not behave as a true gentleman would, but it was due to the tremendous effect you have upon me, an effect which I am now equally certain I have upon you." *Admit it, Anne, please admit it, for if you only knew how much I need you to tell me you love me. . . .*

"Mr. Danby, I deeply regret what took place, and if you are indeed a gentleman, I trust you will put the entire matter from your mind." The noise of the pony and trap was growing louder.

"I cannot do that."

"Then you will not be welcome here again." She met his eyes squarely, for she meant every word. Too much depended upon the betrothal for her to do anything now except deny her own heart.

He saw how implacable was her determination and gave in—for the time being. "As you wish, Miss Willowby."

"Do I have your promise that no word of tonight will ever pass your lips?"

"I am offended that you need my pledge."

"Please, sir, for no matter how intimate we were a few minutes ago, the fact remains that we do not know each other at all. I certainly do not know anything about you, not even if you have a wife." This awful possibility suddenly struck her, and her hand crept awkwardly to her throat. The misdemeanor would be bad enough with a bachelor, but with a *married man*!

"I am a free agent, just as you are, so the only offense committed tonight was against propriety."

"I'm not a free agent, sir, as we both know full well."

He reached out suddenly to raise her left hand. "I see no binding proof that you are another man's possession."

"I am bound by my word," she replied, wresting her hand from him and glancing uneasily toward the door as the dim light from the trap began to shine beyond the courtyard archway.

"What of your heart? What of your future happiness?"

"I don't wish to discuss this any further, Mr. Danby," she replied, achieving a cold detachment that belied the passionate emotion within. "I ask again—do I have your word that my indiscretions will remain secret?"

"You do." There was such an air of finality about her that he was afraid she didn't intend to receive him again. He had to make sure she did. "May I remind you that I have not completed my inspection of the ledgers?"

"I need no reminding, sir. You are welcome to examine them again, but I must ask you not to call unannounced. There must be advance warning of your next visit, so that Mrs. Jenkins can be present at all times. Do I make my position completely clear?" Her uneasy glance moved toward the courtyard, where the clatter of the pony and trap was suddenly loud.

"Only too clear, Miss Willowby." How would any seduction be achieved in the face of such a restriction?

"Now I wish you to leave."

Gervase inclined his head. "I will see myself out, Miss Willowby," he murmured, then went from the kitchens to the hall to collect his hat and gloves. As the servants entered by one door, he left by the other, so they knew nothing of the second visit of the mysterious Mr. Danby.

Mrs. Jenkins was dismayed by the disagreeable news that there had apparently been a felon of some sort in her kitchens. She was tired after all the cleaning up at her sister's house, and, truth to tell, had taken a large measure of soothing elderberry wine when she decided to check that the upstairs fires had been made safe for the night. First she went into the study, where the empty brandy glass immediately told a tale of which she would have preferred to remain in ignorance. Whoever may or may not have knocked things over in the kitchens, there had certainly been an identifiable but equally unwelcome visitor up here! She didn't doubt who the caller had been, and as she went into the drawing room, she wondered how best to broach such an exceedingly delicate subject of the handsome but questionable lawyer, whose motives for coming here were either devious or simply improper. Then she noticed something very odd, or at least *thought* she noticed something very odd. The lampholder was without its wooden naiad, or nad, as Mrs. Jenkins was wont to call it. Stretching out a hesitant hand, she slid her fingers over the carved surface, feeling for the splintered parts where someone had wrenched the nymph away. But there were no jagged edges, just smooth polished wood. And the candle tray was on the table!

Suddenly uneasy, Mrs. Jenkins drew back sharply. It was the elderberry wine, she told herself. "You've had more than you should, Gwen Jenkins, so it's bed for you," she muttered to herself, then without further ado hurried up to her room on the next floor.

Chapter Seventeen

The sun was shining the following afternoon when Hugh and Kitty arrived at the White Boar, having spent the previous night at a hostelry high on the Cotswold hills. Hens scattered before the horses' hooves, and a tethered dog began to bark as the coachman brought the vehicle to a standstill. The hostelry commanded a fork in the road from Peterbury, one route swinging away toward Monmouth, and the other to Goodrich, which had a splendid ruined castle on a crag above the Wye. The inn was an unremarkable gray stone building, with a wide dusty area serving as a yard in front of the main entrance, but its accommodation was clean and comfortable. Later in the summer it would be frequented by sightseers eager for the fashionably picturesque scenery of the valley, but at the moment trade was so quiet that the appearance of a smart London traveling carriage was cause for the landlord himself to come out in greeting.

He was a tough ex-pugilist who had used the fruits of his considerable success to purchase the inn. His eyes were set close together above a broken nose, and he was very tall and broad, although his once hard muscle was now soft. He was all smiles as he wiped his hands on his apron, then opened the carriage door for Hugh to alight.

"Welcome to the White Boar, Mr. er . . . ?"

"Oadby," Hugh replied smoothly, for he and Kitty had already decided upon false identities, and Oadby in Leicestershire was her hometown.

Hugh glanced around, then eyed the man. "I trust you have suitable accommodation for my sister and me?"

"Oh, indeed so, sir," the landlord replied, glancing disbelievingly at Kitty. Sister? Pigs would swim down the Wye first! These two were a gentleman and his trollop, but if they paid well, who was he to care?

"We require two rooms, but adjacent, for Miss Oadby is afraid of intruders." Hugh smarted a little, for he could read the man's insolent thoughts. The original plan had been to pose as Mr. and Mrs. Oadby, but a quarrel during the latter part of the journey had led to Kitty's taking umbrage and insisting upon separate rooms.

The landlord met his gaze. "Certainly, sir."

"Are your best rooms available?"

"The second bedchamber is certainly available, sir, but the principal bedchamber itself will soon be required by Sir Thomas and Lady Fanhope."

The Fanhopes? Hugh's smile became fixed, and in the carriage Kitty gave a sharp intake of breath, for this was a circumstance neither of them could possibly have foreseen. The last thing they wanted was the arrival of someone who knew exactly who they were, especially one of Kitty's most recent lovers!

Hugh cleared his throat. "When are they expected?"

"In a week's time. I understand from Sir Thomas's message that they will be en route for Bristol, from where they intend to take passage to America."

Hugh recovered. "My sister and I will take the rooms in question, for we will have left before they arrive." Until now he hadn't decided exactly when and how to dispose of tiresome Anne Willowby, but the landlord's information concentrated the mind most sharply. The Fanhopes had to be avoided at all costs, therefore the lady's extinction had to be achieved swiftly, although how he would do it remained uncertain.

Hugh turned to hold his hand out to Kitty, but as she began to alight, the team moved forward a foot or so, and she lost her balance. With a squeal she fell heavily onto Hugh, who fell as well, and in a moment they were both sprawled in dust where the inn's hens had more than left their mark. As the dismayed landlord helped them to their feet, a loud mocking bleat drifted from a stable door farther along the inn. Hugh turned to see a goat standing on its hind legs to peer out at the commotion, and from the way it bleated again, showing yellow teeth, he was certain it was laughing.

Anne had no idea that her future husband had arrived in the vicinity, or that she was in danger from him. Troubled about her astonishing misconduct with Charles Danby, she avoided the servants all morning, and in the afternoon decided to go for a walk by the river. Putting on a blue-and-white gingham gown and a light shawl, she went downstairs in so preoccupied a mood that she didn't see Mrs. Jenkins in the hall.

The housekeeper, who was suffering a little from the after-effects of the further glasses of elderberry wine she'd taken after discovering the strange business of the disappearing nad, was polishing a table. The nad was where it should be this morning, and the housekeeper put the whole thing down to alcohol, but she knew that the empty brandy glass had been only too real. Something had to be said to Anne. But what? It was very delicate. When she saw her young mistress coming downstairs, she decided to seize the moment.

"Begging your pardon, Miss Anne, but may I have a private word with you?" she said.

Anne gave a start, for she hadn't realized anyone was there. "A-a word? Yes, of course. What is it? Is something wrong?"

"That may be for you to say, Miss Anne," Mrs. Jenkins replied quietly.

"Me? I don't understand."

"Well, unless you have taken to consuming Mr. Willowby's cognac . . . ?"

The glass! Anne had forgotten all about it.

The housekeeper drew a long breath. "The kitchen intruder wasn't the only stranger here last night, was he? Mr. Danby was here as well."

Anne couldn't meet her eyes.

"Oh, Miss Anne, what *were* you thinking of?"

"I didn't know what to do, Mrs. Jenkins. I'd told him that it would be in order for him to call again, and that he did so when I was alone in the house put me in some difficulty."

"Maybe it did, but I'll warrant there was nothing accidental about his arrival. He *knew* you were alone."

"Knew? What are you suggesting?"

"That Mr. Charles Danby is definitely *not* a gentleman. Miss Anne, I must warn you against him. I may be only a servant, and therefore presumptuous in speaking my mind at all, but for all that he says he is a man of the law, it is my opinion that Mr. Danby is not to be trusted in any way at all."

"You are very free with such a sweeping judgment, Mrs. Jenkins."

"I have the evidence before me. His manner toward you

since arriving has been too forward by far, and I cannot help but be aware that he puts you all of a fluster. You were like an open book to me that first night when he took his leave, and now I learn that he has been here again. It will not do, Miss Anne. You are to be the Duchess of Wroxford, and the duke is about to come here, so no hint of scandal must touch upon you."

"You think I do not know that?" Anne turned away slightly, gripping the handrail as she struggled to recoup her lost composure. She'd hoped that last night's visit would remain a secret, but it was clear she'd hoped in vain.

"I've been giving his motives considerable thought. At first I wondered if he was simply intent upon seduction for seduction's sake, but then I discounted that because if his activities were discovered, his firm would lose the duke as a client, and a junior partner would very swiftly be thrown out on his handsome ear. That leaves another motive entirely for his persistence. I'm sorry, my dear, but the only conclusion I can reach is that you are being tested to see if you are indeed suitable to be a duchess."

Anne's dismay was complete, for was that not exactly what she herself had thought?

Mrs. Jenkins searched her face. "You've gone very pale, my dear. Could it be that Mr. Danby took liberties last night?"

"Oh, Mrs. Jenkins, please don't ask," Anne whispered, close to tears.

The housekeeper put a concerned hand on her arm. "Did he . . . ? I mean, you didn't . . . ?"

"I am still chaste, if you is what you fear to put into words," Anne replied, mastering her emotions sufficiently to speak levelly.

"But something happened, didn't it?"

"Yes."

"Oh, Miss Anne . . ."

"It will not happen again, for I have told him so. I have also told him that he will not be received in future unless he sends word in advance, so that I may have you in attendance at all times."

"You would have done better to forbid him to come at all."

"I cannot do that, for he is here in connection with my betrothal. Oh, Mrs. Jenkins, whether or not he is false-hearted, I would find it very easy to love him." Anne's eyes shone with tears, and she gathered her gingham skirts to hurry across the hall and out into the courtyard, leaving the housekeeper to gaze sadly after her.

Anne hardly realized her decision to go into the maze. It wasn't until the cool shade of the high hedges made her pull her shawl closer that she knew, but she walked on anyway, and at last the maze splayed back to reveal the rotunda—and the statue. As she gazed at the latter, she knew why her subconscious had brought her here. The marble figure was so like Charles Danby that it drew her like a moth to a candle.

Gervase was very aware of her the moment she appeared, and when he saw the way she looked at his face, he was again afraid she had guessed the truth. If she looked at his hand and saw the scratch Mog had left, she *would* know! His marble heart tightened as she studied him intensely for a moment, before going to sit on the stone bench. His initial relief was almost immediately swamped by further apprehension, for his clothes—only too recognizable as Charles Danby's—were hidden in the thick ivy growing all over the bench. Had he concealed them well enough? His only consolation was that at least Sylvanus was nowhere to be seen, for the faun was sleeping in the temple, having only come to the rotunda briefly just before the dawn in order to acquaint Gervase with his success with Penelope—for success he had certainly had.

But Anne didn't notice anything as she clasped her hands in her lap and continued to gaze at the statue. She knew she should turn her back completely on her feelings for Charles Danby. He had awakened emotions she had never experienced before, and awakened them so passionately it was as if she had slumbered her life away until now. If only things were different, and she could not only be sure of his character and intentions, but have been at liberty last night to declare her true feelings; if only she could be sitting here now, waiting for him to come openly to her. But things *weren't* different, and it was best if she forgot all about him, and certainly best if Mrs. Jenkins remained present at all times should he decide to call again. She prayed her trust would not be broken, and that if nothing else, Charles Danby would stand by his promise not to say anything of what took place last night.

She continued to gaze at the statue, taking in the lean but muscular body, slender hips, and well-shaped legs. And taking in too that part of the male body that had pressed so ardently against her when she'd been in Charles Danby's arms last night! She'd felt wonderful, and to have given herself completely would have been to enjoy the perfect initiation—well, almost, for to lie with him in a cornfield beneath the summer sun would be the most perfect initiation of all. . . . She lowered her glance. Was it really possible to feel this way about someone who was as false as Mrs. Jenkins feared? Could one's heart be so misguided?

With a sad sigh she got up, but as she passed the statue, she halted to put a hand to Gervase's cold face. "I wish you *were* my wickedly handsome lawyer," she whispered, reaching up to kiss his marble mouth. There were tears in her eyes, and suddenly she linked her arms around his neck and kissed his lips more ardently. She pressed against him, remembering the joy of being embraced by a flesh-and-blood lover.

Imprisoned in marble, he ached to return the embrace, but was unable to do anything except feel the sweet yearning in her lips. If only she would whisper more, if only she would say the three words that would release him! Say them! *Say them!*

But after clinging to him for a long moment, she gradually became mistress of herself again and slowly drew back and left the maze.

As Gervase looked helplessly after her, he felt as if his marble heart were breaking.

Chapter Eighteen

Hugh wasted no time about making his first visit to Llandower. He hired a horse at the White Boar, and after asking directions of an ostler, set off along the winding country road that was flanked by meadows of cowslips and hawthorn hedges that frothed with white blossom. He hardly glanced at the beautiful scenery; indeed he might have been in the dingiest quarter of the port of London for all the notice he took. He was preoccupied with how he was going to dispose of his unwanted bride, but as he at last rode across the Peterbury road bridge over the Wye, his own words to Kitty suddenly echoed in his head. *I'm going to make you the Duchess of Wroxford, and if I have to drown Anne Willowby in the River Wye in order to do it, then I will.* He reined in to gaze at the shining water, and a cold smile played briefly about his lips as he rode on. Yes, a simple drowning would do very well!

Anne was writing to her parents in the study when a highly flustered Mrs. Jenkins came upstairs to tell her who had called. Anne was hugely dismayed to be caught at such a disadvantage. She had intended to be elegantly turned out for Hugh's first call, but instead of sending word ahead, he had just arrived at the door! There was no time to change out of the simple blue-and-white gingham into something more suitable for receiving a duke, so all she could hope was that she wouldn't create too provincial an impression. Taking a deep breath to steady nerves that were suddenly all over the place, she went downstairs with the housekeeper.

Her first impression on seeing Hugh's tall figure in the hall was that he bore an astonishing and welcome resemblance to Charles Danby, although on drawing nearer she realized it was only superficial. However, she would have liked him well enough simply because he reminded her of the lawyer, so that when he smiled warmly and drew her hands to his lips as if they were friends already, she was sure they could get along together. He didn't seem to notice her country gown or the simple way she'd attended to her hair, for he looked intently into her eyes when she spoke, and was gifted with the sort of easy conversation that removed all hint of awkwardness. Yes, she thought with relief, she would be able to get on well enough with Hugh Mowbray, but the thought was detached, lacking the fire and emotion that from the outset had marked her dealings with Charles Danby; Hugh kissed her hand politely, Charles scorched her very skin.

Hugh's thoughts were very different in those first moments. He judged her unremarkable in every way, and his inner dislike and resentment was so great that he had to concentrate upon maintaining a semblance of interest and charm.

After the somewhat stilted and awkward introductions, he opened the conversation with an obvious politeness. "Are your parents not at home, Miss Willowby?"

"I fear not, sir. They are in Ireland."

"Ireland? I had no idea." Excellent, for he had expected their presence to supply his crime with two more potential witnesses; now it seemed he did not have to concern himself about that particular problem. He smiled. "No doubt I will meet them in due course."

"Oh, yes, you will." She thought it a little peculiar that he was ignorant of her parents' absence; after all, Charles had known, and both had recently been in conversation with Mr. Critchley, to whom her father had apparently written.

He glanced around. "What a charming home you have, Miss Willowby. I fancy my ancestors were unwise to leave it for grander pastures."

She smiled. "I'm glad they did, sir. I mean, Your Grace . . . for I have certainly always loved it here." She had no idea at all how to speak to him. Her mind was blank, and she couldn't recall how she'd addressed his late uncle last year.

He smiled. "That is a little formal, don't you think? As we are to be man and wife, would it be too heinous a crime against propriety if we used our first names? Or would that offend etiquette too much? What do you think, Mrs. Jenkins?" With a gallantly convincing smile he suddenly turned to the housekeeper, who gave a surprised start on being solicited for an opinion.

"Sir, I would not presume to . . ."

He continued to smile winningly, for instinct told him that the woman would be an invaluable ally. "Oh, come now, I am sure a *ménagère* of your admirable experience and qualities can judge in an instant."

Mrs. Jenkins wasn't quite sure what a *ménagère* was, but as the remainder of what he said made her feel most flattered, she felt certain the foreign word wasn't anything insulting. "Well, I do not know that my view is of any consequence, sir . . ."

"Of course it is. So, what is it to be? Formality, or congeniality?"

"Why, I suppose the latter, sir," the housekeeper replied after a moment.

Anne couldn't help giving her a surreptitious glance, for if Charles Danby had asked the same question, the answer would have been very different!

Hugh smiled at Anne again. "I trust you do not mind such a decision being made for you?"

"I have no objection, sir."

"I have no objection, *Hugh*," he prompted.

"I have no objection . . . Hugh," she repeated obediently.

Mrs. Jenkins looked inquiringly at her. "Begging your pardon, Miss Anne, but should I prepare some refreshment?"

Hugh intervened hastily, for he had promised Kitty he would dine with her. "There is no need, for I intend to eat later at the inn."

"The Salmon's Leap in Peterbury?"

"Er, no, at the White Boar," he replied reluctantly, for the question caught him off guard.

Anne looked swiftly at him. "Indeed? Then no doubt you have encountered Mr. Danby?" She felt Mrs. Jenkins cross gaze upon her, but under the circumstances, not to mention Charles would surely appear odd.

"Danby?" Hugh looked blankly at her.

"Of Messrs. Critchley, Faulkner, Oliver, and Danby. Your lawyers, I believe?" she added with a smile.

Hugh was alarmed, for he didn't want one of Critchley's cohorts in the very inn he was staying with Kitty! But then he remembered something. "Forgive me, er, Anne, but there is no Mr. Danby at the inn. On my arrival I had the pick of rooms because the landlord specifically mentioned there being no other guests at the moment."

"Oh." Anne looked away. "Well, I expect he has returned to Monmouth, for he did say he had other business to attend to."

Hugh prayed this was indeed the case, but he was still curious about the apparent visit. "Are you *sure* this Mr. Danby is from the lawyers?"

"Quite sure. He came to examine the ledgers."

"I find this most intriguing, because when I spoke to Mr. Critchley a few days ago, he knew I was coming straight here, so I would have thought he would have told me if one of his partners had left on such an errand."

"It must have slipped his mind," Anne replied.

"Yes, I suppose so," Hugh conceded, but privately determined to ask the landlord about this Danby fellow, for something didn't feel quite right about it. An awkward silence had descended over the hall, and Hugh galvanized himself into returning things to the former state of relative bonhomie. Besides, he wanted to examine the boats at the willow-hung jetty he'd spied while riding up the drive. "Shall we stroll in the sunshine, Anne? I vow it is too pleasant a day to stay inside, and it looked most agreeable by the river."

"Why, of course."

Again Hugh turned to the housekeeper, whom he wished to lull into as false a sense of trust as Anne herself. "Mrs. Jenkins, I'm sure correctness and other such things will be best served if you come too."

"Accompany you, sir?"

"You are clearly a person of unquestioned propriety, and apart from that, why should you not enjoy the sunshine too?" He smiled into her eyes.

The housekeeper was won over completely. "If you wish me to be there, sir, I will go for my shawl." Her skirts rustled and her shoes tapped as she hastened up to her bedroom on the third floor.

Alone with him for a minute or so, Anne felt quite uncomfortable, although she could not have said why. He appeared to be everything she could wish, and yet there was something—she could not have put her finger upon what, exactly—that made her wish to draw away from him. He caught her eye and smiled, and for a fleeting second, oh, so fleeting, she thought she detected a chill behind the apparent warmth.

Hugh guessed he'd been less than guarded, and was at pains to rectify the slip by reassuring her. At the same time he gave in to the conceit of painting himself in as noble a light as possible. "I have a confession to make, Miss Willowby. Unlike you, I am under no compulsion to proceed with this match."

She was shaken. "You aren't? But I thought—"

"My late cousin was indeed obliged to bow to his father's wishes, but it seems I *can* escape if I so wish, there being no actual provision for Gervase's death and my succession to the title. True, it would be a little complicated to get out of but not impossible. However, I *choose* to proceed because I wish to be settled and married, and since you are still bound by the exact terms of the will, I believe we will do well together." Even the Archangel Gabriel would have been taken in by such noble sentiments, he thought.

In spite of her momentary reservations, Anne was taken in too. "I am relieved you feel that way," she replied, lowering her eyes quickly as Charles Danby's face seemed to hover before her.

"Then the marriage will proceed," he said quietly, taking her hand and raising it to his lips. He didn't want to kiss her fingers—he wanted to sink his teeth ferociously into them.

Mrs. Jenkins returned, and Hugh offered Anne his arm. They crossed the courtyard, then walked alongside the maze as they made for the river. Something pattered on the gravel path the other side of the high hedge of the maze, and, thinking it was Joseph's lurcher on the roam, Mrs. Jenkins frowned as she remembered the currant buns cooling on a rack on the kitchen table. "That Jack—Joseph swore he'd take him with him to the east woods today," she muttered beneath her breath, vowing that if a single currant was missing on her return, she'd tie a knot in the thieving dog's tail.

But it was Sylvanus, not Jack, on the other side of the hedge. The faun had slipped out of the temple not long before in order to see Gervase, and had just been on his way back to his hidey-hole—intending to go by way of the kitchen, and then, if possible, his beloved Penelope in the drawing room— when he'd been appalled to recognize Hugh riding into the courtyard. Sylvanus didn't dare try to eavesdrop in the castle itself because he'd have to pass young Martin, who had suddenly appeared with a ladder to clean a second-floor window, so he waited just inside the maze to see what happened in order to report back to Gervase. As Anne, Hugh, and Mrs. Jenkins at last emerged from the courtyard and came within earshot, the listening faun accompanied them on the other side of the hedge.

Mrs. Jenkins turned to call out to be boy up the ladder. "Martin, you keep an eye out for that dratted mongrel! He's in the maze, and if he goes anywhere near my currant buns . . . !" Her voice faded on a dire note.

Martin looked down in puzzlement. "Jack can't be in the maze, Mrs. Jenkins; he went with Joseph this morning."

"He's in there, I tell you, I can hear him. Just keep a look-out."

"Yes, Mrs. Jenkins." With a shrug, Martin went on polishing the window.

Anne glanced at Hugh. "I trust the cuisine at the White Boar meets with your approval, for it is considered excellent, especially the Wye salmon."

Only three feet away, Sylvanus's pointed ears pricked. The White Boar?

Hugh murmured something about liking salmon no matter from which river it came, then he nodded toward the jetty. "I, er, notice you have rowing boats. Do you often go on the river?"

"Not as often as I'd like." Anne smiled as fond memories of past jaunts and picnics flitted briefly through her mind.

Hugh observed the nuances on her face. "What are you thinking?"

She told him all about the excursions on the river and even mentioned the next day's omission of the annual moonlight picnic and trip downstream to St. Winifred's Well.

Hugh listened with grim delight as she innocently presented him with a heaven-sent opening. "It is your birthday tomorrow?" he repeated.

"I fear so."

"I had no idea. We must observe it, of course."

"Oh, there is no need . . ."

"Forgive me for presuming, but maybe you and I—and Mrs. Jenkins, of course—could celebrate your birthday picnic after all?" he ventured, turning to smile conspiratorially at the housekeeper.

Anne was so agreeably surprised by his thoughtful spon-

taneity, that she felt ashamed of her earlier unease. "Oh, I
would like that," she replied gladly.

"Perhaps you would also like to be rowed across to the
well?"

She smiled. "Yes, I would, very much, and I'm sure Mrs.
Jenkins will too."

Mrs. Jenkins was flattered to be included, but had certain
reservations. "It will be most agreeable, sir, but I have a dread
of boats, so will remain on dry land if you don't mind."

Mind? It suited him most excellently! Hugh could have
laughed out loud that his plan seemed to be falling into place
so ridiculously easily. They would have the picnic on the
jetty, then he and dear Anne would cross in the darkness to St.
Winifred's Well. How charming she would look seated in the
stern of one of those boats; how easy she would be to render
unconscious and tip into the water the moment an opportune
moment presented itself. His frantic but unsuccessful attempts
to rescue her would be dimly witnessed from the shore by the
housekeeper, who already thought him everything that was
admirable, and who would be further taken in by his exhibi-
tion of anguish and guilt because he had persuaded dear Anne
to go out on the water with him in the first place. . . .

He felt so arrogantly confident as they walked on toward
the jetty, that it amused him to indulge in more small talk. "I
trust your parents' visit to Ireland is proving agreeable? As a
country it can be so very *wet*, don't you agree?"

"As it happens I haven't heard from them since they left,
but I don't think the climate will have much bearing on their
particular situation." she replied.

Her next words were lost to Sylvanus, for they passed out
of hearing as they struck across the park toward the jetty.
After a precautionary glance at Martin, whose back was safely
turned toward the maze, the faun made his way swiftly to the
rotunda to acquaint Gervase with all he'd learned.

Gervase was dismayed to learn that his loathed cousin had
arrived. *"Damn it, I was hoping he'd take longer."*

"So was I."

*"I wish you could turn me to flesh right now, so I can face
him as he should be faced!"*

"Well, I can't, it only works after dark. Besides, you need
Anne to tell you she loves you *before* you confront Hugh."

"How do you arrive at that conclusion?" Gervase demanded.

"Because Bacchus has decreed that she must tell you of her love without knowing who you really are. By confronting Hugh too soon, you run the risk of being identified by him, which will mean remaining half-man, half-statue for the rest of your existence," the faun warned.

Gervase knew the advice was wise, and so strove to quell the bitter rage that burned through him. *"Is Hugh staying here at Llandower?"* he asked after a moment. That would be too much!

"No, he's at the White Boar."

Gervase thought swiftly. *"I trust to God Charles Danby's name doesn't crop up in conversation, for Hugh is sure to say that there is no such person staying there. I wish now that I'd thought of some other false identity. Hugh is bound to have visited Critchley, and will be very curious—if not to say suspicious—that he wasn't informed of Danby's business here."*

"It's too late now," the faun replied pragmatically.

"Thank you, I do realize that!" Gervase responded sharply.

Sylvanus gave him a look. "Well, I see no point in worrying about something you can't rectify."

"Just as you didn't worry when Baccus knew you'd misused your power on Anne and me, I suppose?" Gervase supplied in the sort of unhelpful tone the faun was only too frequently wont to use.

Sylvanus chose to ignore the remark. "Your cousin is supposed to bring the diadem here, so I think I'll go to the inn tonight and see what I can find."

"I'd quite forgotten about the diadem."

"I certainly haven't," the faun muttered, sitting on the bench and swinging his hooves thoughtfully.

"Don't forget that you are bound by Bacchus's conditions too. Hugh has to give the diadem to you willingly." Gervase reminded, fearing Sylvanus might be tempted to steal it on the spur of the moment.

They were both silent briefly, then Gervase said, *"So Anne intends to go out on the river with him?"*

"Yes. Something about a birthday picnic in the moonlight, and then rowing across the river." Sylvanus's hooves stopped swinging. "Actually, I thought he was a little odd when he suggested it. Too eager by far, if you know what I mean."

"No, I don't know what you mean."

"He's up to something."

"Of course he is, he's intent upon stealing my name, my fortune, and the woman who is supposed to be my wife!"

"Is he? About the third of those things, I mean?" Sylvanus looked slowly up at Gervase's motionless marble face. "I know I'm irrationally frightened because I nearly drowned, but there was something about the way your disagreeable cousin mentioned rowing across the river that made my fur creep."

The faun's meaning was borne in on a horrified Gervase. Without a bride, there could be no marriage. Anne's life might be in danger!

Sylvanus rubbed a horn uneasily. "Well, if he *does* intend to try something—and I'm not saying he does—it won't be until after dark tomorrow, so we'll be able to keep an eye on things, eh? Besides, there is still tonight." The faun gave a reassuring grin.

"Tonight?"

"You can call upon her again, and this time Penelope and I won't disturb you."

"She won't receive me, and besides, the dragon house-keeper is there as well. As far as I can see, it's an impossible situation."

"Look, if you want to escape from what's happening to you at the moment, you'll find a way. You had better, because I want to go home, *and* I want to see if my master will let me take Penelope with me. If she'll come," Sylvanus added.

Chapter Nineteen

Later, as Hugh rode swiftly back to the White Boar, his first purpose was to find out about the apparent visit of Mr. Charles Danby. At the inn the first sight to greet him was the goat tethered on the grass verge opposite. The goat looked at him with another undulating bleat, and as he dismounted, Hugh's mind raced back to those dreadful moments in the Italian grove. He shook the unpleasant memories aside as he sought the landlord, who was in the cellar, making a detailed record of his stock.

A shaft of slanting light fond its way through a cob-webbed window, and the air was cool but dusty as he turned on hearing Hugh's steps. "Good evening, Mr. Oadby—what brings you down here?"

Hugh glanced around a little nervously, for the shadows seemed to gather, and the goat called again outside. The landlord's stolid Monmouthshire accent brought him back to the present. "How may I be of service, Mr. Oadby?"

"I'm curious about a recent guest here, a Mr. Charles Danby."

The burly landlord looked blankly at him. "Mr. who?"

"Danby. A London lawyer on business at Llandower Castle."

"I know of no London lawyer, sir." The landlord picked up a dusty bottle and examined the label. "Someone has got it wrong, sir. If this Mr. Danby was in the neighborhood, he must have stayed elsewhere. He probably lodged locally, for there are many folks in these parts who take in guests. Too many, for they take my business," he added resentfully, replacing the bottle.

"I'm told he stayed here."

"Mr. Oadby, trade has been so unusually quiet of late that if a London lawyer had stayed, I'd remember. There was no one here of that name." The landlord's tone became labored.

"You're quite sure about this?" Hugh pressed.

The landlord, who was already irritated with Hugh's "sister" for inconveniently demanding a hot bath in her room, wasn't prepared to keep repeating his answers. He drew himself up in a manner only too suggestive of his pugilistic past. "Are you questioning my truthfulness, Mr. Oadby?"

Hugh climbed down swiftly. "Er, no, of course not, it's just . . . Oh, it doesn't matter."

The landlord smiled coolly. "Dinner will be in an hour, sir. I trust that will be in order for you and er, Miss Oadby?"

"Quite in order."

As the landlord deliberately picked up another bottle to continue his task, Hugh turned angrily on his heel and left the cellar. He went straight up to Kitty, whom he found dressed only in a diaphanous cream muslin wrap, which she had deliberately left untied at the waist. She was anxious about his meeting with Anne and intended to make sure of her hold upon him.

But he was too preoccupied to notice as he took off his coat and flung it over a chair. He didn't want to quarrel now, not when he had so much else on his mind. "Something's wrong," he said after a moment.

"Wrong? What do you mean? Doesn't your Miss Willowby find you to her liking?"

"Oh, I promise you she finds me very much to her liking; indeed we got along famously."

Kitty's smile faded. "Really?" she said coolly.

Hugh didn't notice. "She told me that Charles Danby has been to Llandower, and that he stayed here at the White Boar, but the landlord has never heard of him."

"Neither have I. Who is Charles Danby?"

Hugh explained.

Kitty was mystified. "What does it matter? Danby clearly told her he was staying here, when in fact he was elsewhere. No doubt he was doing exactly what you are—dallying with a lady brought secretly with him."

Hugh hadn't thought of that. "I suppose it's possible," he conceded.

"More than possible, it's highly probable," Kitty said.

"But why didn't Critchley mention sending him here?"

"Is it compulsory to keep you informed of everything?"

"No, but I would have thought . . . Oh, I don't know, but I can't help feeling decidedly uneasy. I'd have sworn Critchley would tell me such a thing as this, but he didn't."

"Oh, forget it—besides, I want to know how you and Miss Primness went on. Is she pretty?"

"No."

Kitty relaxed a little. "So she wasn't to your liking?"

"You are the only one who is to my liking," he said softly, his glance at last moving to her figure, so clearly visible through her muslin wrap.

"When will you see her next?" Kitty asked, moving a little closer.

"Tomorrow. It's her birthday, and in her parents' unfortunate absence, I am going on the river with her instead. It's some sort of rustic family tradition, but I fear this will be the last time dear Anne enjoys it." He told her his plan. "The housekeeper will think I am valiantly striving to save her, when all the time I will be holding my tiresome bride down."

Kitty's eyes shone with excitement as she came close enough to touch him. "I still can't believe you really mean to do it," she breathed.

"I must be rid of her if I am to make you my duchess," he reminded her, stretching out a hand to touch one of her up-turned nipples.

Slowly she discarded the wrap and put her arms around his waist. "So you and Miss Willowby got on, did you?" she whispered, moving her hips to and fro against his.

"Well enough," he murmured, closing his eyes.

"As well as this?" She stretched up to put her lips to his.

He felt weak, and his concern about Charles Danby faded into oblivion as other emotions began to grip him. He cupped her full breasts in his hands, and she allowed him to caress her nipples for a moment before she drew away. "To the bed, I think," she whispered, catching his hand and leading him across to the ancient four-poster, the blue hangings of which were sun faded on the side nearest the window.

Kitty watched as Hugh took off his clothes. He was more than ready for her, but she felt nothing as he took her. Her soft noises of delight were deceiving, for her gaze was upon the diadem, which she had left on a chair. She smiled. Soon she would wear it at Almack's.

As darkness approached, Sylvanus left the security of the temple, to which he had returned for a nap, and visited the stables to inquire of the horses which way to find the White

Boar. Then he returned to the house, and listened at the door to the kitchens passage. He wanted to get Penelope so that they could slip away to the inn and search for the diadem as soon as Gervase had been brought to life for the night. The faun could hear Joseph lecturing Martin in the kitchens, because the unfortunate boy had cracked a windowpane earlier in the day. Mog and Jack sensed the faun's presence and scratched frantically at the courtyard door in an effort to escape.

The faun was about to risk going into the passage when footsteps approached and Mrs. Jenkins swept past with a tray upon which stood an untouched cup of chocolate and an equally untouched scone filled with cream and strawberry preserves. The housekeeper placed the tray crossly on the kitchen table. "Oh, for heaven's sake, Martin, let those foolish animals out before they break the door down."

As Martin got up to obey, Mrs. Jenkins surveyed the tray. "Well, now, wouldn't you think Miss Anne would be pleased after what happened today? The new duke is as fine a gentleman as any young lady could wish, yet instead of thanking fate for sending Master Hugh instead of Master Gervase, she sits there as if all the troubles in the world were on her shoulders. Look at this tray. She hardly glanced at it."

"I'll have the scone, Mrs. J.," Martin offered hopefully.

Joseph was too quick for him. "Oh, no, you don't my laddo. First come, first served, and I was on this earth before you." There came the slight sound of a china plate sliding across a wooden surface, and a few minutes after the appreciative sound of Joseph licking his fingers. "By all the powers, Gwen Jenkins, you always did make a grand scone."

"Thank you, I'm sure." She sat down with a sigh. "Oh, I knew there'd be trouble from the moment I clapped eyes on him," she muttered then.

"Clapped eyes on who, Mrs. J?" Martin asked curiously.

The housekeeper drew herself together. "Oh, no one. Pay no attention."

Sylvanus gazed toward the arc of light from the kitchen. He knew to whom the housekeeper was referring, for that same gentleman was at this moment reposing in a casing of fine white marble in the rotunda. As silence descended on the room, the faun went softly toward the hall, then up the staircase as fast as he could. He hoped to pass Anne in the study again, but to his dismay, she was in the drawing room, reading by Penelope's light.

At least she was trying to read, for she was so deep in thought that the volume of *Waverley* had lain open on her lap at the same page for half an hour now. She wore a long-sleeved primrose wool gown, and her curls were dressed up neatly, for she had no intention of being caught unprepared should Hugh decide to call again without warning. Not that she really expected him to; indeed if she was honest with herself, it wasn't Hugh she anticipated might call, but Charles Danby. At least, deep inside she hoped he would call, for she simply could not help herself where he was concerned.

She leaned her head back wearily. Mrs. Jenkins was right to scold her, for Hugh was a vast improvement upon his late cousin, and any other bride making an arranged match with such a bridegroom would have been over the moon with relief. And Anne would have been too, if it weren't for a continual intrusion of Charles Danby upon her thoughts.

She swallowed as conflicting emotions brought a lump in her throat. Maybe he'd obey the wish she'd expressed so vehemently when last they parted and would herald any future call in advance as demanded, but right now, when he filled her consciousness like the very air she breathed, she wished he would defy her. Her whole being ached to be in his arms, ached to submit to an attraction that was so fierce and consuming that if it hadn't happened to her, she would never have believed it possible. Suddenly, she closed the book with a snap that made Sylvanus start in the shadows of the passage. Moping here wouldn't do any good; what she needed was another breath of fresh air. It was dark now, but the moon was out and the riverbank beckoned.

Sylvanus pressed swiftly into the shadows as she set the book aside and hurried from the room. He lingered close to the staircase as she went up to the next floor, and he saw her hurry down again with her plaid shawl around her shoulders. She was going out! In a moment the faun had scurried back to the drawing room, transformed Penelope, then grabbed her hand to hasten after Anne, who had already slipped secretly out into the courtyard from the entrance hall rather than the kitchen, in order not to face Mrs. Jenkins again. From the archway the faun and nymph watched Anne cross the grass to the jetty, where she lay back in one of the rowing boats to watch the stars through the willow fronds. Sylvanus led Penelope into the maze, and freed Gervase from the marble.

"You have a chance to get Anne alone. She has come outside on her own, and is at the jetty at this moment," the faun explained after examining the scratch Mog had left on his hand the night before, as Gervase began to dress.

Sylvanus hopped impatiently from one hoof to the other. He was anxious to get to the White Boar to see if he could ascertain whether Hugh had really brought the diadem with him, but felt obliged to stay until Gervase was ready. "Oh, do hurry up, for you may not have much time before she goes back inside again."

"I'm being as quick as I can!" Gervase was none too pleased about Penelope's presence, for it was bad enough to be stark naked and on display while made of marble, but it was ten times worse when he was a living man.

Penelope smiled. "I much prefer gentlemen with cloven hooves, so there is no need to feel embarrassed in front of me," she whispered.

Gervase felt his face redden a little in the darkness. Was nothing sacred? Ever since this incredible nightmare had begun that night in Naples, he'd had no privacy whatsoever!

Sylvanus looked disapprovingly at Gervase's clothes. "You don't look as elegant as your cousin did earlier," he judged after a moment.

Gervase was further piqued. "Thank you very much, but it isn't exactly easy to be a sartorial paragon when one's only set of togs has been worn and worn again, and when a certain faun has ruined one's greatcoat beyond all redemption!"

"There's no need to be like that," Sylvanus replied huffily.

"Oh, yes, there is. You've just had the gall to criticize my appearance, yet *you* are the one who treated my best coat like a rag!"

Sylvanus's lower lip jutted peevishly, but before he could respond Penelope tactfully intervened by taking Gervase's hand. "Don't worry, for I am sure Miss Willowby will not spurn you."

"Would that I could be so sure."

"I know she feels a great deal for you."

"Yes, she does, but can she be induced to admit it? We are another Beauty and Beast—our tale cannot have a happy ending until she breaks the spell, but because I'm forbidden to tell her the truth about myself, she will continue to believe that choosing me will mean turning her parents out of Llandower. She is far too loving and loyal a daughter to ever contemplate that, and so we will remain trapped, I fear."

"Something will happen to put everything right," Penelope said earnestly.

Gervase softened then and drew the nymph's little hand to his lips. "You're far too good for that obnoxious faun," he murmured.

Sylvanus glowered and pulled Penelope away. "There isn't time to dillydally on all this nonsense—we should be looking for the diadem," he said huffily.

Gervase was further annoyed. "And when you're struggling for a way to induce my cousin to willingly hand it over, I will make a point of being as helpful and understanding as you've been tonight."

"I *have* been helpful and understanding!" Sylvanus cried, his tone threatening to become a bleat of considerable ire.

The faun's reaction caused Gervase much satisfaction. "Well, at least 'getting someone's goat' is now a phrase to savor!" he declared with alacrity.

Penelope spoke up swiftly. "Stop it, both of you—allies shouldn't fall out. Now then, Sylvanus, you and I will go to the White Boar without further delay and leave Gervase to handle his meeting with Anne in his own way." Taking the faun firmly by the arm, she steered him out of the rotunda.

Ally? Sometimes Sylvanus seemed more like a hindrance than a help! Gervase calmed down a little as soon as the fractious faun had gone. He tried to concentrate on the more important obstacle of Anne's sense of right and wrong. The coming minutes presented him with what might be his last opportunity to be alone with her. At any moment she might to return to the castle, where the watchful Mrs. Jenkins would be only too clearly at hand. He drew a deep breath, for in one thing at least Sylvanus was right—there wasn't time to dillydally. Taking a deep breath, he followed the faun and nymph out of the maze.

Chapter Twenty

Anne didn't see Sylvanus and Penelope slipping away toward the Peterbury road bridge, nor was she aware of Gervase approaching across the park. The night air was scented with flowers, and high above, myriad stars glimmered in an indigo sky. The Wye washed softly against the jetty, and the light breeze rustled the willows and reeds, familiar and comforting sounds to someone who'd spent her entire life in this one beloved place.

Lying back in the rowing boat, she trailed her fingers in the water and stared up through the willows. It wasn't the stars she saw, but the light in Charles Danby's eyes! And it wasn't the gentle breeze that stirred the little curls framing her face, but his fingertips brushing through them as he caressed her! She closed her eyes in a vain attempt to quell the tumult of emotion, but nothing could defend her from the assault that was battering her poor heart. Why had fate to be so cruel? Why couldn't he have come into her life before now?

She tried to remind herself that she knew nothing of him, that his conduct thus far had at the very least been open to question, but it made no difference, for the effect he had upon her was so piercing and intense that it was as if her whole life hitherto had been meaningless. She tried to think of Hugh instead, but in comparison he was a pale shadow, for Charles Danby was her first love, and would remain her greatest.

Suddenly, Gervase spoke. "Anne?"

She gasped, and the boat swayed a little as she sat up to see him standing on the jetty.

He stretched out a reassuring hand. "Please don't be alarmed . . ." he began.

She stared mutely at him, but then found her tongue. "I thought it was still understood that you would send word in advance of your next intention to call; yet here you are, and at night again too. Your dishonorable motives are only too clear, sirrah!" Her voice trembled with feeling.

"I think too highly of you to harbor dishonorable motives," he replied.

"Oh? Then why have you come straight here to me like this? Why didn't you go to the house?"

"Are you so sure I didn't?"

"Yes, because Mrs. Jenkins would *never* permit you to come out here to be alone with me."

He met her eyes. "Very well, I admit that I didn't go to the house, but came straight over when I noticed you. I know that the duke has arrived," he added.

"From which I take it that you have returned to the White Boar?"

He ignored the question. "How impressed are you by His Grace, the ninth Duke of Wroxford?" he asked.

"That is no business of yours."

"He has an easy way with him, I'll grant him that, although some might say it is too easy by far."

"It ill becomes you to speak like that of one of your firm's most important clients."

"There is a great deal you do not know about him." Gervase was dismayed. Was she defending Hugh? Did she feel warmth toward him?

"I'm sure there is, just as there's a great deal I don't know about you—except, of course, that you are not a gentleman."

"So you approve of the duke?" He couldn't help pressing, for the fear that Hugh might succeed with her after all was almost too much to bear.

"He has revealed himself to be a thoughtful, charming, and amusing man."

"Without blemish, I suppose," he said acidly.

"So far, yes. We are to celebrate my birthday tomorrow by going on the river in the moonlight—with Mrs. Jenkins, of course."

"Who approves entirely, no doubt."

"Why do you dislike him?"

Gervase's unease intensified. She *was* defending Hugh! His anxiety made him rash. "I dislike Hugh Mowbray because he is a maggot of the first degree!"

She was shocked, not only by the words, but by the vehemence with which they were uttered. "I doubt very much if

Mr. Critchley would approve of his junior partner expressing such sentiments," she said, wondering why he despised Hugh so much.

"Critchley isn't here."

Something struck her then. "How did you arrive? I heard no horse."

"I rode slowly; maybe the sound didn't carry."

She didn't reply.

"Anne, we must talk—" he began.

"Please don't use my first name, Mr. Danby," she interrupted.

"How can you ask me to be formal when we—?"

"Don't speak of it!" she cried, rising agitatedly to her feet. The boat lurched alarmingly, and she would have lost her balance if it weren't for Gervase's swiftness. He reached down to catch her hand and pull her up to safety. Her carefully pinned hair caught in the willows and tumbled down in profusion around her shoulders. As soon as she was on the jetty, she pulled angrily from him. "Please leave, Mr. Danby!"

"Not until we've spoken properly." Her shawl had fallen, and he bent to retrieve it.

"There is nothing to say."

He didn't return the shawl, but glanced down at the beautifully knotted fringe. How like her to make even a simple shawl so very much her own, he thought absently, but then looked at her again. "Nothing to say? On the contrary, there's a great deal. Please, Anne, can't we at least discuss how things are between us?"

"There is nothing between us," she insisted.

"That is a patent untruth, and we both know it."

"Very well, what I'm saying is that there *cannot* be anything between us," she corrected.

"So you do admit to feelings for me?"

"I admit nothing."

"Oh, Anne, we're alone, so why can't you at least be honest with me?"

"Because I have given my word that I will marry the Duke of Wroxford, and I mean to stand by that word."

"Even though *I* am the one you love?" He held his breath, but still she didn't say the words he needed.

"My decision was made before I met you, and nothing will change it."

He was anguished. "Oh, Anne, what have I done that you have not shared?"

"That was ill said."

"Maybe it *was* ill said, nonetheless it was the truth. We *shared* those caresses, Anne."

She was in turmoil. "Why are you doing this? What possible good can come of your interference?"

"'Interference'? That word suggests a lack of sincerity, and—"

"'Sincerity'? Well, since you mention it, I do still wonder what your purpose really is, because if you are directly responsible for preventing me from marrying the Duke of Wroxford, you will certainly forfeit your partnership in Mr. Critchley's firm, and thus, presumably, your livelihood. You also know that the ending of my betrothal will mean impoverishment for my family and the loss of this estate, yet *still* you importune me. Neither of these things suggests true honor or sincerity, and since you are not a fool, sirrah, I have to conclude that you still have some ulterior—and probably dishonorable—motive."

Oh, if only he could tell her he was the real Duke of Wroxford, and that none of her fears would be of any consequence at all if she would say only she loved him!

She met his gaze. "Please leave, Mr. Danby."

"Anne—"

"Leave me alone!" she cried then, her agitation so great that she could have burst into tears. Her emotions were tugging in such opposite directions that she felt as if she would tear in two, with one half of her wanting to be in his arms, conceding her heart with every kiss, the other half bidding her keep her distance for the sake of the match that she had to put before all else.

"Oh, Anne," he whispered, putting his hand to her cheek.

"Just go," she breathed.

"No."

"Then I will." She began to walk past him, but he dropped the shawl in order to catch her wrist and force her to face him.

"I'm not going to let you do this, Anne. There is something between us that neither of us can ignore!"

"I can, and I will!" she cried, struggling to wrest herself free.

"No, Anne," he replied, tightening his hold and pulling her toward him. "I'm going to *make* you admit the truth," he said, putting his other hand to her chin and raising her lips toward his.

"Please, don't. Please . . ." she begged tearfully, for she knew her weakness only too well.

"I must, don't you see?" he murmured, and his mouth brushed hers as he spoke.

Her body was taut and anxious as he slid an arm around her waist, and his kiss allowed her no quarter at all. Never before had he used his experience so passionately, or so deliberately. He didn't merely *want* her to respond, he *needed* her to, and he resorted to every sexual wile to achieve his aim. His relentless lips teased and caressed hers with warm yearning, and his desire enveloped her like a cloak. The sensuous onslaught was skilled as he held her against him in a way that left her in no doubt as to the extent of his arousal.

The tears were wet on her cheeks, but although she tried not to give in, she could feel her resistance deserting her. She was again consumed by the passion that had kindled from that first moment she'd seen him. Dismay failed to douse the riot of desire that tingled bewitchingly through her, and with a soft moan she gave in, returning the kiss in a way she knew was wrong. His hands moved lovingly over her, and she instinctively stood on tiptoe to link her arms around his neck. As she stretched up, he eased his hips forward so that his masculinity pressed urgently against her. New, more imperative sensations caught her up, sweeping her along on the current of pleasure she'd always longed for, but hadn't known until this man.

He lifted her gently from her feet, so that she sank against him even more intimately, and as he kissed her again, he could feel a new softness in her lips, a new warm pliancy in her body. He felt the ripples of ecstasy that passed through her and heard her gasp as the sensations continued for several long, sweet seconds. His own need was great, but his only thought in those seconds was of her pleasure, and when at last he set her gently down on her feet again, he took her face in his hands and kissed her once more. She was warm and almost drowsy, still in the tender grip of gratification, but her lips responded with the natural ease that told of the absolute perfection he could share with her.

But gradually the carnal shackles fell away, and the truth stared her in the eyes again. Her cheeks were wet with silent tears as without another word she caught up her skirts and fled toward the house.

"Anne! Come back!" he called.

But she didn't look around, and he knew it would be wrong to pursue her. He picked up the shawl again and inhaled her lingering perfume. "Oh, Anne," he whispered sadly, the softness of his voice lost amid the rustle of the willows and reeds.

Chapter Twenty-one

Sylvanus and Penelope crept toward the White Boar, but suddenly the faun stopped to sniff the air. "There's a goat somewhere nearby," he whispered.

Penelope was already wrinkling her nose. "One doesn't need to be a faun to realize *that!*"

Sylvanus was put out. "Are you implying that goats smell?" he demanded.

"I'm not *implying* it—I'm stating it as a fact," she replied.

"Then you think *I* smell?"

"Fortunately, you smell of human."

At that moment the goat in question reared up on its hind legs to peer out of the stable about six feet away from them. Penelope gave a start, but Sylvanus greeted the startled animal in its own tongue. After a moment the faun exhaled with some satisfaction. "I now know exactly where to find the man called Hugh, *and* the woman with him," he added meaningfully.

"Woman?" Penelope asked quickly.

"It seems Gervase's horrible cousin is with someone supposed to be his sister, they have adjacent rooms on the second floor, and are calling themselves by the name of Oadby."

"Adjacent rooms? Well, maybe she *is* his sister."

"Gervase told me his cousin was an only child."

The main door of the inn opened just then, and a rather drunken farm laborer staggered out before the faun could dodge out of sight. The man stared, then hiccuped and grinned. "By God, Harry, I didn't recognize you! That's a spanking good fancy dress you've got there; reckon you'll be a riot come May Day!" Chuckling approvingly, the man wove his unsteady way up the road toward the lights of a cottage.

Sylvanus was furious. "Fancy dress? How *dare* he make fun of me like that!"

The goat laughed, but was silenced by Sylvanus's bleat of dire warning. "I can turn anything to marble, so don't offend me!" As the goat hastily disappeared from the doorway, the faun caught Penelope's hand again. "Come on, let's find a quiet way in."

"What if we're seen? If we're inside the inn, it might not be easy to escape."

"You forget my power," Sylvanus pointed out quietly, then smiled. "I mean to use it on Hugh as soon as he's surrendered the diadem."

"You mean to turn him to marble?"

"He doesn't deserve anything less." Without further ado, Sylvanus led her toward the rear of the inn. There was no one around as they made their way up an outside staircase to a gallery that ran along the entire building. After climbing through an open window into a darkened room, they listened carefully at the door at the precise moment Hugh and Kitty returned from dining.

The meal had not gone well, for Kitty had wanted to wear the diadem, but Hugh had prevented her. She had eventually given in, but with exceedingly bad grace, and very little had been said at the dinner table. As Kitty haughtily prepared to go into her own room without a word, Hugh caught her arm. "Please don't let's part on a sour note."

"Then apologize. All I wanted was to wear the diadem. I thought you'd be pleased, not disapproving."

Sylvanus and Penelope exchanged glances behind the nearby door.

"I *was* pleased—it's just that London togs would have looked a little too much in a place like this." Hugh glanced along the deserted passage. "Look, I want to talk."

"About what?"

"I can't get this Danby business out of my mind."

Sylvanus and Penelope looked at each other again.

Kitty hesitated, then nodded. They went into her room, and the door closed behind them.

The faun and nymph immediately emerged to cross the passage to eavesdrop. The voices inside were muffled, but perfectly audible. Kitty tossed her reticule upon the dressing table. "Oh, do stop worrying about nothing! It simply slipped Critchley's mind that this Danby person was coming here, and Danby had his own reasons for lying about where he was staying. Besides, if we should worry about anyone, it's the Fanhopes, who might arrive earlier than expected. You are supposed to be here in order to see Miss Willowby, yet you're using a false name and have me in tow as your 'sister.' Lady Fanhope may not know either of us, but Fanhope himself certainly does, and he has no reason to hold his tongue."

"I've been thinking about that. He's not going to say much in case we tell his wife a few things I'm sure he'd rather she didn't know! His liaison with you, for instance."

Kitty thought for a moment. "Yes, I suppose you're right," she said then.

"Of course I am. Forget them, for they will apparently soon be on the way to America." Hugh was thoughtful. "Don't you think it a little odd that they are to stay here?"

"Why? *We're* staying here," Kitty pointed out.

"Yes, but only because I must visit Llandower. What possible reason could Fanhope have? Sportsman he may be, but tourist he isn't, nor is his wife, nor is this place exactly en route to Bristol."

Kitty shrugged. "I neither know, nor care what their reasons are."

"Well, I find it most curious, if not downright odd."

"Oh, for heaven's sake, let the matter lie." He was sometimes like a dog with a bone, and Kitty found it boring in the extreme.

Her tone got under his skin. "You're perfect, are you?"

"I beg your pardon?"

"What exactly did Gervase find out about you that disgusted him so?"

She flinched. "Find out? I don't know what you mean."

"Oh, yes, you do—it's written all over you."

"You're wrong, because there is nothing to find out." Kitty trembled within but managed to conceal it.

Hugh still didn't believe her. Gervase had learned something, and one day he would find out what it was!

She found defense in attack. "Your Miss Willowby is more to your liking than you've said, isn't she? Now you wish to find an excuse to back out of marrying me! That's it, isn't it? I'll warrant you wish you'd never given me the diadem, so that you can give it to her instead!"

Sylvanus and Penelope stared, and the faun's brow darkened. That the Lady Ariadne's wedding crown should have fallen into Hugh's hands was bad enough, but that such a doxy should be wearing it was too much!

Hugh tried to calm things. "You're wrong, I'm *glad* you have the diadem. You're also wrong about my feelings for Anne Willowby. Believe me, I intend to consign her beneath the Wye tomorrow night. Her body will be found somewhere downstream, and I will be exonerated because I will have gone to such visible lengths to rescue her."

The eavesdroppers were appalled. Consign Anne to the Wye? Her body found downstream?

Hugh spoke again. "Then, when the sensation dies away, I will marry you, Kitty. I promise." He added the last two words in the soft tone of a man hoping to wheedle his way into a woman's bed for the night.

Kitty decided the time had come to be warm and loving again. "Oh, Hugh, I find it so *exciting* that you are going to do this just to have me."

"Then let me make love to you now. Give me your hand— let me place it somewhere that will prove how ardent is my need for you."

"Why, sir, how flatteringly rampant you are, to be sure," Kitty murmured huskily.

In the ensuing silence Sylvanus and Penelope drew back across the passage and entered the darkened room opposite. The nymph was frightened as she looked at the faun in the darkness. "Oh, Sylvanus, do you think he *really* intends to— to do away with . . . ?" She couldn't finish.

Sylvanus remembered what Hugh had done to Gervase in the grove and nodded. "Oh, yes, he intends to do it—there's no mistake of that. Come on, we must return to Llandower to tell Gervase! I only hope he's managed to make Anne say she loves him, because if *that* has happened, it's all over anyway."

But as they slipped swiftly out of the inn and began to run back along the road toward the bridge and the riverside meadows, Gervase was seated forlornly in the rotunda with his head in his hands. Tonight he'd resorted to all the wiles in his sexual repertory, but still Anne had refused to confess her heart. Never had he encountered anyone who could adhere so resolutely to the very last letter of her principles, or who could suffer such tortures of the flesh without whispering a few unguarded words. He knew only too well how passionate she was, for the fire in her nature had seared his very soul, but if she was so determined to turn her back on her true self in order to keep her word, there was nothing else any mere man could do.

Chapter Twenty-two

When Anne ran tearfully back to the house, her intention had been to avoid all chance of encountering any of the servants—who knew nothing of her sortie—by going directly upstairs, but on the landing she was dismayed to see candlelight approaching from the direction of the drawing room. A moment later, Mrs. Jenkins appeared. The housekeeper was pale and anxious, and her hand was shaking so much that the candle flame shook and shadows reeled over the landing. Anne's first guilty thought was that the meeting on the jetty had been observed from an upper window, but it soon became apparent that something else had upset Mrs. Jenkins.

"Oh, Miss Anne, I think I'm going mad!" she said in a shaking voice, too distracted even to notice her mistress hastily wiping away tears of her own.

Anne concernedly put an arm around the woman's plump shoulders. "Whatever is it, Mrs. Jenkins?" she asked.

"You will indeed think me mad if I tell you."

"I'm sure you're perfectly sane. Please tell me what is upsetting you like this," Anne urged gently.

"It—it's that nad."

"Nad? Oh, you mean wooden naiad on the lamp stand?"

"That's it, the nad. Well, twice now I've gone into the drawing room to tend the fire for the night, and both times the nad hasn't been there."

"But it was there earlier."

Mrs. Jenkins looked warily into Anne's eyes. "The *stand's* there now, Miss Anne—it's the nad that isn't, and what's more, there's no damage to the wood, and the tray she holds has even been put on the table, for all the world as if she just upped and went."

Anne stared at her. "That can't possibly be," she said after a moment.

"There, I *knew* you'd think I was mad!" The housekeeper's voice choked.

"No, Mrs. Jenkins, I just think there must be some mistake, a trick of the light, perhaps. Come on, we'll go and look together." Anne took the candle and led the way.

But Mrs. Jenkins halted nervously at the drawing room door. "I don't know whether I want the wretched thing to be there or not. If it's there, then I'm imaging things and should be locked away; if it's not there, well, it will be more than passing strange, won't it?"

Leaving the housekeeper in the passage, Anne went inside. As she drew closer to the smooth, undamaged lamp holder, she saw there was no sign of Penelope, and that the candle tray lay on the table, just as Mrs. Jenkins had said. Her eyes widened with shock as she halted right by the deserted stand. "You'd better come here, Mrs. Jenkins, for your eyes didn't deceive you. She's gone."

"You're sure?" came the wary response from the passage.

"Yes."

Slowly, Mrs. Jenkins came in to join her, and they both stared at the lamp holder. Anne drew a long breath. "It is indeed as if she just put down her tray, then upped and went," she murmured.

"But how, Miss Anne? It's simply not possible for part of a carving to just disappear without leaving some sign of having been broken off. We both knew that Joseph made her from one piece of walnut, not three."

"You say it happened before?"

"Yes. It was after I'd helped clear up at my sister's. I came in here to see if the fire was safe for the night and saw the nad was missing." Mrs. Jenkins cleared her throat uncomfortably. "Now, as you well know, ordinarily I'm not one to partake of too much alcohol, but I have to admit that on that occasion I *had* taken a sip or two of elderberry wine, so that's what I put it down to. Anyway, I thought nothing more of it because the nad was there again the following day. Now it's gone again, and you're here to see as well, so this time it's not elderberry wine *or* imagination, is it?"

"No."

"What shall we do?"

"I really don't know," Anne confessed, for it wasn't exactly the sort of situation to which she was accustomed. She managed a weak smile. "Maybe she'll be back in the morning, and we can convince ourselves we didn't see anything out of the ordinary."

Mrs. Jenkins smiled sheepishly as well. "Maybe."

Anne thought for a moment. "Actually, there were other odd things that night. Mog got in a terrible state in here and knocked things over, including that little Cupid, which not even Joseph could mend. Then later there was that strange business in the kitchens, which couldn't have been Mog because the courtyard door was open. Actually, I'd feel happier if it *had* been Mog the second time, for at least that would mean there wasn't a stranger poking around in the kitchens, and possibly the rest of the house too." Anne shivered a little, for it wasn't a pleasant recollection that while she and Charles were in the study, someone else had clearly entered the house.

"Mr. Danby was here that night, and it wouldn't be the first time he's pried uninvited," Mrs. Jenkins observed darkly.

"He was with me," Anne replied uncomfortably.

"Maybe so, but if you ask me, he's as mysterious as the rest of this."

"I didn't ask you, and anyway, he's *not* mysterious." But he was, and Anne knew it. There was something undeniably odd about the way he simply appeared from nowhere. She hadn't once heard him ride up, or even seen his horse, come to that. She drew herself up sharply. This was foolish, for he had always offered perfectly logical explanation for everything. She was simply allowing her imagination to be carried away by the present undeniably eerie situation.

Mrs. Jenkins gave a sigh. "Well, whatever the rights and wrongs of Mr. Danby's presence here, it's still a fact that someone else came in that night, and Joseph is convinced they were hiding somewhere here on the premises."

"'On the premises'?" Anne repeated uneasily.

"Yes. Mog isn't the only creature behaving oddly at the moment; that mangy lurcher is too. Joseph reckons the dog has scent of someone nearby. He's going to see if Jack can pick up any trail." The clock on the mantelpiece began to chime the hour, and the housekeeper gave a start, then laughed nervously. "Dear Lord, I'm all of a pother now! Let's go downstairs."

"I think I'll just go straight to bed," Anne said quickly.

Mrs. Jenkins looked at her properly for the first time. "Are you feeling unwell, Miss Anne?"

"I have a headache. I went out for a walk in the fresh air, but it hasn't helped."

"Then you go to bed right now. You'll feel as right as rain for your birthday tomorrow, and you'll look as fresh as a daisy for the duke," the housekeeper added with a smile.

Anne had to look away. After what had happened on the jetty tonight, she didn't know how she was going to look her future husband in the eyes. She had betrayed both him and her conscience in Charles Danby's arms.

Mrs. Jenkins misunderstood. "The duke is as fine a gentleman as any young woman could wish. You're very lucky, indeed, and I know he'll soon make you forget all about that rascally lawyer. Just you wait and see. After tomorrow night's picnic and trip on the river, you'll have changed your mind completely about both of them."

In the maze Gervase roused himself a little from his despondency as swift footsteps approached through the maze. He began to straighten uneasily, but then realized that it was only Sylvanus and Penelope returning. As the nymph and faun hurried exhaustedly into the rotunda, it was plain that they'd come from the White Boar without pause. He looked anxiously from one to the other. "What's wrong? What's happened?"

Penelope sank onto the bench, and Sylvanus tried to gather his breath before speaking. "First I must know how you progressed with Anne."

Gervase exhaled slowly and shook his head. "She'll never confess her true feelings to me."

The faun sighed too. "Well, that's a pity, because we found out something dreadful tonight. To begin with, your cousin is calling himself Oadby." He began to relate what they'd overheard.

Gervase interrupted at the mention of the so-called sister. "Kitty? Are you sure that was her name?"

"Yes."

"Hugh hasn't got a sister, but I certainly suspect I know who she is." It had to be Kitty Longton, who hailed from Oadby in Leicestershire, if his memory served him well. So the scheming denizen of Drury Lane was still hot in pursuit of a fine title, and Hugh had the gall to bring her to within a few miles of Llandower! Renewed dislike and contempt sliced through Gervase, for he could never think of Kitty without recalling what she'd done to her helpless little brother. She was a fitting leman for the likes of Hugh Mowbray!

Sylvanus looked curiously at him. "Hugh seems to think you know something terrible from her past."

"I do." Gervase related the story of the terrible orphanage.

Sylvanus drew a long, disapproving breath. "Well, your cousin is set to make this monstrous woman his duchess."

Gervase stared at him. "He can't. My father's will restricts him to marrying Anne in order to gain the title."

"Well, he's thought of a way around that particular obstacle." The faun told him what Hugh intended to do.

Gervase was alarmed. "Are you *quite* sure that's what you heard?"

"Sure beyond all doubt. We could hear quite plainly through the door, couldn't we, Penelope?"

The nymph nodded. "There's no mistake. He intends to make it seem like a terrible accident, and in order to fool Mrs. Jenkins, he will go through all the motions of trying to save Anne, but all the time he'll be making sure she drowns. It's horrible."

Gervase leaned weakly back against the pillar and closed his eyes. Sweet Jesu, Anne . . .

Chapter Twenty-three

Kitty slept alone in the White Boar's principal bedchamber, Hugh having returned to his own room in order to preserve the story of Mr. and Miss Oadby. The actress's brow was clear as she dreamed of the jewels, silks, and privilege that would be hers once Hugh had disposed of Anne. She stirred slightly as the sound of an approaching carriage disturbed the silence of the country night, and she stirred a little more as the vehicle halted at the inn, but she didn't awaken.

In the next room, however, Hugh sat up with a start. He flung the bedclothes back and got up to see what had awoken him. He was naked, and the night air was cool upon his hot skin as he looked down at the newly arrived carriage. Its lamps pierced the darkness, and the only other light came from a lantern held by the sleepy landlord as the coachman lowered the steps for the occupants to alight. Hugh saw them only from above, a gentleman in a top hat and a lady with her hood raised, but he was struck by the immense concern the lady showed regarding a padlocked chest that was lashed to the rear of the carriage. The rest of the luggage could be brought up in the morning, she declared in an affected, nasal tone, but the chest had to be taken to their room without further ado. After instructing two grooms to attend to the matter, the landlord led the new arrivals into the inn, and they passed out of sight.

Hugh was most curious as to what such a weighty and apparently important item of luggage might contain—something valuable, that was certain. The contents of the mysterious chest faded from his thoughts as he reached for a cigar from the pocket of his coat, which had been left over the back of a chair. His lucifers were there too, and a moment later a curl of smoke drifted past the window as he gazed up at the starlit sky. By this time tomorrow night, he would be free of Anne

Willowby, and the future he had always coveted would be his once and for all. "Hugh Mowbray, ninth Duke of Wroxford." He murmured the title aloud and smiled. How gratifyingly grand it sounded.

He was brought back to the present by the sound of voices in the passage as the landlord conducted the new arrivals to a nearby room. The heavier footsteps of the two grooms followed as they staggered beneath the weight of the chest. Candlelight flickered beneath the door, and the lady's nasal whine was only too apparent as she complained that the accommodation was not as specifically requested, but it wasn't until her husband added his comments that Hugh froze, for the voice belonged to Sir Thomas Fanhope! A door opened, there was a terse exchange, then the door slammed, and the irritated innkeeper stomped past once more, muttering something under his breath about damned unreasonable nobs.

Hugh was so dismayed that he forgot the cigar, but he was reminded very abruptly when some hot ash fell into the forest of hair at his loins. With an alarmed gasp he dashed the ash away, but with little burning pinpricks it scattered over a certain exceedingly tender and vital organ instead. Holding himself and stifling little yelps of pain, he stubbed the cigar on the plate next to his unfinished bread and cheese supper, then hurried to the washstand to scoop cold water over the area in question. He dabbed himself dry with a towel and examined himself as carefully as he could in the darkness. He breathed out with relief, for his masculinity didn't seem to have suffered too greatly.

He tossed a dark look toward the door. God *curse* Fanhope and his miserable spouse! Why couldn't they have kept to their original timetable? Would they still be here tomorrow night when he did away with the Willowby creature? Damn it, he wasn't even sure if they knew of Gervase's enforced betrothal, and if they did, would they know the lady concerned was Anne Willowby of Llandower? This was a complication he could do without! His mind raced, and then he became a little more calm. No one at the White Boar knew that Oadby and the Duke of Wroxford were the same person, and since the Fanhopes were en route for Bristol and then for the other side of the Atlantic, they would most likely have departed by the time news of the Duke of Wroxford's unsuccessful rescue efforts reached the inn. Their presence in the meantime still made things awkward, though, and Kitty had to be told before morning, so that a contingency plan could be formed to explain the use of the false identities.

Putting on his dressing gown, Hugh listened at the door before slipping out into the deserted passage. He could see candlelight shining from beneath the Fanhope's door further along, but apart from that all was quiet as he went to Kitty's room adjacent to his own and tapped stealthily. "Kitty?" he whispered, but she didn't respond, so he raised his hand to knock again.

Suddenly the door of the Fanhopes' room opened, and to Hugh's further dismay a resentful Sir Thomas emerged with a candle. Fashionably dressed in a pea-green coat and cream trousers, he was thirty-five years old, of medium height, with blond hair and the sort of complexion that flushed easily. His figure, formerly spare and in the peak of condition, had softened since his marriage, but he hadn't lost his much admired looks, which Hugh had always jealously dismissed as overrated. He was clearly under instructions to remonstrate yet again with the landlord, and didn't perceive Hugh until the last moment. His china blue eyes widened. "Good God! Mowbray!" he cried, halting in amazement.

"Er, Fanhope, fancy meeting you here." Hugh lowered his hand and summoned a smile of sorts. There was no love lost between them, but they had always been civil.

"What in God's name are you doing here? I thought you had accompanied Gervase to Italy so that he could postpone his betrothal to that Elmley woman. Was it Elmley? Maybe it was Beechley. Some tree or other, anyway, and she lives in the depths of Scotland or some other far-flung corner." Sir Thomas eyed him again. "Here with a piece of muslin, eh?" he asked, having perceived that Hugh had been knocking at the door, which clearly wouldn't happen if it was his own room.

"Yes. Someone we both know, actually." The damned fellow had to be confided in to some extent; there was no other course.

Sir Thomas became still. "Are you saying it's Kitty?"

Hugh nodded, and the other glanced hauntedly back along the passage. It was an action that spoke volumes of how much he dreaded his wife. Hugh thought quickly. "Look, can we talk in my room for a moment?"

"Talk? Well, I suppose so, but it had better not take long. I'm supposed to be putting the landlord in his place. We ordered the best room, but a Miss Oadby has taken it, and my wife is not pleased."

Once inside, Hugh closed the door, and they faced each other. "Clearly you have not heard that Gervase is dead," he said bluntly.

Sir Thomas's jaw dropped. "Eh?"

Hugh told him the doctored version of events in Italy, and his accession to the title. He carefully omitted all mention of Anne Willowby, of whom it seemed Sir Thomas knew very little, and he trod very carefully when it came to the matter of Kitty. "You know how I've always wanted Kitty, but she wouldn't glance at me because I didn't have a title or fortune? Well, I have both now, and I'm enjoying the benefit, if you know what I mean."

After his initial shock about Gervase's fate, Sir Thomas gave a wistful grin. "Oh, yes, I know what you mean," he murmured, noticing the unfinished bread and cheese and helping himself to a portion of the latter.

Before he realized it, a sudden question leapt to Hugh's lips. "I don't suppose you know why my cousin ended things so abruptly with her?"

Sir Thomas paused. "She told me *she* was the one who ended it. Not that I believed her, mind you, for she wanted to be his duchess, so nothing on God's earth would have induced her to give him his congé. Besides, when she took up with me, it was clear she was afraid he'd tell me about something in her past. He didn't, but she certainly thought he would. By Gad, this is a tasty bit of goat's milk cheese," he declared with relish.

Hugh stared at him. "*Goat's* milk?" he repeated with a shudder. "Are you sure of that?"

"Oh, yes, I'd know it anywhere."

Hugh felt ill.

Sir Thomas licked his fingers, then looked at him. "Is there anything else, or can I toddle off to find that damned landlord?"

Hugh pushed the plate of cheese away. "I haven't quite told you everything. As far as the landlord is concerned, Kitty and I are Mr. and Miss Oadby, a brother and sister."

"So *Kitty* has the principal room?" Sir Thomas's brows drew together. "Why in God's name didn't you simply pretend to be Mr. and *Mrs.* Oadby?" he asked.

"Because we quarreled during the journey, and she decided it would teach me a lesson if we were in separate rooms."

"Rations, eh?" Sir Thomas was pleased to think that Hugh wasn't getting full helpings of the dish he himself still craved.

"Look, Fanhope, you and I have got to handle this situation with care. It would be most awkward for Kitty if our little deception were to become known. She doesn't want *any* slight upon her reputation, now she's set to become titled and respectable, and I'm sure you wouldn't wish to be the cause of her unhappiness. Besides, if your wife should learn about your past with an actress, it would be the doghouse for you, so I think it sensible all around if we keep each other's little secrets, don't you?"

Sir Thomas's smile had faded. "Are you threatening me?"

"I'm only pointing out the disadvantages to us both. Your wife is a most, er, chaste lady, or so I understand, and her father does still control the purse strings, does he not?"

Sir Thomas's eyes narrowed. "I never did like you, Mowbray."

"The feeling's mutual, but in this we're forced to be allies, don't you agree?"

After a moment Sir Thomas nodded. "Yes, I suppose we are."

"We will all be strangers at the breakfast table, agreed?"

"Agreed. Is there anything else?"

"Just one thing. If we are strangers, you still cannot know about Gervase's death, so don't go back now and tell your wife all about it."

"Eh? Oh, yes, I take your point."

The other was about to go out when Hugh spoke again. "By the way, I was at the window when you arrived. What in God's name is in that padlocked chest?"

Sir Thomas shrugged. "I haven't the faintest notion."

Hugh stared. "But you must have!"

"My dear wife's lips are firmly sealed, and if I so much as mention it, she threatens to tell Papa I have been mistreating her. It's not a threat to take lightly, because, as you so kindly reminded me, he controls the purse."

"Upon which I've heard the duns are closing in."

"If they are, I've seen no evidence."

With that Sir Thomas went out, and as the door closed behind him, Hugh leaned his hands on a table and bowed his head with relief. All that had to be done now was warn Kitty. Taking a huge breath, he went again to try to wake her. He tapped constantly on her door until at last she admitted him.

Chapter Twenty-four

Anne's birthday dawned fine and clear, and when she left her room, wearing a yellow-and-white striped muslin gown, with her willful hair painstakingly pinned and ribboned, she was determined to banish Charles Danby entirely from her thoughts. Today she had to devote herself to thoughts of Hugh Mowbray.

Mrs. Jenkins had already told her that Penelope was back in her rightful place, but Anne still wanted to see for herself, and so she went to the drawing room before going downstairs. The lamp holder was complete again, and in the cold light of day the only sensible explanation—admittedly a weak one—was that she and the housekeeper had both been more upset the night before than they'd realized and had somehow allowed themselves to be carried away. What else could it have been?

Everyone was in the kitchens, even Mog and Jack, who tolerated each other when it suited them. The cat reposed on Mrs. Jenkins's sunlit chair by the fire and looked so sedate and relaxed it was impossible to imagine her being hysterical enough to do the damage she had in the drawing room, and maybe here in the kitchens as well. Jack—ever hopeful—was eyeing the table, where stood the birthday cake Mrs. Jenkins had baked, but the housekeeper had determined that not a single crumb would pass his thieving canine lips.

The cake was not the only gift awaiting Anne, for Mrs. Jenkins had also embroidered a set of handkerchiefs for her. Joseph's secret woodwork was revealed to be a beautiful carving of her favorite roan mare, and Martin had walked to the woods at dawn to gather her an armful of bluebells. Her parents had left a present in Mrs. Jenkins's keeping, and everyone gathered around as the housekeeper placed a large flat cardboard box on the kitchen table. It contained a costly cream silk evening gown that was fashionable and elegant enough for the Duchess of Wroxford to wear at Almack's, and Anne's eyes filled with tears, for she knew her father really could not afford it.

The gifts were then set aside, and while Anne sat down to a leisurely birthday breakfast, Mrs. Jenkins began to prepare the picnic, determined to show the new duke that good Monmouthshire food was every bit as good as that "Frenchified stuff" to which he was no doubt accustomed. Martin was despatched on his morning tasks in the stables, and Joseph had just begun to don his gardening boots, when through the open door he suddenly noticed something odd across the courtyard by the cellar trapdoors. He paused in astonishment. A snake? Surely not. Taking a walking stick of Mr. Willowby's that was awaiting repair, he advanced cautiously in his socks to attend to the reptilian intruder and found it to be merely a serpentine length of rope. Tutting with annoyance that he'd been taken in, he picked it up and shoved it in his pocket, for if nothing else, it would do to tie a rambling rose that needed cutting back, but which he couldn't touch because it was Mrs. Willowby's favorite.

Still tutting, he returned to the kitchens, passing Mog in the doorway. She was lazily contemplating an inspection of her territory in the grounds and immediately caught the faint scent of the "snake" from which she'd so wisely steered well clear. What she detected at these close quarters certainly wasn't snake but goatman! Arching her back and spitting at the startled gardener, she dashed toward the archway and vanished from sight. Joseph—no lover of cats at the best of times—frowned after her. "Miserable darned feline," he muttered, resuming his place on the stool. Jack was highly intrigued by the cat's reaction and came to sniff interestedly at the pocket. Disagreeable memories were aroused of being kicked on the rump by a horned man with hooves, and the peeved lurcher padded over to the trapdoors to investigate further. As the horrid scent became very strong indeed, he raised the alarm by barking for all he was worth.

With a sigh Joseph finished attending to his boots. "Leave off, you old fool!" he shouted, but Jack took no notice.

Mrs. Jenkins went to the door. "You don't think it could be rats, do you?"

The gardener was offended. "Rats? I'm most particular about controlling vermin, and you know it."

"Well, there's clearly *something* bothering that mongrel of yours."

Anne had a thought. "I heard something in the rotunda, and it crossed my mind that it might be a rat."

Joseph had other things to do and didn't want to be bothered with dark cellars, but he knew he had no choice. Devil take Jack! "All right, I'll go and investigate," he muttered reluctantly.

Mrs. Jenkins caught his sleeve suddenly. "Maybe it's that intruder! You did say he might be hiding somewhere here, and it's true that neither of us saw anyone hurrying away when we returned the other night."

Joseph blinked. "What are you saying? That you reckon there's a *person* down there?"

"I suppose I am," the housekeeper replied, turning to cast an uneasy look at Anne, who had come to join them at the door.

Joseph drew himself up purposefully. "That does it. I'm not having anyone on these premises what isn't supposed to be here. Where did I leave that there blunderbuss?"

Mrs. Jenkins's eyes widened. "Oh, you will be careful, won't you?"

"I'll do what has to be done." He took the formidable gun from its place on the wall above his woodworking shelf, and after lighting the lantern to take with him, he marched across to where Jack was still barking hysterically. Anne and Mrs. Jenkins remained nervously at the entrance of the kitchens as the trapdoors were opened and the angry lurcher leapt down into the darkness below. Joseph followed more cautiously, then held the lantern aloft to look around. The dog had disappeared into the most shadowy recesses, where he began a loud clamor as he found the hole that gave into the temple below. The intensity of the scent wafting up warned of the creature's close proximity, but the lurcher didn't care to confront it without Joseph and the blunderbuss.

Sylvanus was rudely awakened by the barking at the top of the temple steps. Alarmed, he scrambled up from his bed on Gervase's coat and hid behind the altar, for there was no way of escape. He saw the swaying glow of the lantern as the gardener came to see what the dog had found.

"Good God above," Joseph gasped as he saw the opening revealed by the removed stone flag. He crouched to hold the lantern down in order to see more, then stared as the ancient steps were revealed. "Good God above," he gasped again and began to go warily down into subterranean darkness. Still barking, Jack brushed past him and rushed toward the panic-stricken faun. Sylvanus had no option but to use his powers. He cried the magic words. Jack's noise was cut off midbark; there was a thud, then absolute silence.

Joseph halted uneasily at the foot of the steps and raised the lantern to try to see what had happened. "Jack?" he called. There was no reply, and he called again. "Jack? Come here, boy." Still there was silence. Placing the lantern on a ledge, the gardener held the blunderbuss at the ready, but as he stepped purposefully forward, he was shocked to see the white lurcher lying motionless on the floor. Almost immediately there was a soft sound, and he whirled toward the altar. For a split second he saw an ugly bearded head, horned and snub-nosed, and in his shock he fired the blunderbuss. Fragments of the ceiling scattered, and the report reverberated like thunder in the confined space.

Sylvanus bleated with sheer terror and used his power again, this time upon the old man. As Joseph turned to marble, the faun scrambled up the steps to the cellars. There he froze with further alarm, for the two women had come running as soon as they heard the blunderbuss. Pressing back behind some empty casks, he watched as they descended the ladder. They saw the beam of lantern light reaching up from below, and the faun waited until they'd hurried past him before he whispered the incantation that would return the gardener and dog to their true selves, then he clambered up the ladder and fled to the maze as if an entire pantheon of outraged gods were on his goat tail.

Joseph was sitting up dazedly as Anne and Mrs. Jenkins came anxiously down into the temple. The gardener's face had drained of all color, and he shook like a leaf as he patted Jack, who'd crawled over to him on his belly and was whining pathetically. Both man and dog kept a nervous eye upon the altar, for fear whatever it was might still be there.

Anne gazed around the temple in amazement, then took the lantern and hurried over to the gardener. "Are you all right, Joseph?" she asked.

"I think so. Just shaken, that's all." Joseph tried to clear his mind, for the past few seconds didn't bear thinking about.

Mrs. Jenkins came over and knelt next to him. "What happened?" she inquired, putting a concerned hand on his shoulder.

He hesitated, but then drew back from a truth that would surely see him pass through the doors of the nearest bedlam. "I just tripped and fell."

"Should we send Martin for the doctor?" the housekeeper asked.

"No, I'd much rather not. I'm just shaken up, that's all," Joseph said uncomfortably.

Mrs. Jenkins looked around with some relief. "Well, at least there doesn't seem to be anyone down here. When that blunderbuss went off, I was afraid . . ." She didn't finish.

Anne noticed how swiftly Joseph lowered his gaze and suddenly knew he wasn't telling the truth. He hadn't simply tripped and fallen; there had been something else. She glanced at Jack, whose cowering fright surely resulted from more than just the blunderbuss going off. Maybe someone *had* been down here. She was uneasy, for if there had been, then she and Mrs. Jenkins must have passed the person.

The housekeeper continued to look around. "What *is* this place?" she asked.

"I think it's a Roman temple," Anne replied.

"And it's been right here under Llandower all this time?" Mrs. Jenkins shivered and got to her feet. "Let's go back up into the daylight," she said, holding out a hand to help Joseph.

As the housekeeper assisted the unsteady gardener out of the temple, with Jack at their heels, still belly low on the ground, Anne picked up the lantern and glanced around again. She was about to follow the others when she noticed what seemed to be a pile of crumpled old cloth on the altar. On investigation she was startled to find not rags, but a fashionable greatcoat someone had been using as bedding. So a fugitive *had* been hiding down here. Her pulse quickened unpleasantly, for it was a very unsettling thought. Still, she could prevent any return by bolting the door to the kitchens' passage and padlocking the trapdoors from the courtyard.

Her attention returned to the coat, which she decided must have been stolen. She ran a curious fingertip over the gleaming silver buttons, only one of which was missing. Why would a thief fail to remove and sell such costly items? As she looked, she suddenly recognized the maze badge of the Mowbrays and recalled that the old Duke of Wroxford had buttons like these. Surely, the vagrant couldn't have been hiding down here as long ago as that? Almost immediately she discounted the thought, for this was a young man's coat, stylish and bang-up to the latest mark. It was a winter garment, and therefore far too heavy and warm for this time of the year, but who else could it belong to except Hugh? He hadn't brought it with him when he'd called, but that didn't signify because the thief could have stolen it from the White Boar. She'd ask him about it. Taking the coat with her, she made her way out of the temple.

Chapter Twenty-five

Sylvanus was still so unnerved by the closeness of the call in the temple that on reaching the rotunda he flung himself among the thick ivy behind the bench, his hands clasped over his head and his furry posterior up in the air.

Gervase gazed uneasily at the faun's trembling little tail. *"Sylvanus? Are you all right? Is Anne still safe—?"* His fear for the woman he loved was almost too much to bear.

"Yes, she's all right." Sylvanus peeped timidly over the bench.

"I thought maybe my damned cousin had come early, and . . ." The coming evening weighed heavily upon Gervase's heart.

Sylvanus lowered his eyes. "She's quite all right," he said again. "Well, when I say that—"

"What happened?" Gervase interrupted anxiously, for clearly something had occurred that involved Anne.

"My rope snake must have been removed, because the dog found me. Then the gardener came down with his blunderbuss, and I could only escape by turning them both to stone for a few moments. It was either that or be caught. I'd dearly have liked to leave that wretched dog as a statue, though," the faun added, recovering sufficiently to sit weakly on the bench.

"What of Anne?"

"She and the housekeeper came down, but they passed me in the darkness. They'll have had a shock about finding the temple, but that's all, because I'd turned the man and the dog back from marble by then."

"Did the gardener see you?"

"Yes, but it was over in seconds, and he will probably think he imagined it. The dog realized more, but he can't speak to humans."

Gervase didn't say anything, for he could well recall his

own feelings when he'd first been turned to marble. Joseph might think he imagined it, but he'd never forget it all the same.

Sylvanus looked uncomfortably at him. "There's just one thing. I forgot to bring your coat with me. If they find it and recognize the buttons . . ."

"They might show it to Hugh." Gervase finished.

"He's bound to recognize it and wonder how on earth it comes to be here."

"Well, what's done is done."

At that moment Anne had just placed the coat in question in a corner of the kitchens, then she turned toward Joseph, who was seated with a drink of something to steady his nerves. Jack was at his knee, and the lurcher was still quivering. "Right, Joseph, I think you should tell us the truth now," she said quietly.

He sat forward guiltily. "I've already said what happened, Miss Anne."

"You haven't," she replied patiently.

"I have, I swear it!" he cried.

Mrs. Jenkins looked closely at him and realized Anne was right. "Joseph Greenwood!" she said sharply.

He eyed them both unhappily. "Look, I just *can't* tell you!" he said then.

"Why not?" the housekeeper asked.

"Because it's too mad, that's why."

Anne and Mrs. Jenkins exchanged glances, each thinking of the strange business of the disappearing nymph. Anne looked at him again. "Just tell us, Joseph, because believe me, there have been some strange things going on around here recently." Briefly she told him about Penelope's comings and goings.

The old man stared at her. "But that's impossible," he said.

"More impossible than whatever it was that happened in the cellar?"

He hesitated, then shook his head. "Maybe not. All right, I'll tell you, but you must *promise* you won't say a word of it to anyone. I don't want to end up in a bedlam." He cleared his throat and stroked the lurcher's head. "There were three things really. Firstly, I saw Jack all turned to stone, as white and stiff as that statue in the maze; then I saw something like a man, except it had horns and a billy-goat's beard. The last thing I remember was feeling myself turning to stone too. It lasted only a few moments, then I was myself again, but it's the truth, I swear it upon my mother's grave. Look at Jack— can't you *see* that something mighty frightening happened to him?" There was silence, and the gardener got up from the chair. "Right, I've told you what happened, and now I want to forget it. I'm going to go out to the garden and get on with the jobs I intended to start earlier, and I'm not going to mention a single word of this ever again."

No one said anything as he clumped across the kitchens in his heavy boots. Jack followed him out, and as man and dog crossed the courtyard, the two women looked at each other. Mrs. Jenkins spoke first. "There's something very odd going on around here, isn't there, Miss Anne?" she observed with masterly understatement.

"I fear there is, Mrs. Jenkins." Joseph's words echoed disturbingly through Anne's head. *As white and stiff as that statue in the maze.*

The housekeeper sat down unhappily. "What with the nad, and now horned men in the cellar . . ."

Anne remembered her decision to make the cellar secure. "Where is that old padlock from the outhouse that was demolished last autumn?"

"In that drawer over there, Miss Anne."

"Will you bolt the door from the passage into the cellars? I intend to make absolutely certain he doesn't get in again."

The housekeeper nodded, then hesitated. "May I say something, Miss Anne? I know you won't like it, but I have to say all this has only started happening since Mr. Danby came here."

Anne had also begun to wonder if there was a connection, but she wasn't about to admit it. Without replying, she left the kitchen to put the padlock on the trapdoors, then she straightened and glanced through the archway toward the maze. Could it really be just coincidence that Joseph described Jack as being like the statue? And was it also coincidence that she herself thought the statue was the image of Charles Danby? She swallowed, for her thoughts were drifting toward too incredible conclusions.

Suddenly, a figure appeared beneath the archway, and there came the loud clanging of a handbell. She gave a frightened start, but then almost laughed aloud, for it was only the letter carrier, and he'd brought a letter from Ireland. Thoughts of Charles Danby were temporarily set aside as she immediately broke the seal and began to read.

Ballynarray, Monday, May 6th, 1816.

My dearest child,

This letter comes with all our love and sincere hope that you enjoy(ed?) your birthday. Your dear mother spent many an anxious moment deciding upon the exact form of our gift, but I think you will agree her efforts were not in vain. I will not mention what it is, for fear this letter arrives *before* the event!

Now to other things. I have made my peace with my brother, whose health is now very frail but who is thankfully no longer in danger, and I am writing this in the hope that you will accept and understand the momentous decision to which your mother and I have come. To be brief and to the point, when you become Duchess of Wroxford, we intend that Ballynarray, which is my birthright once more, will be our home.

Anne stared at the last sentence for a long moment before reading on.

Having no doubt shaken you with this revelation, allow me to explain. In recent years my secret longing for my homeland has become more and more difficult to ignore. Now that I have returned to Ballynarray and found that not only is it mine again, but my name has at last been cleared of all supposed past crimes, so great has my happiness become that I can no longer pretend that I wish to remain at Llandower for the rest of my days. Your mother understands, and is happy to live here—after all, without you, what is Llandower to us? I think that once you have recovered from the shock of this letter, you will understand how I feel. Your marriage and my brother's illness have combined to create a watershed in all our lives, and I intend to return to my roots. You have only known Llandower, and I do not doubt that you will always regard it in the same light that I regard Ballynarray, but you are soon to be the Duchess of Wroxford, and Wroxford Park will be your home. Besides, the duke owns Llandower, so you will not be completely parted from it. Forgive me if I seem to be putting my needs before yours, my dear, but I have yearned for Ireland ever since I left. At Llandower I have always had to struggle to balance the books, but Ballynarray is prosperous, and offers me the degree of security and independence I have always wanted. I will own this land, my dear, not merely be the tenant, and that means a great deal.

Please understand, and be happy for us, as we are happy for you. We still do not begin to understand about your match with the duke, but as it is clearly what you wish, then we are content for you. I will not write more now, because I do not doubt that I have given you enough to think about. We will return within the month, because my tenancy soon falls due, and I will have to see Mr. Critchley about its termination. There is also the matter of the servants. We do, of course, intend to offer Mrs. Jenkins, Joseph, and Martin places with us here in Ballynarray, although whether or not they choose to leave England is another matter. However, that remains to be seen.

Until we see you again, my dearest daughter, I am, your loving

Father.

Hardly able to absorb what she'd just read, Anne slowly folded the letter. Her hands were trembling, and she could have laughed out loud at the irony of the situation. She had thought Llandower meant everything to her father, when all the time he longed to be free of it! If she'd known the truth, she would *never* have entered into the contract with Gervase Mowbray, never felt obliged to continue the match with Hugh Mowbray, and above all, never have considered her feelings for Charles Danby to be wrong!

Suddenly, the implications were borne in on her. She'd been released from the old duke's pressure, and Hugh had told her he could get around the terms of the will, so the match could be abandoned! Gathering her skirts, she ran back to the kitchens, where Mrs. Jenkins was continuing to prepare the picnic food. All at once, it seemed entirely inappropriate for Hugh to come tonight; indeed it seemed inappropriate that the picnic should proceed at all. Anne's mind was made up in a moment. "Mrs. Jenkins, there isn't going to be a picnic tonight; in fact I'm about to write a note to the duke to tell him that the betrothal is at an end. Martin must deliver it to the White Boar without delay."

The housekeeper dropped the plate she was holding. "You—you what, Miss Anne?" she said faintly.

Anne smiled. "Don't look like that, Mrs. Jenkins, for I am happy. Please read this." She held out her father's letter.

Slowly, the housekeeper took it, and her eyes widened as she read, especially when she reached the suggestion at the end that she, Joseph, and Martin might like to go to Ireland. "Oh, my Lord above," she said weakly and sat down. Then she looked earnestly at Anne. "But what of becoming Duchess of Wroxford? Do you really want to turn your back upon such a fine husband?"

Anne crouched beside her and took her hands. "I've never really wanted the match; I only entered into it because if I'd refused, the old duke would have turned my parents out of Llandower." She explained exactly how the match had come about in the first place.

The housekeeper listened in silence and held her gaze. "So you're telling me that the new duke doesn't really want the match either, nor his cousin before him?"

"That's exactly what I'm saying, especially of the late Gervase Mowbray, who *certainly* resented the whole thing."

"And now I suppose it is Mr. Danby who is uppermost in your thoughts?"

Anne drew back a little. "I admit I feel a great deal for him, Mrs. Jenkins, even though I hardly know him."

"I suspect you know a great deal more than you should," the housekeeper observed shrewdly.

Anne colored.

Mrs. Jenkins exhaled. "Oh, what a day, and it's hardly past breakfast," she declared.

Anne smiled. "A memorable birthday, indeed."

"Indeed."

Anne got up. "I'm going to write that note now," she said firmly.

"But what on earth will you say? Surely it's best to speak to the duke face-to-face?"

"I intend to, Mrs. Jenkins, but the birthday picnic doesn't seem the proper occasion. It will be far better if I speak to him on neutral ground at the White Boar, and since—what with one thing and another—I admit to being a little overwrought at the moment, I think I will go tomorrow." Anne lowered her eyes. *And in the meantime, please come to Llandower again, Charles, please . . .*

Chapter Twenty-six

At the White Boar Hugh was taking breakfast with Kitty. The actress had donned her best pink lawn morning gown for the benefit of Sir Thomas and his wife and was in a good humor because it amused her that she probably knew far more about Sir Thomas's predilections between the sheets than his sour-cat spouse ever would. She wouldn't have been in such an amiable mood had she realized that her appearance wasn't quite as elegantly proper as she thought. Her short-sleeved, exceedingly décolleté gown was intended to be made respectable for daytime by the addition of long muslin sleeves and a carefully tucked scarf, but in her vanity she had chosen not to wear either, of which glaring omissions Hugh first learned when she joined him at the table. He was tastefully and discreetly turned out in a plain brown coat and fawn trousers, perfect attire for breakfast at a country inn, and he was dismayed by her lack of discretion. Suddenly, he found himself recalling Gervase's observation in Naples. *A daring expanse of bosom is embarrassing and vulgar outside the confines of the bedchamber.* How disagreeably true.

Kitty sensed nothing of his thoughts and fully expected to be the object of Sir Thomas's renewed desire and his wife's envy. The former she was to enjoy, but the latter was certainly not forthcoming. Sir Thomas entered, his clothes pitched at exactly the same level as Hugh's, except that he wore a gray coat and cream trousers, but when he turned for his wife to enter as well, the contrast with Kitty could not have been greater. Lady Fanhope was a thin, flat-bosomed woman with a sallow complexion and primly pursed lips. Her light hair was tugged back into a tight knot at the back of her head, and her long-sleeved gown—costly bottle green silk—had a starched lace ruff high around the throat. She was so busy lecturing her husband in her unpleasantly nasal voice that at first she did not notice the only other persons at the inn, but she fell ominously silent as her disapproving glance at last fell upon Kitty. Her lips pursed still more, her pointed nose seemed to visibly turn up at the end, and her gaze became withering as it encompassed the alarming plunge of the pink lawn. Then, without acknowledging her fellow guests in any way, she sailed grandly to an unlaid table in the farthest corner of the room. As the flustered inn maids hurried to lay crockery, cutlery, and a fresh cloth, Sir Thomas paused awkwardly. On the one hand he was mindful of Hugh, but on the other hand his purse dictated that he had to bow to his wife, so after glancing yearningly at Kitty's offending décolletage, he cleared his throat and hastened after his spouse.

Kitty accurately interpreted the incident, and myriad savage expressions crossed her beautiful face. Hugh smarted as well, for by snubbing Kitty so completely, Lady Fanhope had snubbed him as well. One day he would make Fanhope's piece of Staffordshire earthenware very sorry indeed! He looked across at the other table, where Sir Thomas's face was an embarrassed study, and his wife looked as if she had just drunk a glass of vinegar. This was a sample of things to come if Kitty became his duchess, and it wasn't a feeling he enjoyed. Quite suddenly, all desire was extinguished, and the thought slid into his head that maybe he would be better off without her.

Lady Fanhope observed them, then sniffed disdainfully. "How can she sit there at the breakfast table in such a state of undress? Has she no discretion at all? I am put in mind of cream blancmange, although thankfully we are spared the sight of the cherries on top."

Had any other woman passed such a comment, it would have been meant to amuse, but Lady Fanhope did not possess a sense of humor, so Sir Thomas said nothing as he applied himself to the bacon, eggs, and sausage a maid placed before him. He stole a surreptitious glance at the cream jellies. Oh, for a goodly helping, *and* a nibble on the cherries!

Lady Fanhope allowed herself another covert inspection of the other table. "I'd hazard she is very well acquainted with the demimonde."

"I really could not say, my dear," he replied uncomfortably.

"And her companion can be no better than he should be, for

a person of true quality would not *choose* to be seen with such a low creature."

Sir Thomas's neck went very red, and he ran a finger nervously around his collar.

"I will not, under any circumstances, tolerate their society while we are here. When we dine tonight, I will cut them both again, and you are to do the same, is that clear?"

"Perfectly, my dearest one," he replied, making a mental note to plead with Hugh for understanding on such a delicate point. Oh, God, women! Men were cursed with *and* without them!

Lady Fanhope observed Kitty a little longer. "One wonders what she will deem suitable for dinner. She'll be ablaze with cheap paste, of that I'm quite certain."

It was midmorning when Anne's note arrived at the inn, where, of course, nothing was known of the Duke of Wroxford. Encouraged to hope that perhaps this exalted aristocrat would soon grace the premises with his presence, the landlord left the note on a shelf in the entrance hall while he went to instruct the maids to clean the next best bedroom from top to bottom.

The note lay on the shelf for the remainder of the day, and Hugh knew nothing of it as the evening wore on, and at last it was time to prepare for Llandower. He looked very much the duke, in an indigo coat and rose-and-white striped waistcoat, with white trousers and gleaming Hessian boots, and he was utterly calm as he tied his starched neckcloth in the elaborate style he favored most. In his mind he had gone over and over how the coming hours would proceed, and he was confident that he was prepared for what must be done. Anne Willowby's demise was as good as accomplished.

Kitty was ready to dine at the inn and wore a kingfisher taffeta gown that exposed as much of her bosom, if not more, as the pink lawn. The diadem graced her head, for it was her intention to show Lady Fanhope that she possessed something that would eclipse anything in her ladyship's jewelry box, but as she left her room to go to Hugh's, she came face-to-face with the Fanhopes. She paused, holding her head high and looking scornfully at Lady Fanhope's discreet diamond necklace. Sir Thomas's jaw dropped when he saw the diadem, for its intense glitter told him it was only too real, but his wife's glance was as withering as Kitty's. Twitching her maroon silk skirts aside, her ladyship again swept past without a word, and after smiling longingly at his former mistress, Sir Thomas hurried obediently after her.

Kitty believed herself to have triumphed, but she halted at Hugh's door as Lady Fanhope's nasal tones drifted mockingly from the staircase. "I told you she'd be ablaze with cheap paste! Did you ever see such a fairground bauble in your life?"

Sir Thomas replied, "My dear, I think you'll find those stones were the real thing."

"The real thing? Thomas, I *recognize* the item in question."

"You do?"

"Yes. It was brought to the London jeweler only the other day when I was waiting for the senior partner to return. Don't you recall? I had to make a serious complaint about being expected to wait in that poky backroom."

"Oh, yes, dear, I recall," Sir Thomas muttered long-sufferingly.

"Well, a gentleman—a male person, anyway, presumably the very same who is staying here now—brought that trinket in. I couldn't see him, but a mirror afforded me an excellent view of what he wished to have priced. As you, he clearly believed it was valuable, but he was soon disabused of that misconception, for it is worthless."

The story rang only too true, and Kitty's eyes hardened. *Worthless?*

"My dear, you cannot possibly be sure it was the same piece."

"Thomas, if I tell you it was the same, then it was the same!" she replied sharply. "Besides, I'd recognize it anywhere. Some of those glass stones are unusual, both in shape and color."

"My dear, I still can't help thinking their glitter seemed genuine," Sir Thomas ventured again.

"It is a gewgaw, Thomas, and a vulgar one at that."

Kitty remained in frozen fury as their voices faded down the stairs. The truth stared her in the eyes. What a fool she'd been, for if Hugh was prepared to fob her off with paste, he was also prepared to lie about marriage! He'd clearly never had any intention of making her his duchess! She'd been used! Rage, incredulity, and humiliation engulfed her, and wisdom had no place either as she snatched the diadem from her head and burst in upon him.

Hugh whirled around in alarm as the diadem flew past his ear, struck the drawn curtain, and rolled onto the worn rug by the bed. "What in God's name—?" he cried.

"How *dare* you attempt to fob me off with paste!" she cried.

"Paste?" He tried to evince astonishment, but the flicker of his eyes told her differently.

"You know it's worthless, and you lied to me in order to get me between your sheets! Well, I've warmed your bed for the last time, for I'm no longer the fool you took me for!"

"Keep your voice down!" He strode across to drag her into the room, then he slammed the door. Still gripping her arm, he looked coldly down at her. "What is all this about?"

"I've just overheard Lady Fanhope! She was there that day the jeweler told you the diadem was worthless!"

"She what?" Hugh was startled.

"She didn't know it was you, but she recognized the diadem!"

Hugh dissembled smoothly. "Lady Fanhope may have been present when *someone* took *something* to *a* jeweler, but it wasn't me."

But Kitty had seen the initial dismay in his eyes and knew who was telling the truth. Her fury made her foolhardy. "You're lying, and I'll make you pay!" she cried.

Until that moment he hadn't realized exactly how much he now despised her. Breakfast had been an embarrassment he never intended to experience again, and as to permitting her to threaten him . . . His hold on her arm became cruel. "Have a care, Kitty, for I'm not a man to cross! One word out of place, and you'll be sorry—is that clear?" Like lightning he put his other hand to her throat. "Just remember I make a very dangerous enemy," he breathed, stroking her skin with his thumb.

A deadlier truth stared her in the eyes now, and the blood froze in her veins as she saw that the fate planned for Anne Willowby could as easily be assigned to her. From the depths of her acting soul she clawed a mien that was both conciliatory and humbled. "F-forgive me . . . it's just that I'm always foolish when I'm angry. You don't honestly think I'd betray anything, do you? Besides, we are in this together, aren't we?"

Satisfied that he'd frightened her into submission—albeit

temporarily—he slowly released her. "Yes, of course we're in this together," he said softly.

"I should go down to dinner . . ."

"By all means." But as the door closed behind her, his eyes glittered coldly. Kitty had become tiresome, and certainly could not be trusted to hold her tongue. She would have to go—permanently.

Just on the other side of the door, Kitty was shaking like a leaf. Her fate had been written only too large and clear in Hugh's eyes, and she knew she had to get away from the White Boar as quickly as possible. She'd be long gone before he returned from the vile deed at Llandower! Fortified by decision, she was about to return to her own room when she heard a scraping sound coming from the Fanhopes' room. Curious to the last, she gathered her skirts and hurried to peep through the keyhole.

She saw Sir Thomas dragging a small but heavy chest from beneath the bed. He unlocked it with a key he took from a secret compartment in his wife's jewelry box, and Kitty's eyes widened when she saw that the chest contained a hoard of golden guineas that shone richly in the light of the setting sun. Sir Thomas was startled too, for he drew back with a gasp, but then his brow darkened with anger, and he rose to his feet with an air of what Kitty could only interpret as simmering resentment. Intuition told her that what she'd just witnessed could be turned to her advantage, and without further ado she opened the door and went in.

Sir Thomas gave a fearful start, expecting to see his wife. His shock was almost as great as he saw it was Kitty, her lips curved in the sort of seductive smile he'd conjured in his dreams ever since he'd had to set her aside in favor of money.

"Well, Thomas, what have we here?" she murmured, closing the door and leaning back in a pose that outlined her figure to perfection.

His glance moved over her, and when he met her eyes, he was her prisoner once more. He didn't mince his words where his marriage was concerned. "What you have here is a husband who is apparently not to be trusted with anything, but who can be compromised most shamefully when it comes to breaking the law," he replied.

"Breaking the law?"

"I'll warrant you've heard the rumors about my father-in-law's finances?"

"A little."

"Until now I've never seen anything to either confirm or deny the whispers. I wondered what was afoot when my wife was despatched upon this visit to America, and I became downright suspicious when she brought this chest with her. She claimed it contained nothing more than books for her New York cousin, but since she always keeps the key with her, I couldn't take a look. Tonight, however, she forgot, and I made an excuse to leave her in the dining room and return here for something. *Et, voilà!*" He indicated the gleaming hoard. "Clearly, the duns are snapping at his heels, so dear Papa Pottery has despatched his daughter with as much of his wealth as he can before his debts catch up with him. I have been dragged along and made accessory."

"You have been used most vilely, Thomas, and so have I, for tonight it has become clear that Hugh has no intention of marrying me," Kitty said softly. "Oh, Thomas, would it not serve them both right if we took our revenge?" She smiled and glanced meaningfully at the gold. "I presume passage has already been booked to America?"

His lips parted. "Eh? You mean . . . ?"

She shrugged. "If the coins have no business being sent away at all, I hardly think your wife will dare set the authorities after us, do you? We could live very well indeed." She raised a cunning eyebrow.

He hesitated, then smiled.

Hugh had temporarily dismissed Kitty from his mind. He was confident that her ambition for a title would keep her close by, so it simply did not occur to him that she would slip from his clutches. Ready to set out for Llandower, he paused to retrieve the diadem from the floor, and was about to toss it onto the bed when he recalled how delighted Kitty had been with it at first. He smiled. How ingratiatingly perfect a birthday present it would make for Anne Willowby! It would make him appear even more charming and thoughtful. He cast around for something in which to wrap it and on the bedside table saw the small tablecloth that concealed old wine stains. Carefully, he wrapped it around the matchless piece of jewelry, then tucked the resultant package in his pocket and left the room.

As he crossed the entrance hall, he was startled as the neat handwriting on Anne's note leapt out at him. *The Duke of Wroxford.* Realizing immediately that it could be only from Anne, he glanced swiftly around to see if there was anyone to observe Mr. Oadby purloining a message meant for the Duke of Wroxford. No one seemed to be near, so he took it and withdrew to a quiet corner to read. The formality of the opening greeting warned him immediately that something was wrong.

> Your Grace, (For such I believe I should address you from now on.)
>
>   I am sure that in spite of your reassurance, in your heart you would prefer to abandon our match, so it will be welcome tidings indeed to learn that I am now free of any compulsion to proceed. Word has reached me from Ireland that my parents intend to make their home there, thus Llandower ceases to be of any consequence in the scheme of things. In view of this I feel it would be inappropriate for our picnic plans to continue, or for you to come to Llandower for a celebration which would not be of any interest to you were it not for our enforced betrothal. Accordingly I will attend you at the White Boar at noon tomorrow, when I trust we will be able to discuss our situation, and then part as amicably as we met. I will not communicate with Mr. Critchley until you and I have addressed the entire matter to our mutual satisfaction.
>
>   Sincerely, Anne Willowby.

Hugh was so shaken that he almost dropped the note. She was withdrawing from the match? In a flash he saw the destruction of his dreams. By lying that he could avoid the terms of the will, he'd allowed her to think he would not suffer at all if the match was ended. Why, oh *why* had he gilded the lily like that? That moment of conceit had proved his downfall.

Then he paused as it struck him how easily he might have walked past the note and arrived at Llandower none the wiser. He could still do that! It was imperative that he see her tonight, because now she *had* to die before it got out that she'd changed her mind. The old glitter returned to his eyes, and he ripped the note into tiny fragments, which he tossed into the empty fireplace before strolling out into the late evening light, where an ostler waited with his horse.

The inn goat did not make a sound as the rider disappeared toward Llandower.

Chapter Twenty-seven

Anne believed she had successfully canceled Hugh's visit, and so had spent the day picturing the various ways the following day's meeting at the White Boar might go. Her concentration upon Hugh had been very determined indeed, because the alternative was to dwell endlessly upon her increasing disquiet regarding the statue. The strange events of the morning, coupled with Joseph's insistence that he and Jack had fleetingly been turned to marble, left very little option but to wonder about the impossible.

All day she'd stayed well away from the maze, and the fading evening light found her reading in her bedroom, but her gaze kept wandering to the open window, beyond which lay the dark-hedged maze. Birdsong echoed across the park, and the scent of spring flowers was almost beguilingly heady as she at last went to the window to gaze down at the rotunda. It seemed the remnants of the sunset shimmered with a different light from usual, and that the hazy evening was unseasonably warm and drowsy. The cupola of the rotunda rose from the center of the maze with an air of mystery it had never possessed before, and she could just make out the head of the statue. All day she had wondered might be so much more than it seemed.

She'd kept telling herself she was allowing her imagination to run wild, but if that was so, then Joseph and Mrs. Jenkins were doing the same. Had the occupants of Llandower Castle been bewitched of late? Or were they suffering from shared hysteria? It was hard to accept either explanation, for the gardener was a down-to-earth countryman, not given to an overactive imagination, and Mrs. Jenkins hadn't invented the mystery of the disappearing naiad, for Anne herself had witnessed its absence and subsequent return. She wished she could blame it all on the vagrant who'd been sleeping in the temple, but although that would explain away the theft of food and the knocking over of pots and pans, it didn't explain the comings and goings of the naiad. Nor did it account for the apparent transformation of flesh into marble. . . .

Suddenly, she knew she couldn't ignore things any longer. Every instinct urged her to allay her wild and totally unlikely suspicions by finding something that proved the statue *wasn't* Charles Danby! But as she left the room to do just that, she wondered what she would do if the very opposite happened. What if she was about to *confirm* the impossible? What then?

She hurried into the maze, the atmosphere of which was eerily different tonight, but when she reached the clearing in the center, she hesitated before facing the chimera that had tormented her more and more all day. As she at last took another step forward, a sound somewhere behind made her whirl about. Her heart lurched because she hoped to see Charles, but there was nothing there, just the tall, dark hedges, silent in the breezeless air, and the gravel path disappearing among them. Then she remembered hearing a similar sound on the stormy night when she'd first found the statue. On that occasion it had come from the bench at the back of the rotunda, and she'd thought it was rats, but now she knew rats had nothing to do with it. Was it the intruder? Had he taken refuge here now that he'd been found out in the temple? Her heart quickened unpleasantly as her uneasy glance moved from lengthening shadow to lengthening shadow, but as the seconds passed and there was no further sound, she gradually relaxed and turned to face the rotunda again.

Behind the hedges Sylvanus was down on all fours, making himself as small as possible in order to avoid detection. Deprived of his comfortable temple, the faun had spent a very disagreeable night in the open air on the bench and had been on the point of leaving the maze on the lovesick and rather risky errand of trying to see Penelope before the light had properly faded, when he realized Anne was coming. Concerned as to why she'd come here when—as he thought—she must be expecting Hugh at any moment, the faun had hidden down one of the maze's blind alleys until she passed, then followed her back into the heart of the maze. The sound she'd heard came when he'd caught a hoof in a root and stumbled against the hedge, and now, as he peered uneasily through the tight-packed greenery, a sixth sense told him something was wrong. Surely she could not have begun to guess the truth about the statue? He tried to keep her in view, but as she stepped forward again, the density of the hedge hid her from view.

Gervase knew she was there, for he heard the lightness of her tread on the gravel. He thought she still expected Hugh and longed to stretch out his hand to draw her safely into the protection of his embrace, but until darkness fell, he was helpless.

Anne forgot her fear as she approached the rotunda, which had an almost unearthly appearance in the lazily warm shadows. She wondered if she'd feel foolish because the statue wasn't the image of Charles Danby after all, but as she gazed up at the finely chiseled face, she knew the opposite was true, for the white marble seemed to be him down to the very last detail. The eyes were his, so were the lips, and if the hair were brushed back . . . Yet it couldn't actually *be* him—it couldn't! Could it? If she inspected its hand, would she find the scratch Mog had left that night in the kitchen passage? She swallowed as this struck her. The scratch had been a bad one, requiring bandaging with a handkerchief, and would still be evident now, even in marble.

She was afraid to look, for if the scratch was there, the impossible would become cold sober fact, and fantasy would not only invade the safe haven of logic, but triumph decisively over it. Yet she had no choice but to look. This had to be settled once and for all, and the presence of the scratch would provide all the evidence she needed. Taking a deep breath, she looked at the hand. Her breath caught, and an enervating weakness swept over her, for there, defined unmistakably across the marble knuckles, was the mark of Mog's frightened leap from the shelf. Logic was vanquished. This *was* Charles Danby!

As her shaking fingers brushed his rigid, unyielding skin, Gervase knew his secret was out, and a maelstrom of helplessness spun through him. Trapped in his marble cocoon, he could only watch the incredulous emotions on her face. He saw how pale she went. What was she feeling? Was she horrified? Repulsed? Did she think she had gone mad? Dear God, what else *could* she think, for the truth was beyond reason. He wanted the moment to stop, and all he could think of was appealing to the faun for help. *"Sylvanus? Are you still here?*

Can you hear me? Don't let this go further! She must tell me she loves me, not be frightened into believing her wits have deserted her!"

Unable to watch because of the thickness of the hedge Sylvanus had been taking comfort from Gervase's silence, but as the anguished plea rang silently out, the faun was startled into hasty action. He scrambled to the edge of the central clearing and was dismayed to see Anne's ashen face as she stared down at Gervase's hand. The horrified faun's only thought was to petrify her, but in his panic he applied instead his forbidden power to cause irresistible attraction. He realized his mistake almost immediately and glanced up fearfully at the sky, but there was no flash of lightning, just a shooting star that signaled that Bacchus acknowledged the extenuating circumstances. Sylvanus's reassured glance flew back toward the rotunda, for he needed time to think, so it really didn't matter which power he used, and in his decidedly earthy opinion, there had always been much to gain from a little sexual bewitchment.

Anne was aware of the fading of all fear and confusion. What did the impossible matter? What nonsense it was to fight facts when all that was really of consequence was how she felt about Charles Danby. She gazed at the statue, but instead of marble saw the warm, flesh-and-blood lover who'd held her in his arms and made her feel as she'd never felt before. It had been wonderful when he'd held her in the study, and again when he'd gently lifted her from her feet on the jetty and allowed her to sink against the hard exciting contours of his body. Her beloved Charles, ruggedly handsome, tanned from the sun, with eyes as clear and blue as the heavens, and lips that could sweep her to ecstasy, was with her again now. With a sigh she linked her arms around his neck and put her mouth adoringly to the smooth white marble.

There was such sensuous seduction in her kiss that Gervase felt almost as if he were coming to life in her arms, but it was only a cruel illusion, for his flesh remained cold and hard. Desire engulfed him as her breasts pressed sweetly to him, her aroused nipples tangible even to a man of marble. He loved her so much that the agony of feeling he knew now was the most remorseless pain imaginable. If she would only whisper those three words, he would be liberated and able to consummate the passion that burned through them both.

Anne's exhilaration was totally wanton. She neither knew nor cared what was happening; all she could think of was Charles Danby. To her his lips were warm and responsive, and as she moved against him, the pleasure was intoxicating. This was the realization of the yearning that had beckoned her through the long nights, the final clarification of the half-captured images that had flashed fragmentedly through her days. This was enlightenment, ravishment itself . . .

The sound of hooves came from beyond the maze, and Sylvanus tore his interested gaze from the rotunda to turn perplexedly. Who could be arriving? Gervase was lost in Anne's beguilement and heard nothing, but after a few minutes Mrs. Jenkins's flustered voice penetrated his joy with words that shattered his magic.

"Miss Anne! Oh, Miss Anne, please come, for His Grace is here!"

Sylvanus withdrew his power from Anne, then scampered back to his blind alley, where he pressed down beneath the hedge and curled up into the tightest of balls so that she wouldn't see him when she hurried past.

She awoke in a state of utter confusion. The rotunda seemed to be spinning. Or maybe the maze was revolving around it. Whatever it was, she felt giddy and uncertain of what was real and what was fantasy. Her memory was wiped clean from the moment she'd seen the telltale scratch on the statue's hand, so she knew nothing of what had passed during the past few minutes. As she glanced again at the scratch, the true implications surged through her, and she could not even begin to comprehend what was going on in this peaceful Monmouthshire backwater that until now had always been so placidly ordinary. She looked at Gervase's face. "I'm not going mad, am I? It really *is* you, Charles?" she whispered.

"Yes, it's me! Say what's in your heart, my love!" he begged.

"Miss Anne? The duke is here!" Mrs. Jenkins called again.

Anne's lips parted in dismay. Hugh? But why had he called after all? Surely she'd made her wishes plain in her note? There was no time now to think of the whys and wherefores, for somehow she had to speak to him. She really didn't know how she was going to achieve it with decorum after the astonishing discovery here in the rotunda, for she felt more like giving way to hysteria. She closed her eyes for a moment, then hurried from the rotunda.

"Anne! Just say you love me and this will all be over! Beware of my cousin, for he means you the greatest harm imaginable!" Gervase's agonized imploration winged desperately after her, but did not even begin to touch upon her consciousness. She neither sensed nor heard anything, and as she passed the end of the blind alley, she didn't see Sylvanus in his hiding place either.

At the edge of the maze she paused to compose herself, then walked sedately toward the castle, where Hugh, sinister behind a smile, was waiting in the hall.

Chapter Twenty-eight

"Good evening, Anne, may I waste no time in wishing you the very happiest of birthdays?" Hugh murmured as he took her hand and drew it warmly to his lips.

She looked urgently behind him at Mrs. Jenkins, seeking a hint as to why he had called after all, but the housekeeper, who was hastily lighting candles because the daylight had now quite gone, could only spread her hands perplexedly, for the note had been taken to the White Boar in ample time. Anne withdrew her hand a little distractedly. "Your Grace, I—"

He interrupted with a gentle reproof that could not have sounded more warmly sincere. "I thought we had agreed to dispense with disagreeable formality?"

"Yes, but—"

He broke in again as he held the cloth-wrapped diadem out to her. "Please accept this, not only as a birthday gift, but as a token of my regard. I have no doubt that in the coming years I will take great pride in seeing you wear it."

Anne stared at him in increasing dismay, for this unexpected development was a great strain, coming as it did so hard on the heels of her incredible discovery in the maze. "Sir, I sent word to you which I fear you cannot have received."

He didn't seem to hear as he pressed the diadem into her hands. "I chose it especially for you."

Unable to think what else to do, she unwrapped the cloth, and as the diadem's glory caught the candlelight, her parted lips betrayed reluctant admiration.

Mrs. Jenkins gasped. "Oh, my, what a beautiful thing," she declared.

Anne turned the wedding crown gently so that the jewels flashed. "It's exquisite," she murmured.

"Exquisite indeed, and you are more than worthy of it," he said gallantly.

She gazed at the matchless workmanship. That it was very valuable she did not doubt, just as she did not doubt that she could not accept it. Slowly, she rewrapped it and held it out to him again. "Greatly as I find it to my liking, sir, I fear I cannot accept."

"Cannot? I don't understand." At last he pretended to notice what she was saying.

"I sent you a note today, sir, but it is clear that you cannot have received it." She continued to hold out the diadem.

"What note was this?" he asked, ignoring the returned gift.

As she placed the diadem on the table, she struggled to find the right words. "This is a little awkward, sir . . ."

"Maybe you would find it easier if we went for a walk? To the jetty and back, perhaps?" he suggested.

"Th-the jetty?" She smiled with relief. "Yes, I think that would be best."

He offered her his arm. "Er, what of you, Mrs. Jenkins?" he inquired, for he needed the housekeeper to witness his apparent heroism.

But Mrs. Jenkins cast an unhappy glance at Anne and shook her head uncomfortably. "I think not this time, Your Grace."

"As you wish." Damn! Still, he had no choice; he *had* to proceed tonight, because by tomorrow a letter would surely be on its way to Critchley, advising of her withdrawal.

As they went out, the housekeeper gathered her skirts and hurried up to Mr. and Mrs. Willowby's bedroom, from where she observed as best she could through the telescope, although in the encroaching darkness it wasn't easy to make out any detail.

Anne didn't speak as she and Hugh walked past the maze, but time and time again her haunted glace stole toward the soaring hedges, which to her were now so very much more mysterious than before. She could not know that from within those high leafy walls, Gervase was watching anxiously. Brought to life again by Sylvanus the moment the last of the sunset had disappeared, he was at the entrance to the maze as they went by. The impulse to step out and save Anne by confronting Hugh was almost overwhelming, but he was mindful that Anne had to confess her love *without* knowing who he really was. Hugh was certain to identify him and thus the chance of escaping from Bacchus's magic would be lost forever. So, for the moment at least, all he dared do was appoint himself her determined guardian, revealing himself to Hugh only if her life was in peril.

He waited impatiently for Sylvanus, who had stolen into the castle to get Penelope, and the moment the faun and nymph returned, unseen by Mrs. Jenkins, whose attention was on Hugh and Anne, all three hastened stealthily across the park to some thick bushes on the riverbank close to the jetty. As they crouched low among the leaves and reeds, a trick of the night breeze carried the sound of the rapids downstream, an ominous roar that echoed the emotion engulfing Gervase now that he saw Hugh properly for the first time since Naples. Here at last was the despised cousin, who not only threatened his beloved Anne, but had usurped his title and position by the foul means of leaving him to drown. No, it was more than just leaving him to drown! Gervase recalled that moment in the grove when his helpless fingers had been cruelly crushed by the heel of Hugh's riding boot. There hadn't been any hesitation, just the unspeakable act that would gain Hugh Mowbray a few seconds more in which to escape, and which would also bring him the dukedom he'd always craved. Now Anne stood in the way too, and her life was only too dispensable. Hugh's decision in the grove had been made on the spur of the moment, but this was cold-blooded premeditation. It was often said that everything was easier the second time, and from Hugh's relaxed manner and easy smile, the old adage was only too true, for no one looking at him now would guess that he had murder in mind.

Sylvanus sensed Gervase's justifiable rage. "For Jupiter's sake, don't do anything rash. If need be, we can see she comes to no harm."

"Would *you* be calm if Penelope were the one in danger?" Gervase demanded resentfully.

The faun didn't answer, but Penelope leaned across to put a soothing hand on Gervase's arm. "We won't let anything befall her—truly we won't.

"I just want to go up to my cousin and knock that evil smile from his face!" Gervase breathed as he looked at Hugh again.

"And so you will, at the proper time," the nymph said

quietly. "Remember that Anne must tell you she loves you *without* realizing who you really are."

"I know, but I'd still like to tear Hugh Mowbray's head from his shoulders," Gervase breathed.

Sylvanus gave him a reassuring smile. "If we keep *our* heads and think everything through properly, we'll *both* meet Bacchus's conditions."

Penelope had been watching the jetty, and suddenly her breath caught. "Oh, no! They're getting into one of the boats!"

As Hugh untied the rope and then took up the oars, Gervase's heart almost stopped with dread for Anne. "We can't let her go with him!" he cried.

Penelope put a hand on his arm again. "Yes, we can. I'll swim after them."

"Swim? But—"

"I can call out if he does anything!" Without further ado, the nymph dove silently into the Wye and swam down into the weed-laced depths, which were as much home to her as the open air.

The occupants of the rowing boat had no idea at all that she was cleaving through the water only a few feet away, nor did they see Gervase and Sylvanus slipping from bush to bush on the shore, keeping the boat in sight all the time. The distant thunder of the rapids carried on the breeze as Anne tried to reason with Hugh, who had been prolonging their moments alone together by arguing passionately in favor of keeping the match. He was so convincingly dismayed that when he begged her to accompany him on the river, claiming that rowing would provide him with a welcome distraction, she felt obliged to agree. His evident distress puzzled her, for she could see no reason for him to want her as his bride-to-be. On his own admission he wasn't compelled to take only her, and as Duke of Wroxford he could have his pick from the length and breadth of England, so why on earth was he almost *begging* her not to withdraw?

Confused, and becoming a little discomforted by his vehement defense of a contract she certainly had no desire or need to preserve, she began to wish she'd stayed on the shore. She lay back uneasily in the stern of the boat, trailing her fingers in the water and gazing fixedly toward the far shore, where St. Winifred's Well had now come into view. She hadn't looked directly at Hugh for several minutes because she was embarrassed, and so she wasn't really aware that he had ceased to row. He kept talking as he shipped the oars and then stood, and it wasn't until the boat swayed as he stepped forward to seize her that she at last began to look around to see what was happening. Someone shouted from the shore. She thought it was Charles, but there was no time to heed the warning because Hugh lunged at her. She tried to scramble away as he grabbed her, his hands at her throat. Her screams were choked and terrified, but then someone, or something, reached up from the water and began to rock the boat so fiercely from side to side that the oars fell overboard.

Another shout rang from the shore, and Hugh hesitated as he thought he recognized the voice. The boat was rocked even more violently as he half turned to look, and he staggered, lost his balance, and with a cry was pitched headlong into the river. He fell against Penelope and in spite of his shock was aware as she tried to squirm away. His clawing fingers twisted instinctively in her long, flowing hair, and she gasped with pain as her head was wrenched backward. His murderous resolve wasn't diminished as he thought that Anne must have been thrown overboard as well, and as he began to hit the diminutive nymph furiously with his clenched fist, it was Anne he believed he was knocking unconscious in order to more easily hold her under the water.

From the moment Hugh had shipped the oars, the boat had begun to be carried downstream, and as he fell into the water without succeeding in his monstrous plan, Gervase began to run desperately along the shore. The dull roar of the rapids could now be heard clearly in the darkness ahead, and from the thunderous sound he realized the flimsy vessel would not survive them. He knew nothing of Penelope's plight, for his thoughts were all of Anne, who had to be saved before the drifting boat reached the gorge.

Sylvanus's alarmed attention remained fixed upon the threshing water where Hugh was attacking Penelope. The faun began to dash helplessly up and down the shore. He knew Penelope needed him, but he was terrified of the river. The desperate struggle went on, though, and then he heard the little naiad sob his name. It was too much. His love for her overcame his dread, and with a silent prayer to Bacchus, he leapt into the river.

At first his panic was almost overwhelming, but then knowledge came from nowhere, and he began to swim like a dog. His limbs moved swiftly and rhythmically, and his life-long fear was suddenly vanquished as he began to close the gap between himself and the nymph he adored so much. "I'm coming, my love! I'm coming!" he bleated so fiercely that he felt as if his heart would burst.

Penelope was frightened. She had always thought naiads would be indestructible in water, but now it was clear she was as vulnerable to drowning as any human. She struggled with all her might, but Hugh merely held her hair more tightly, and all the time rained blows upon her. Suddenly, Sylvanus was there, kicking and punching as he hurled himself upon his beloved's assailant. Caught unawares, Hugh had to release Penelope in order to defend himself properly, and the moment she was freed, the battered, barely conscious nymph dove like a fish into the depths of the Wye.

Hugh pulled back, unable to withstand such a frenzied attack, and at last he saw the faun's horns and snub-nosed face. A scream of terror was wrenched from his lips as the horror of the Neapolitan grove returned. With a bleat of triumph Sylvanus delivered an upper cut to his jaw that was worthy of a trained pugilist. Dazed, Hugh floated away in the boat's wake toward the maelstrom of the rapids.

Sylvanus trod water and glanced around desperately for his adored nymph. "Penelope? Where are you? Are you safe?" Suddenly, she floated limply up into his arms, and the devastated faun bore her back to the shore, where a shingle bank made it easy for him to carry her to safety in the cloak of bushes. There he cradled her in his arms and showered her poor bruised face with kisses, but she didn't stir. Not by so much as a flicker of her eyelids was there any sign that she was alive.

Chapter Twenty-nine

The pounding of the rapids shook the air as Anne lay in dazed confusion in the drifting boat. She was hardly able to believe that Hugh had just tried to murder her, and yet there was no doubt that was what he would have done if someone hadn't saved her. She remembered hearing a man shout from the shore—Charles, she was sure of it. At the same time she'd seen small feminine hands reaching up out of the river to shake the boat in order to unbalance Hugh.

Gradually, she became aware of the rapids and with a frightened whimper pulled herself up to stare into the darkness ahead, where the sheer wooded cliffs of the gorge marked the rocky descent that surely spelled death. Then she heard someone shout again and saw a man standing on the boulders that forced the river through the first rapid. *Charles!* She tried to call his name, but no sound passed her frightened lips. Tears stung her eyes, and she continued to cling to the edge of the boat, grasping the damp spot left by Penelope's fingers.

Gervase had sprinted along the bank. The current was much more swift as the river neared the confines of the gorge, and he knew he stood no chance of being able to swim out to the boat. Once on the rocks, he would be about four feet above her, and his only hope would be to pluck her from the boat. But did she have the strength, and the wit, after what had just happened? His heart pumped exhaustedly as he scrambled onto the damp stone and began to shout and wave. He saw her pale face looking toward him. The roar of the Wye was deafening as he lowered himself above the shining water and held his hand down.

"Take my hand!" he called, but his voice seemed lost in the racket of the river.

She knew what she must do, but her muscles seemed to

have lost their strength. All she could do was cling to the side of the boat.

"Anne!" Seeing her frozen immobility, he shouted her name like a command.

His tone cut through her fear, and suddenly she found the will to move. Somehow she made herself let go of the side of the boat and braced herself to reach up to him. The current was racing now, and she was skimming toward him so quickly that she knew she would have only a split second in which to catch his fingers. Tears stung her eyes, and she felt more daunted than she ever had in her life, but she found the courage somewhere in the depths of her soul, and as the boat shot between the rocks, she stretched up with all her might. His fingers closed firmly around hers, and suddenly she was swung from her feet.

The boat skimmed on, grating and cracking against the rocks as the river began to claim it, but Gervase had Anne tightly in his grip. It took all his strength to pull her up onto the rock, but at last she was in his arms, precious and safe, her body trembling with fear and relief.

"It's all right now, my love, it's all right," he whispered.

The Wye drowned his words, but she knew what he said, and her arms moved around his waist. As she sobbed and buried her face against him, however, there was renewed danger only a few feet away. While the river's main current sped furiously between the rocks, on both sides just before the bottleneck there was an almost gentle swirl of relatively quiet water, where Hugh, who had recovered sufficiently from Sylvanus's punches, managed to swim. As he looked up and saw someone hauling Anne to safety, bitter disbelief erupted through him that not only had she survived, but there was clearly a witness to what had happened. Now both she and her rescuer had to die if he was to save himself! Her hem trailed within his reach, and he lunged up to grab it.

Anne screamed as she was jerked back toward the waiting water. As she tried to kick free, she saw Hugh's hate-filled face and the whiteness of his knuckles as he pulled with all his might.

Gervase pitted all his strength against his cousin. "No, Hugh!" he cried, gripping Anne tightly as his boots slithered a little on the rock.

At last Hugh realized with whom he was dealing, and his face changed as he stared up at the man he thought had died in the Italian grove. The moment of distraction cost him dear, for the main current snatched at him, and had it not been for his hold upon Anne's hem, he would have been whirled into the rapids. Desperate to save himself, he clung to the lifeline, and Gervase felt himself being dragged down. Unless Hugh let go, they would all three drown in the Wye!

"For pity's sake, Hugh!" he cried.

But Hugh's hold did not weaken. Anne was suddenly his only hope for survival, and even though he knew he stood little chance of succeeding, he began to use her in order to haul himself out of the water.

Gervase's boots slipped a little more, and he shouted desperately. "You're going to kill us all!"

Hugh hesitated. Moments from their shared childhood glimmered in the darkness before him, good moments, of which there had been many, and at last he realized the enormity of what he had done. His eyes changed, and he reached up desperately—whether in hope of miraculous rescue or simply to touch for a last time the cousin he had wronged so much would never be known, because the Wye finally plucked him into its watery depths. For one heart-stopping second the cousins looked at each other, then Hugh was swept away through the rapids and dashed so ferociously against the rocks that he was dead before reaching the calmer water a hundred yards downstream.

Gervase was numb, for no matter what, Hugh had still been his cousin, but then his attention was snatched back to Anne, who was still suspended perilously above the eager current. Pulling with all his strength, he at last managed to drag her to safety, then he carried her to the shore and laid her gently in the lee of the rocks, where the noise of the rapids was much more dull.

There he held her to his heart while she sobbed. "It's over, sweetheart, it's over; he's gone forever now," he whispered, resting his cheek against her hair and exulting in the joy of her heartbeats next to his. After a long while he cupped her tear-stained face in his hands. "Are you all right?" he asked.

She managed to overcome her tears and nod. "Why did he do it?"

Gervase touched her hair gently. "Look no further for a

reason than that Hugh Mowbray was a monster without principle."

"I thought he was so sincere. At least . . ." She recalled that brief moment in the entrance hall when she perceived a chill behind Hugh's smile. She searched Gervase's face. "What was he to you? I mean, you called him by his first name, so your relationship could hardly be one of duke and lawyer."

Oh, how he wanted to tell her everything, but even now he was afraid to break Bacchus's condition.

She took his hand and indicated the scratch. "You are the statue, aren't you?" She could hardly believe she was actually putting the question to him, but she was so sure that his answer would merely be confirmation.

"Yes."

She stared at him, for much as she had expected it, that single word despatched common sense into oblivion.

He drew her fingers to his lips. "I can't tell you about it yet, but I will as soon as I can, I promise." *The moment you tell me you love me . . .*

"Why can't you explain now? Surely we can trust each other after all that has happened tonight? Or am I perhaps dreaming everything? Will I shortly awaken? Is that it?"

"No, of course not, and trust has nothing to do with it, for I would trust you with my very soul. Believe me, when I beg you to be patient, it is for a very vital reason."

"Vital? You make it sound as if—"

"As if my life depends upon it? Maybe that's because it does." He looked away, for what else but a form of death could he call his fate if she did not confess her love for Charles Danby? He pulled her close suddenly, putting his lips over hers in an agony of emotion that made him brutal, then he drew back. "That is all the answer I can give now, but it tells you what is in my heart."

She was about to speak again when something on the riverbank upstream made her gasp and shrink against Gervase, who followed her glance and saw Sylvanus. The sobbing faun was holding Penelope in his arms, and the nymph was limp and seemingly lifeless. His tail drooped forlornly, and his cloven hooves slithered on some shingle as he gazed imploringly at Gervase.

"Please help! I think Penelope is dying!" he called, his love for the naiad overriding all other consideration, even Anne's presence.

Gervase took Anne by the shoulders and looked urgently at her. "His name is Sylvanus, and he means you no harm; in fact I suppose I claim him as my friend." Then he got up to run to the distressed faun, who placed the unconscious nymph on the ground and then cradled her battered head on his furry but still rather wet lap.

For a moment Anne was too bemused to move. This time her eyes *must* be deceiving her. She couldn't possibly be looking at a faun and a decidedly unwooden water nymph! And yet, was it any more incredible than her discovery about Charles Danby? Shaking off her shock, she rose to her feet and hurried over to them.

Gervase was examining Penelope's injuries as best he could in the darkness. He had taken one look at the nymph and known the faun was right to fear the nymph was dying, for her pulse was very faint indeed, and her face was drained of color. "What happened?" he asked Sylvanus, who was rocking to and fro and making soft crooning sounds.

Tears streamed down the faun's cheeks as he related what had happened when Gervase had run after the drifting boat. "He just kept hitting her and hitting her, and I think she hurt herself even more on something when she dove down to the bottom of the river," he finished, pointing to a nasty gash in the nymph's side.

After looking in dismay at the wound, for Penelope was losing a great deal of blood, Anne glanced urgently at Gervase. "Am I right in thinking this is the same Penelope who is a lamp holder in the castle?" Yet another incredible question to ask anyone, but then this entire situation was incredible.

Gervase nodded.

"Then somehow she's turned from wood into flesh, and then back again?"

Gervase nodded again. "Sylvanus has the power."

Anne met his gaze, realizing that this power was used upon him too, but then she turned back to the faun. "Sylvanus, you must turn her to wood again immediately, before she loses any more blood."

For a moment Sylvanus didn't seem to comprehend, but then realized what she was saying. "Why didn't I think of that?" he bleated in dismay, wondering how much worse he'd made the situation by carrying Penelope to find Gervase.

Gervase gave him a reassuring look. "Just do it, mm?" he said gently but firmly.

The faun said the words, and Anne stared as before her eyes the nymph slowly became wood again, but this time there were marks upon her shining surface, scratches and splintered damage that had never been there before.

Sylvanus bleated distractedly. "Oh, look at her! She's going to die, I know she is!"

Anne hesitated, but then ventured to put a kind hand upon his arm. "Wood can be repaired," she pointed out quietly.

The faun stopped midbleat. "Repaired?"

"She was badly damaged once before, but the man who made her—Joseph, the gardener—mended her so well that I'll warrant you never knew she'd been damaged at all."

"No, I didn't." Sylvanus's face brightened with hope. "Can Joseph mend her again now?"

Anne glanced at Gervase. "Yes, I'm sure he can, but that means taking her back to the castle, and letting Joseph *and* Mrs. Jenkins in on a little of what's been happening."

Gervase drew a long breath. "Well, I'll warrant that after all that's gone on of late, they already think they're losing their wits, so an explanation for it all might help restore their faith in their own eyes."

"Yes, but what an explanation," Anne murmured, picturing the housekeeper's reaction.

She was right, although as the strange party entered the kitchens half an hour later, Mrs. Jenkins didn't at first notice the faun or what he was carrying. Joseph noticed, however. The gardener was seated at the table with his woodworking things laid out lovingly before him, and he stared directly at Sylvanus. "Well, *that* explains a few things," he observed. Jack noticed too and slunk out without further ado, having no intention of risking another confrontation with the hooved man.

Mrs. Jenkins's baleful gaze had been drawn instantly to Gervase. "I might have known *you'd* be here! Where is the duke? What has happened? Miss Anne?" But then she saw Sylvanus and his precious burden of carved wood and gave a squeal. "Oh, my good Lord above, it's a two-legged billy goat with the nad!" she cried, and fell in a faint.

Chapter Thirty

Anne hastened to the swooning housekeeper, and Gervase wasted no time about informing Joseph what was needed, not that the gardener needed much telling, for he could see the catastrophe that had befallen his handicraft. Nor was Joseph inclined to ask other questions, for as far as he was concerned, Sylvanus was explanation enough for anyone. Repairing the damaged nymph was the sort of challenge in which he reveled, and as he set to with his tools, glues, oils, and waxes, he assured Sylvanus that when he'd finished, Penelope would be as good as new. Sylvanus hovered nearby in an agony of worry and grief, and there was nothing Gervase could say to ease the faun's suffering.

As Anne tended to Mrs. Jenkins, she was surprised at her own calmness; after all, she had almost been murdered tonight! On top of that she was with a lawyer who was sometimes a marble statue, a wooden nymph who was sometimes alive and who was being repaired by the gardener, and the odd company was completed by a lovesick faun whose power it was that transformed the others in the first place. It was bizarre, credulity stretched so far beyond normal bounds that it had virtually come full circle, to the point that she almost felt it would be strange *not* to be in such company!

Mrs. Jenkins came around, and on seeing Sylvanus parted her lips to squeal again, but Anne addressed her very sharply. "Don't you *dare* have the vapors, Mrs. Jenkins!"

The housekeeper was shocked into silence, but gazed warily at the faun's horns and cloven hooves.

Anne straightened, feeling a little guilty for having been so harsh. "I'm sorry, Mrs. Jenkins, but the poor creature is upset enough already."

"B-but what *is* it?" whispered the housekeeper.

Gervase glanced across. "Sylvanus is a faun, Mrs. Jenkins. He comes from Roman mythology."

Mrs. Jenkins blinked. "Mithulgy?" she repeated blankly.

He smiled a little and nodded. "Yes."

"A-and the nad is from mithulgy too?"

"The what? Oh, yes, she is."

As Gervase returned his attention to Joseph's ministerings and to Sylvanus, the housekeeper looked quizzically at Anne. "What is all this about, Miss Anne? Where is the duke?"

"I'm afraid the duke is dead, Mrs. Jenkins."

The housekeeper went even more pale than she already was. "He's dead?" she repeated faintly.

Anne hastened to the pantry to pour her a glass of elderberry wine, which she pressed gently into the woman's trembling hand before telling her, to the best of her knowledge, what had happened on the river.

"But why did he do it?" Mrs. Jenkins asked.

"I don't know."

"You don't know? Not even what Mr. Danby's part in it all might be?"

"No. I accept what I see now, and what I feel." Anne glanced at Gervase as she said this. "But I don't know the whys or wherefores. When I do, I will tell you."

The housekeeper looked at her. "Do you trust him, Miss Anne?"

"Mr. Danby? Oh, yes, implicitly."

Mrs. Jenkins eyed him. "Then I must too, although as God is my witness, it will not be easy."

"There is nothing easy about anything that's gone on here of late," Anne observed dryly.

"That's true," muttered the housekeeper with feeling. "What a birthday for you, Miss Anne."

"One I'll never forget, and there's more I must tell you yet, I fear. You see, fauns not only still exist; they have the power to turn people and things into marble and back again. He's the one who turned Penelope from wood into a living nymph." Anne drew a long breath. "He also turned Mr. Danby into a statue," she said at last.

Mrs. Jenkins's jaw dropped, then her interested gaze swung to Gervase. "Well, I never," she murmured, and downed the rest of her glass in one mouthful.

Anne looked at Gervase too. He had referred to Sylvanus as his friend, and certainly seemed to hold the faun in affection. How could that be if Sylvanus was responsible for making him into a statue? Oh, how she wished she knew the whole story, but until Charles felt it was the right moment, she would clearly have to wait.

Things had been happening at the White Boar as well, for Kitty and Sir Thomas had quit the inn with the chest of gold and had made good their escape in Sir Thomas's carriage—or rather his wife's. Their departure had been hasty but stealthy, and they'd crossed the landlord's palm with silver to fob Lady Fanhope off with falsehoods for as long as he could. All he had to do, they advised, was say he knew nothing, except that Sir Thomas had felt unwell and had gone for a long walk in the cool night air. This was Sir Thomas's idea, since he often resorted to this in order to get away from his wife for an hour or so. The landlord agreed, believing that Mr. Oadby's doxy had merely transferred her affections, and that Sir Thomas could not be blamed, seeing what manner of wife he had. That they were stealing a hoard of gold remained unknown to him, for Sir Thomas told him the chest contained books for his cousin in America. As they drove off into the night, the only thing the landlord knew was that their destination was Bristol, because he heard Sir Thomas instruct the coachman.

Lady Fanhope was unperturbed at first when she returned to the bedroom after dining alone. She encountered the landlord on the staircase, and he dutifully informed her of her husband's nocturnal perambulation, so that it did not cross her mind to look under the bed to see whether or not the chest was still there. But as time ticked by and she prepared to retire, Sir Thomas's failure to return began to concern her. It was then that she looked in the wardrobe and saw that his belongings were gone. With a horrified gasp she darted to the bed and found the precious chest gone as well.

Sir Thomas and Kitty were wrong to suppose the money was being illegally removed from all reach of her father's duns, for there was nothing wrong with that gentleman's financial affairs; indeed, contrary to rumor, his purse continued to bulge most agreeably. The money was to fund his purchase of an estate near New York and was being transported to America in the trunk simply because he was too mean to transfer it through a bank, which would charge heavily for its services. So instead of remaining silent about the theft of the gold, Lady Fanhope let out a shriek fit to awaken the occupants of Peterbury churchyard.

Then, still making more noise than a fox in a crowded henhouse, she ran to find the landlord, who was hugely dismayed to realize he'd been party to such a theft. Anxious to exonerate himself, he immediately confessed all he knew, that Sir Thomas had run off to Bristol with Miss Oadby, and within the hour the local magistrate had been alerted. A warrant was soon out for the arrest of Sir Thomas Fanhope and his lady companion.

After that, just Lady Fanhope was recovering with a fortifying glass of brandy, a local man who had been fishing at night on the banks of the Wye came rushing in to say he'd found Mr. Oadby's body floating in the river. Fearing that her ungrateful husband had not only absconded with the gold and a scheming trollop, but had murderously disposed of said trollop's inconvenient lover as well, Lady Fanhope saw scandal looming on a huge scale and collapsed in a fit of the vapors that might have caused graveyard stirring and henhouse panic as far away as Monmouth.

Long after midnight Joseph was almost ready to declare himself satisfied he'd done all he could for Penelope. The nymph's gleaming wood was outwardly flawless again, although not all her glue was entirely dry, but the gardener was sure that if she was turned back into a proper young woman again, she would simply sleep until she was strong enough to awaken. So he just polished her a little more, buffing the shine on her wood so that when she opened her eyes again, she would be as beautiful as possible.

Sylvanus was still not reassured. He hung about wretchedly, shuffling his hooves and wiping away the occasional tear as he watched Joseph at work. His anguish had at last proved too affecting for Mrs. Jenkins, who overcame her alarm to bring the faun a glass of the elderberry wine and some little fruit tarts she'd made for the picnic that never took place. Placing them on the floor by her best fireside chair, she ushered the distressed faun to sit down. "There, you need something to keep your strength up," she declared.

Sylvanus was sufficiently taken aback to forget Penelope for a second or so. "Thank you," he said, and picked up the glass of wine, which he guzzled in his imitable faun way.

The housekeeper was shocked. "Have you no manners, sir? You should not make noises like a drain when you drink!"

Sylvanus was crestfallen. "All fauns do it."

"Not in this house, they don't." A light passed through her eyes. "Well, I think I know now who it was that left that mess before, don't I?"

Sylvanus lowered his eyes. "I'm sorry," he said meekly.

The housekeeper softened. "Oh, go on with you, I suppose you don't know any better," she declared, then busied herself preparing food for everyone, whether or not they wanted it.

There was no sign at all of Mog, who'd made herself scarce earlier when Jack had slunk out, but now the lurcher returned. Unnoticed, the dog observed from the courtyard door, which still stood open to the night. Espying the plate of untouched tarts on the floor beside the faun, the hungry lurcher was sorely tempted. His mouth watered, and at last the temptation became overwhelming, and he slunk in, sidling around behind the chair and then stealing the tarts one by one. Amazed to have gotten away with it right under not only Sylvanus's nose, but Mrs. Jenkins's as well, the lurcher then ventured to sit down in his customary place by the chair, although he kept a careful eye on the faun, of whose powers he was only too aware. He soon sensed Sylvanus's distress and knew it had something to do with the wooden nymph on the table. Much affected by sorrow of any kind, the dog moved a little closer, then a little closer again, and at last could not bear it any more and had to offer a little canine sympathy by putting his head on the faun's knee.

Sylvanus was startled, given the usual state of affairs between his kind and dogs, but there was something so very comforting about Jack's warm presence that after a moment the faun put a tentative hand on the lurcher's silky head. Jack whined a little and wagged his tail. Sylvanus managed a small smile. Maybe dogs were blessed with redeeming features after all.

Shortly afterward, Joseph, cautious to the last, eventually felt he could do no more for Penelope. As wood, she was perfect again, but whether she would be equally as perfect when she was flesh and blood remained to be seen. "We'd best take her up to a bed first, so she'll be comfortable when she awakens," he said, nodding to Gervase to help him carry the nymph.

Mrs. Jenkins hurried ahead of them with a lighted candle, and Penelope was carefully laid in the bed Gervase would have slept in that first night, had he stayed. Then everyone gathered around, even Jack, as Sylvanus said the words that would turn the carved lamp holder into a young woman again. Anne watched in fascination, Mrs. Jenkins made an uneasy little noise as the gleam of polished wood became the soft bloom of living flesh, and Jack whined and put his head curiously to one side, but Gervase lowered his eyes, for he knew only too well what was happening.

Penelope lay there with her silvery hair spilling over the pillow. Gone were the bruises and the wound in her side, and she seemed as perfect as before, except that she did not breathe or open her eyes. Everyone gazed in horrified anticipation, for she seemed quite dead, but then she inhaled deeply, although her eyes remained closed. Sylvanus choked back a sob and caught her hand up to his adoring lips.

Joseph put a reassuring hand on the faun's shoulder. "Now we just have to wait, but I think she'll be fine," he said.

Mrs. Jenkins eyed the gardener with admiration. "Joseph Greenwood, you're a marvel, and no mistake. I shall never again grumble about you, your mangy mongrel, or your horrible potions."

He smiled. "I never thought I'd live to hear you say that, Gwen Jenkins."

Chapter Thirty-one

Sylvanus preferred to remain at Penelope's bedside, so the others respected his wishes. Mrs. Jenkins and Joseph returned to the kitchens, but although Anne expected Charles to accompany her there too, instead he went to Mr. Willowby's study and closed the door behind him. Anne presumed that even after such a night, he remained Mr. Critchley's dutiful junior partner and was diligently attending to the examination of her father's ledgers. Given what she knew of his character, it seemed unlikely, but what other explanation could there be? She did not ask his reasons; indeed, she believed that if she did, he would not tell her—after all, he hadn't explained anything yet. She found it hard to be in such close proximity to him and yet not be trusted with the truth, for in spite of his reassurances by the rapids, it was untrusted that she felt. Tonight they'd all gone through a great deal, and not until Penelope recovered would it be over. No, it would not be over even then, because there would still be so much left unresolved with Charles—if resolved it would ever be.

Too upset to contemplate joining the servants in the kitchens, Anne tiptoed past the study door to the deserted, unlit drawing room. Dawn was not far away now, and the air was fresh as she opened the window to gaze out. The maze was dark and shadowy, and the white of the rotunda stood out with a clarity that was both solid and ghostly. A thin overnight mist had risen from the Wye and hung in delicate veils across the park. The scent of spring flowers was sweet and poignant, and the first bird had begun to sing, a blackbird, she thought, listening to the crisp, intricate notes. Tears stung her eyes, for the night's events, to say nothing of what had gone before, had left her emotionally and physically drained. She hardly knew how to cope with it all, beset as she was by such a momentous sequence of events, but it was her poor battered heart that suffered most.

She glanced up at the deep blue sky. The stars were still bright, but the birth of the new day was just beginning to shine palely to the east. Soon the light would soften the shadows of the maze, and the topmost branches would be touched with green. Another day, but the same heartaches.

"Anne?"

She turned with a startled gasp as Gervase spoke suddenly from the doorway behind her. "How did you know I was here?" she asked, pressing defensively back against the windowsill.

"I didn't. I came here to get something, but I'm glad to find you, because I need to speak to you." He came closer, and she saw that he had a sheet of folded paper in his hand. "Why are you on your own in the dark like this?" he asked softly.

"I needed time to think."

"What about?" He glanced uneasily out the window. The indigo sky had begun to soften to a paler shade of kingfisher, and the first sun rays now lanced thinly up to weaken the glow of the stars. He knew he had little time left before he had to become marble again.

She avoided looking at him. "Oh, not all that much, I suppose," she replied untruthfully.

"Tell me, Anne," he pressed, hoping to prompt her into the confession that would release him.

"Tell you? You decline to explain anything, yet expect me to divulge everything!" Her pain was evident in the bitter words.

"When we were by the rapids, I thought you understood that I would tell you when I could."

"Maybe I did, but understanding is not easy when you calmly remove yourself to my father's study in order to continue going through his accounts as if nothing untoward has occurred!"

"Is *that* what you think I've been doing?" He was startled that his actions could have been thus interpreted, for the last thing on his mind had been those damned ledgers!

"In the absence of any explanation, what else am I to believe?"

He gazed at her. "Oh, Anne . . ."

"Please don't look at me like that." She was glad that the dimness of the light hid the tears that had sprung to her eyes.

His heart twisted with love for her. "When I am eventually able to tell you my reasons, I know you will understand, but in the meantime please take me on trust, for I vow I will not let you down."

"How can I take you on trust when you show no trust in me?"

"I would trust you with my life; indeed, my life is already in your keeping," he said quietly.

Such an odd choice of words made her look intently at him. "What do you mean?"

He felt helpless. The eastern sky was turning to aquamarine, and the maze beckoned. In a few moments he had to return to the rotunda. "Just say what is in your heart," he whispered, his fingers tightening over the paper he held.

The air seemed to become even more still around her. All other considerations suddenly departed, and she knew what she had to tell him. "I love you, Charles—that is what is in my heart," she said softly.

Gervase closed his eyes, for his relief was so intense that he felt weak. Just as another day of marble imprisonment seemed inevitable, she'd given him his freedom! "Oh, my darling, darling Anne, if you only knew how precious those words are to me," he breathed, opening his eyes again to look out at the ever lightening sky. Never had a dawn been more blessed than this one.

His emotion affected her, and she went to him. "Charles?"

He caught her close, finding her mouth in a kiss that made their hearts beat in complete unison. His fingers twined in the warm hair at the nape of her neck, and his lips moved richly and yearningly against hers. She was love itself to him, the embodiment of every sweet feeling, and the justification for his very existence. Without her now, he might as well be marble anyway.

Joy sang through Anne as she returned the kiss, for she could not help but know that no matter how much about himself he held back, his overwhelming love for her was now laid bare. His lips were sensuously arousing, his fingers moved caressingly in her hair, and for a long, exquisite moment his body seemed one with hers, but then he drew back. He was overcome, and for a few seconds could not speak, but then he smiled into her eyes. "I'm myself again at last, my dearest, sweetest, most beloved Anne. As in all the finest fairy tales, the princess has said the three enchanted words that release the prince from bewitchment!"

"Bewitchment?"

"Yes, for now I can tell you who I really am. To begin with, I have never met Mr. Charles Danby, although I'm sure he is a very pleasant fellow." He stepped suddenly to the mantelpiece, selected a letter from the bundle behind the candlestick, and gave it to her, together with the folded sheet of paper he'd held when he entered the room. "Look at them both, Anne. What do you see?"

There was a brief message on the sheet of paper. *Do you recognize my writing, Anne? And having recognized it, do you forgive my past letters? I vow I would not, could not, write them now.* Her lips parted with realization, for the hand was unmistakably the same as that of the letter.

"This is why I was in the study, searching for pen, paper, and ink, and thinking about what words to compose. I wanted to prove my identity, and how better than by my writing, which is surely ingrained upon your memory, albeit in a disagreeable way."

"Gervase Mowbray? You're *Gervase Mowbray*?" Shaken, she raised huge eyes to his face.

"He of the disagreeable manners and character? Yes, Anne, I am."

Mortification swept over her as she remembered what she'd said the second time he'd called. *I confess the advent of Hugh Mowbray gives me cause for some relief, for I cannot pretend to grieve over the passing of his late cousin, whose disagreeable manners and character were only too evident in his letters.* She drew herself up then, for matching handwriting or not, she was again being asked to believe the impossible, and this time it was almost too much to endure. "But you can't be Gervase Mowbray, he's dead!"

"No, Anne, I'm very much alive, and I'm deeply ashamed of my past behavior. All things considered, I probably fully deserved my marble punishment."

She knew he was who he said he was, and her hand trembled as she put the letter and piece of paper down on the heavy table that had once graced the dining room, but which now served to hold the revolving bookstand that held her father's favorite volumes. Then she kept her back turned toward him as she tried to compose herself. "Why did you masquerade as Charles Danby? Why didn't you tell me the truth from the outset? You have not denied that you and the statue are one and same, which alone is hard enough to comprehend, but then there are also Sylvanus and Penelope! I know it is all true, and yet I also know that it is impossible."

"Nothing is impossible, Anne. I know that now, if I didn't know it before." He went behind her, slipped his arms around her waist, and rested his cheek against her hair. Her perfume was all around him, heady and beguiling, like warm summer flowers.

Her fingers crept to rest over his, and she closed her eyes. "Tell me everything," she whispered.

He related the whole story, and she listened with total credulity. She did not doubt that Ariadne's wedding crown was more than just a cluster of stars in the night sky, that Bacchus still mourned his lost love, or that fauns abounded in the hill above Naples, for it was all so patently true, but it failed to occur to her that the diadem in question was at this very moment lying on the table in the hall here at Llandower. She did not realize that the birthday present Hugh pressed upon her was the very thing poor Sylvanus needed so that he too could meet Bacchus's strict terms; indeed, she had forgotten all about the gift.

When Gervase had finished, she told him her own tale, of her reluctant resolve to bow to his father's pressure, her resignation when Hugh apparently succeeded to the title, and about her own father's letter from Ireland. She also told him what had happened on the evening of her birthday, although even then the gift slipped her mind.

On learning of Hugh's arrival after she'd sent word not to come, Gervase smiled. "He received your note, make no mistake of that, but you'd hoist him with his own petard, because contrary to his claims, he *was* still bound by my father's will. I know my cousin, and can put his reasoning together with what I believe to be a high degree of accuracy. He always intended to dispose of you in order to get everything without the inconvenience of a wife he didn't want, but your formal notification to Critchley would mean he could never meet the terms of the will, so you had to be eliminated *before* any letter could be sent to London. Hugh therefore pretended ignorance of the note and arrived anyway in order to despatch you as promptly as possible." He hesitated, for the delicate matter of Kitty's involvement had to be mentioned at some point. "Anne, there's something I've so far neglected to mention in all this. Hugh wasn't staying alone at the White Boar, nor was he using his real name. He was posing as a Mr. Oadby and claimed that his, er, companion, was his sister. He has no sister, and from what I know, I believe this lady to be Kitty Longton, an actress at Drury Lane who coincidentally hails from Oadby in Leicestershire. Hugh was long obsessed with her, for she is very beautiful and can be fascinating when she chooses, but she would have nothing to do with him when he wasn't heir to a title or a fortune. Once he stood in line to inherit *my* birthright, I have no doubt that Kitty would be most, er, obliging."

Anne turned to face him. "Is she the lady with whom your name was once linked?" she asked quietly.

Gervase was taken aback. "You know of that?"

"Even country newspapers stoop to printing gossip."

"Does it make a difference in your regard for me?"

"That you have had at least one mistress in the past? I would be very foolish to imagine you have led the life of a monk, or that Kitty Longton was an isolated case." She smiled.

It was her first smile since learning his true identity, and it lightened his heart. "She wasn't, and one day I will tell you my whole sordid history, but I doubt you wish to hear it right now." His thoughts suddenly turned to the matter of Hugh's demise. "We *should* inform the authorities about what happened tonight, but I don't wish to."

She was startled. "But we have to tell them!"

"Do we? The moment Hugh's death becomes known, it's going to be discovered that he came to dance attendance upon you, that he stayed at an inn under a false name, and that he was in the company of an actress who once happened to be my mistress too. None of these titillating revelations can be avoided, but if you add the further shocking fact that he met with his death while attempting to murder you, the scandal becomes a resounding *cause célèbre*."

She glanced away, for she had not yet considered such consequences.

He went on. "My reappearance will be a talking point as
well. I intend to more or less tell the truth, albeit a version that
is bereft of fauns, Roman gods, and marble statues, since I
have no desire to be thought mad. More prudent by far to con-
fine my explanation to something close to Hugh's. It could be
a simple matter of his attempt to gain my inheritance by attacking me and leaving me for dead on Vesuvius." He looked
intently at her. "Anne, I am determined not to involve you
more than absolutely necessary. There is no *need* to say anything about last night's events. Who is to prove my cousin
ever arrived here last night? We can set his horse loose so that
it returns to the White Boar as if he had a fall somewhere, and
if Kitty should say he set out for Llandower, we can claim not
only that he didn't arrive, but that you had written asking him
not to come at all. Joseph informs me that everything that
passes through the rapids washes up at a certain popular fishing place downstream, so his body is certain to be soon discovered there. That, together with the stray horse, will
convince the authorities that he died accidentally. It's the best
way, believe me."

"You've given this some thought, haven't you?"

"Yes, for I wish to protect you at all costs." He put a quick
hand to her cheek.

"I will go along with whatever you decide."

"Then it is settled; we will insist that Hugh never arrived
here. I take it Mrs. Jenkins and Joseph will support such a
story?"

"Yes, I'm sure they will."

He tilted her chin so that she looked directly into his eyes
again. "Anne, you now know my cousin's motives, but do
you really know mine?"

"Yours?" She was startled. "What do you mean?"

"Well, Hugh may have pretended otherwise, but one way
or another you remained essential to his inheritance, which,
rather embarrassingly, you remain to me as well. I *must* wed
you if I wish to keep my title and estate, but if I do, will you
think my inheritance is my sole motivation? Or will you know
that I do it because I adore you with all my heart? I will give
up everything if you need proof of my sincerity."

Fresh tears sprang to her eyes as she reached up to put her
mouth briefly to his. "You do not need to give up anything. I

would have married you as Charles Danby, and I will marry you still," she said, so choked with happiness that her voice was husky.

His heart surged, and he pulled her swiftly toward him, catching her mouth to his once more.

Chapter Thirty-two

Anne was the other half of Gervase's passion as she went into his arms. Her lips softened and parted beneath the onslaught of his kisses, and as his hands moved desirously over her, she sighed and curved sensually against him.

He felt his body respond. Oh, how he longed to make love to her, to slake the desire that thundered through his veins. He cupped one of her breasts, so firm and eager in the dainty bodice of her gown, and she sank back against the table, drawing him with her. It was a natural movement, innocently knowing, and their lips were still joined as he lay against her. The scent of honeysuckle seemed to fill the air again, and for a moment he thought of cornfields in August, but then it was gone and he was conscious only of the litheness and ardor of her body beneath his. She moved against him, intensifying his pleasure as well as her own. Her passion was wanton and honest, as was his own, for it was love of the strongest and most natural order that governed them both.

He wanted to worship her completely, to sink within the depths of her beloved warmth. It was the perfect moment. They needed each other, their love had been declared, and they would be man and wife. How simple to anticipate their vows. He could make her his right now, but he knew he wouldn't. When he took her for the first time, it would be when she was truly his wife. It took all his willpower to conquer his desire, and although he was still aroused, at last he became master of himself again.

They were still wrapped in each other's arms, too overcome with love to even whisper each other's name, when suddenly there was a commotion from the direction of the staircase. Perhaps it wasn't a commotion exactly, just an overexcited mixture of delighted bleating, hoof stamping, and calling as

Sylvanus summoned everyone to Penelope's bedside because the nymph had awoken.

Straightening hastily, they hurried to the stairwell and found the deliriously happy faun hopping up and down on the landing above. He peered over the wooden balustrade, his face alight with relief as he summoned everyone—anyone— to come see that his adored naiad was well again. Mrs. Jenkins and Joseph had heard from the kitchen and were coming up the stairs as quickly as they could, accompanied by Jack, who was yelping and wagging his tail as if he too knew what had happened. Everyone hastened to the nymph and found Penelope sitting up. She was propped on the mound of pillows Mrs. Jenkins had provided, and she looked as if nothing had ever befallen her. So skilled had Joseph been, there was not even a scratch to show she'd been subjected to Hugh's vicious assault.

Sylvanus was so beside himself with relief that he hardly knew what to do. He talked nineteen to the dozen and kept rearranging Penelope's pillows until she was obliged to tap his hands reprovingly. "You've made me comfortable enough, Sylvanus," she said with a smile.

"Is there anything you want? What can I bring you? Do you want a drink? Are you—?"

"I'm quite all right, truly."

The faun hesitated bashfully. "Am I fussing too much?"

"Just a little," she replied.

The rather bashful Sylvanus was about to say something more when he noticed Gervase and Anne were holding hands. The faun suddenly realized that it was well past daybreak, and Gervase had not had to return to the rotunda. He raised eyebrows inquiringly, and Gervase nodded.

"Yes, my friend, I am free again."

Sylvanus beamed with delight. "I'm so glad for you."

Penelope smiled too. "And so am I, Gervase."

Mrs. Jenkins was startled. "*Gervase*, did you say? But—"

Anne put a hand on the housekeeper's sleeve. "His name isn't Charles Danby at all, Mrs. Jenkins, it's Gervase Mowbray."

The housekeeper stared. "But, I thought Gervase Mowbray died in Italy."

"I will explain in due course, Mrs. Jenkins, but suffice it that nothing could please me more than to be united with him."

"Does this mean you will be Duchess of Wroxford after all?"

"Oh, yes, and it will be a love match, I promise you," Anne replied, smiling at Gervase.

But then Sylvanus's happiness was suddenly extinguished, and with a heartfelt sigh he sank onto the edge of the bed and put his head in his hands. "But what am *I* going to do? Now that Hugh is dead, he can't give me the diadem, and I'll never be able to carry out my task for Bacchus!" Jack whined and rested his head on the faun's knee again.

Mrs. Jenkins and Joseph exchanged bemused glances, for they had no idea what he was talking about.

Gervase stepped forward to put a quick hand on the faun's bowed shoulder. "Hugh gave the diadem to Kitty, remember? You and Penelope overheard at the inn? So *Kitty* is the one who must give it to you, and she is very much alive."

Sylvanus looked up hopefully. "I'd forgotten that. There's still hope then, *if* she can be persuaded."

Gervase drew a long breath, for it would not be easy to part Kitty Longton from anything so valuable.

Mrs. Jenkins looked perplexed at Gervase. "What is this diadem, Mr. Danby? I mean, Your Grace?"

Gervase told her, and the housekeeper turned swiftly to Anne. "But, Miss Anne, isn't that—?"

In a trice Anne realized what she was thinking. *Hugh's birthday gift!* "Wait a moment!" she cried, and gathered her skirts to rush from the room. She positively flew all the way down to the entrance hall, snatched the diadem, and then flew back up again. She paused breathlessly in the bedroom doorway. "Is this what you need, Sylvanus?" she asked.

The faun stared incredulously at the beautiful wedding crown, which seemed to scintillate with flashes of fire in the morning light that now streamed through the east-facing bedroom window. He leapt to his hooves. "Yes!" he cried. "Yes, that's it! But how—?"

"I don't know anything about Kitty having it, but Hugh gave it to me."

"*Gave* it to you?" The faun glanced imploringly at Gervase, who turned swiftly to Anne.

"You own it now, Anne, so if you give it willing to Sylvanus, he will be released, just as I was."

She smiled and pressed the diadem into the faun's hands. "I give it more than gladly."

As Sylvanus's fingers closed relievedly over the precious wedding crown, there was a vivid flash of lightning, followed by a clap of thunder so loud that it shattered the early morning quiet. A gust of wind got up from nowhere, and the window, which was slightly ajar, slammed back on its hinges.

Mrs. Jenkins shrank against Joseph with a squeak of alarm, and Jack crept prudently beneath the bed, whining uneasily, but Anne hurried to the window to look out. Gervase joined her as storm clouds suddenly billowed across the hitherto clear sky, and the approaching sound of laughter and panpipes became gradually audible. An amazing procession emerged from the clouds and began to stream down toward the ground. Bacchus had come for the diadem. Leading his growling panther, he was attended by his troublesome retinue of fauns. The god's golden beauty shone against the darkened heavens, and the fauns danced, played panpipes, and hid in the undulating folds of his magnificent purple cloak. As the deity of wine, happiness, and wild nature alighted upon the northern soil that was so very far away from his warm Mediterranean haunts, he brandished his staff, and his mischievous followers fell silent. They crowded curiously behind him, peering up toward the castle and whispering together as he struck the staff once upon the ground. The sound reverberated across the park.

Still clutching the precious diadem, Sylvanus gave Gervase a brief farewell hug, then held a hand out to Penelope. "Come, we must ask my master now if you are to come home with me, for we will not have a second chance." The naiad flung her bedclothes back, and they both ran from the room.

Mrs. Jenkins and Joseph joined Anne and Gervase at the window as the faun and nymph respectfully approached the god, whose golden light was almost as dazzling as the jewels in the diadem. Sylvanus abased himself and crawled to lay Ariadne's wedding crown respectfully at the stern god's feet, then looked up beseechingly, indicated Penelope, and clearly begged for her to be allowed to return to Italy with him now that he had successfully completed his task. His request made, he pressed his face to the grass, his goat tail aloft in trepidation. Penelope sank to her knees, her hands held nervously to her mouth as she too waited for the god's decision.

Bacchus retrieved the diadem, then jabbed the cowering faun with his staff. The other fauns sniggered, a sound that carried clearly to the watchers at the window. Bacchus silenced them with a glance, then looked at the little naiad for a long moment, as if assessing her worthiness. Coming to a decision, the god said a single word to Sylvanus, who scrambled gladly to his hooves and snatched Penelope's hand. The beaming expression on his snub-nosed face said everything.

Bacchus turned to the castle and raised his staff in salute to Gervase, who smiled. Then the whole incredible procession streamed back into the skies, and the last thing anyone saw was Sylvanus and Penelope turning to wave frantically before disappearing after the others into clouds that a moment later had vanished so completely they might have been a dream.

As the morning sun shone out again, Mrs. Jenkins exhaled slowly. "Well, I never did in all my life," she muttered, turning to Joseph. "Now you'll have to make another nad, and you'll have to be quick about it if we're to go to Ireland."

"Eh? Go to Ireland? What do you mean?" Joseph's jaw dropped, for this was the first he'd heard of it.

"Come downstairs for a cup of tea, and I'll tell you," she said, ushering him from the room.

Alone again, Gervase took Anne's hand and drew her into his arms, but before kissing him, she held back a little. "You do swear that I haven't dreamed all this, don't you? For I vow that even now I cannot believe it had really happened."

"It is no dream, just an incredible truth," he murmured, pulling her close again. "I love you, my duchess-to-be," he whispered, putting his lips lovingly over hers.

Chapter Thirty-three

It was August, and the sun was bright as the newlywed Duke and Duchess of Wroxford rode through the Wiltshire fields not far from the Palladian splendor of Wroxford Park. Skylarks tumbled in the sky, honeysuckle was in full bloom in the hedgerows, and the distant heights of Salisbury Plain shimmered in the heat.

Gervase glanced approvingly at Anne as she controlled her rather capricious bay mount. She wore a corded silk riding habit that was the same color as the poppies that bloomed so freely in the surrounding fields of ripe corn, and her silver buttons bore the maze badge of the Mowbrays. The lace scarf falling from the back of her little gray hat was now the sort of original finishing touch he had come to expect—and adore. As he had begun to realize that first night on the bank of the Wye, her taste in fashion was charmingly unique. She always managed to turn the latest mode into something that was strikingly her own, and the result was always much admired. In London it was already being said that if one wished to anticipate the latest trend, one had only to look to the new Duchess of Wroxford. His quiet, unassuming, enchanting bride had taken the capital by storm. He smiled to himself, for he was not surprised. To know Anne was to appreciate her qualities, although he suspected that she would always find it hard to credit that if on the spur of the moment she decided to carry a pink handkerchief, within the week the drawing rooms of London would flutter with such emblems!

He thought back to the days leading up to their marriage. His sudden return had startled everyone, as he knew it would. There hadn't been any mention of beings from ancient Rome, nor would there be, for as anticipated, Hugh's all-consuming ambition to gain the inheritance by attacking his ducal cousin and leaving him for dead on Vesuvius had proved sufficient explanation. The shocking story soon became one of *the* talking points. Hugh himself was widely regarded to have been very fortunate to have drowned in the Wye, for if arrested, the gallows would surely have awaited him. Foul play was never suspected in his watery demise, and his arrival at Llandower that night had never come to light.

Kitty Longton and the luckless Sir Thomas had been arrested at Bristol and now languished in that city's jail. The trunk of gold had been returned to Lady Fanhope, who was vociferously affronted by her husband's betrayal. One gentleman obliged to sit beside her at a dinner party was afterward heard to remark that her nasal voice put him in mind of an outraged nanny goat.

Gervase glanced at Anne again. She had been at his side throughout the storm. They had arrived in London just before the royal wedding, on the very day Lord Byron was forced into exile in Europe, so that it seemed the Wroxford story might after all slip by without much attention, but that hope had soon been dashed. As more and more details emerged, so interest increased.

Mr. and Mrs. Willowby returned hastily from Ireland on receiving a letter from Anne in which she told them the full story of her betrothal and all that had happened since their departure. She made no mention of things supernatural. The Willowbys were horrified to hear of Hugh's despicable deeds, but delighted to find that their daughter's marriage was to be a love match after all.

The wedding took place on a hot day in late July at fashionable St. George's in Hanover Square, and in importance had ranked second only to the royal wedding. At first society had been condescending toward the new duchess, for she was hardly the sort of bride the *ton* desired for an aristocrat like the Duke of Wroxford, but as the days passed, with few exceptions they were all won around by her gentle ways, quiet humor, and lack of affectation. She was a fragrant country rose in a hothouse of exotic blooms. His rose. His incomparable Anne.

He smiled as he recalled how on the day after the wedding they had danced a waltz at Almack's Assembly Rooms. White, cream, or oyster had become the depressingly uniform colors for ladies at the subscription balls, vouchers for which had been known to be fought over, but Anne had worn lavender. She put matching ribbons in her hair, and her face had been so alight with happiness and fulfillment that she had drawn all eyes. Those who had been prepared to condemn her for failing to conform were grudgingly obliged to admit that she looked exquisite. The younger ladies had long chafed at the dullness of attire, and the next ball had seen a veritable rainbow of color, with lavender being by far the most popular choice. That had been the beginning of Anne's reign.

Her parents had now returned to Ballynarray, taking Mrs. Jenkins and Joseph with them, but Martin had elected to stay behind with his family. Llandower had been Anne's wedding gift from her adoring bridegroom and now had new staff to keep it aired and ready for any whim she might have to stay there. Plans for visits to Ballynarray and Naples were already very much in hand, and there had been so much to do here on this their first visit to Wroxford Park, that Monmouthshire would have to wait just a little while.

All these things were far from Anne's mind now as she savored the summer countryside, which was so very welcome after the heat and bustle of London. She glanced up at the skylarks. "Oh, what a lovely day this is," she murmured.

"Quite perfect," he replied, reining in and dismounting by the open gate of a golden cornfield. Honeysuckle hung down from the hedges, and he brushed against it as he tethered his horse.

She reined in as well and smiled down at him. "I did not think I would like Wiltshire as much as Monmouthshire, but it will do."

"I'm relieved to hear it," he replied, tethering her horse also, then reaching up to help her dismount.

She slid down easily into his arms, raising her lips naturally to his for a moment, before turning to look toward Wroxford Park, so magnificent against the soaring background of Salisbury Plain. "I confess I expected to find Wroxford Park soulless."

"And is it?" he asked, taking off his neckcloth and letting it drop among the poppies that grew so profusely at the edge of this particular cornfield.

"Soulless? No, indeed it has much to commend it."

"Is that the best you can say?" He took off his navy blue riding coat and mustard waistcoat and tossed them idly over the gate.

She laughed and turned. "I reserve judgment. After all, we've only been here a few days."

"So we have," he murmured, beginning to unbutton his shirt.

She watched him in surprise. "What are you doing?"

He placed the shirt on the gate as well, then went to her and tilted her mouth to his again. He kissed her very gently, dwelling upon the moment with complete tenderness before drawing away and whispering softly, "Do you remember telling me something interesting about cornfields and honeysuckle?"

Her green eyes widened a little. "Yes, of course, but—"

"No buts," he said softly, starting upon the silver buttons of her riding habit. "Some fantasies can come true, Anne. This one certainly can."

"But what if we're seen?"

"No one will see. I've issued instructions that no one is to come near this spot today. We are at liberty to do as we please." He slid the jacket back from her shoulders and bent his head to kiss her throat.

As her arms slid around his waist, he deftly removed her hat, which soon joined his neckcloth among the poppies. Next he discarded the pins in her hair so that the willful dark golden curls tumbled down warmly over his hands. He kissed her for a long moment, his tongue toying with hers, then he undid the ties of her riding skirt so that it slithered down to the ground.

She smiled and stepped back, removing her underthings and footwear until at last she was as naked as that other lady had been all those years before.

Gervase's appreciative gaze moved warmly over her, dwelling upon her firm breast, slender waist, and shapely legs. "You are very desirable, Your Grace."

"And so are you, Your Grace," she replied, then smiled again. "We must reenact my fantasy properly." Taking his hand, she led him into the corn, then drew him down. The golden ears swayed above them both as she knelt beside him. Her green eyes shone as she began slowly upon his buttons.

The scent of honeysuckle was heady as the Duchess of Wroxford made love to her duke, and neither of them noticed the sudden breeze that stirred through the corn or heard panpipes in the distance.

Ⓤ SIGNET REGENCY ROMANCE

TALES OF LOVE AND ADVENTURE

☐ **SHADES OF THE PAST by Sandra Heath.** A plunge through a trap door in time had catapulted Laura Reynolds from the modern London stage into the scandalous world of Regency England, where a woman of theater was little better than a girl of the streets. And it was here that Laura was cast in a drama of revenge against wealthy, handsome Lord Blair Deveril. (187520—$4.99)

☐ **THE CAPTAIN'S DILEMMA by Gail Eastwood.** Perhaps if bold and beautiful Merissa Pritchard had not grown so tired of country life and her blueblooded suitor, it would not have happened. Whatever the reason Merissa had given the fleeing French prisoner-of-war, Captain Alexandre Valmont, a hiding place on her family estate. Even more shocking, she had given him entry into her heart.
(181921—$4.50)

☐ **THE IRISH RAKE by Emma Lange.** Miss Gillian Edwards was barely more than a schoolgirl, and certainly as innocent as one—but she knew how shockingly evil the Marquess of Clare was. He did not even try to hide a history of illicit loves that ran the gamut from London lightskirts to highborn ladies. Nor did he conceal his scorn for marriage and mortality and his devotion to the pleasures of the flesh. (187687—$4.99)

*Prices slightly higher in Canada   **RA45**

Buy them at your local bookstore or use this convenient coupon for ordering.

PENGUIN USA
P.O. Box 999 — Dept. #17109
Bergenfield, New Jersey 07621

Please send me the books I have checked above.
I am enclosing $_____ (please add $2.00 to cover postage and handling). Send check or money order (no cash or C.O.D.'s) or charge by Mastercard or VISA (with a $15.00 minimum). Prices and numbers are subject to change without notice.

Card #_____ Exp. Date _____
Signature_____
Name_____
Address_____
City _____ State _____ Zip Code _____

For faster service when ordering by credit card call **1-800-253-6476**

Allow a minimum of 4-6 weeks for delivery. This offer is subject to change without notice.

O SIGNET REGENCY ROMANCE   (0451)

DILEMMAS OF THE HEART

☐ **THE SILENT SUITOR by Elisabeth Fairchild.** Miss Sarah Wilkes Lyndle was stunningly lovely. Nonetheless, she was startled to have two of the leading lords drawn to her on her very first visit to London. One was handsome, elegant, utterly charming Stewart Castleford, known in society as "Beauty" and the other was his cousin Lord Ashley Hawkes Castleford, nicknamed "Beast." Sarah found herself on the horns of a dilemma.
(180704—$3.99)

☐ **THE AWAKENING HEART by Dorothy Mack.** The lovely Dinah Elcott finds herself in quite a predicament when she agrees to pose as a marriageable miss in public to the elegant Charles Talbot. In return, he will let Dinah puruse her artistic ambitions in private, but can she resist her own untested and shockingly susceptible heart?   (178254—$3.99)

☐ **LORD ASHFORD'S WAGER by Marjorie Farrell.** Lady Joanna Barrand knows all there is to know about Lord Tony Ashford—his gambling habits, his wooing a beautiful older widow to rescue him from ruin, and worst of all, his guilt in a crime that made all his other sins seem innocent. What she doesn't know is how she has lost her heart to him?
(180496—$3.99)

*Prices slightly higher in Canada   RR50X

Buy them at your local bookstore or use this convenient coupon for ordering.

PENGUIN USA
P.O. Box 999 — Dept. #17109
Bergenfield, New Jersey 07621

Please send me the books I have checked above.
I am enclosing $_____ (please add $2.00 to cover postage and handling). Ser check or money order (no cash or C.O.D.'s) or charge by Mastercard or VISA (with a $15.00 minimum). Prices and numbers are subject to change without notice.

Card #_____ Exp. Date _____
Signature_____
Name_____
Address_____
City _____ State _____ Zip Code _____

For faster service when ordering by credit card call **1-800-253-6476**

Allow a minimum of 4-6 weeks for delivery. This offer is subject to change without notice.

Ⓢ SIGNET REGENCY ROMANCE

ENDURING ROMANCES

☐ **THE DUKE'S DILEMMA by Nadine Miller.** Miss Emily Haliburton could not hope to match her cousin Lady Lucinda Hargrave in either beauty or social standing. Certainly she couldn't compete with the lovely Lucinda for the hand of the devastatingly handsome Lord Jared Tremayne who was on the hunt for a wife. The duke couldn't see Emily as a wife, but she did manage to catch his roving eye as a woman.
(186753—$4.50)

☐ **THE RELUCTANT HEIRESS by Evelyn Richardson.** Lady Sarah Melford was quite happy to live in the shadow of her elder brother and his beautiful wife. But now she had inherited her grandmother's vast wealth, all eyes were avidly upon her, especially those of three ardent suitors. She had to decide what to do with the many men who wanted her. For if money did not bring happiness, it most certainly brought danger and hopefully love.
(187660—$4.99)

☐ **THE DEVIL'S DUE by Rita Boucher.** Lady Katherine Steel was in desperate flight from the loathsome lord who threatened even more than her virtue after her husband's death. Her only refuge was to disguise herself as the widow of Scottish lord Duncan MacLean, whose death in far-off battle left his castle without a master. But Duncan MacLean was not dead.
(187512—$4.99)

☐ **THE RUBY NECKLACE by Martha Kirkland.** Miss Emaline Harrison was the widow of a licentious blueblood after a marriage in name only. Around her neck was a precious heirloom, which some London gentlemen would kill for. So it was difficult for Emaline to discern the true motives and intentions of the seductive suitors swarming around her. Such temptation was sure to lead a young lady very dangerously, delightfully astray.
(187202—$4.99)

*Prices slightly higher in Canada

Buy them at your local bookstore or use this convenient coupon for ordering.

PENGUIN USA
P.O. Box 999 — Dept. #17109
Bergenfield, New Jersey 07621

Please send me the books I have checked above.
I am enclosing $_____ (please add $2.00 to cover postage and handling). Send check or money order (no cash or C.O.D.'s) or charge by Mastercard or VISA (with a $15.00 minimum). Prices and numbers are subject to change without notice.

Card #_____ Exp. Date _____
Signature_____
Name_____
Address_____
City _____ State _____ Zip Code _____

For faster service when ordering by credit card call **1-800-253-6476**

Allow a minimum of 4-6 weeks for delivery. This offer is subject to change without notice.

SIGNET REGENCY ROMANCE

ROMANCE FROM THE PAST

☐ **THE WICKED GROOM by April Kihlstrom.** It was bad enough when Lady Diana Westcott learned her parents were wedding her to the infamous Duke of Berenford. But it was even worse when she came face to face with him. First he disguised his identity to gain a most improper access to her person. Then he hid the beautiful woman in his life even as that passion of the past staked a new claim to his ardent affection. Now Diana had to deceive this devilish deceiver about how strongly she responded to his kisses and how weak she felt in his arms.
(187504—$4.99)

☐ **THE SECRET NABOB by Martha Kirkland.** Miss Madeline Wycliff's two sisters were as different as night and day. One was bold and brazen and had wed a rake whose debts now threatened the family estate, but the other was as untouched as she was exquisite. Now Madeline had to turn her back on love and get dangerously close to a nefarious nabob to save her sister's happiness and innocence ... even if it meant sacrificing her own.
(187377—$4.50)

☐ **A HEART POSSESSED by Katherine Sutcliffe.** From the moment Ariel Rushdon was reunited with Lord Nicholas Wyndham, the lover who had abandoned her, she could see the torment in his eyes. Now she would learn the secrets of his house. Now she would also learn the truth about his wife's death. And now she would make Nick remember everything—their wild passion, their sacred vows ... their child....
(407059—$5.50)

*Prices slightly higher in Canada   RA48X

Buy them at your local bookstore or use this convenient coupon for ordering.

PENGUIN USA
P.O. Box 999 — Dept. #17109
Bergenfield, New Jersey 07621

Please send me the books I have checked above.
I am enclosing $_____ (please add $2.00 to cover postage and handling). Send check or money order (no cash or C.O.D.'s) or charge by Mastercard or VISA (with a $15.00 minimum). Prices and numbers are subject to change without notice.

Card #_____ Exp. Date _____
Signature_____
Name_____
Address_____
City _____ State _____ Zip Code _____

For faster service when ordering by credit card call **1-800-253-6476**

Allow a minimum of 4-6 weeks for delivery. This offer is subject to change without notice.